HOT TO THE TOUCH

HOT IN CHICAGO ROOKIES

KATE MEADER

Cover: Lori Jackson Design

Cover model and photographer: Zach M. by Wander Aguiar

Editing: Kristi Yanta

Proofreading: Julia Griffis

ISBN: 978-1-954107-27-4

Content Warnings

This book deals with a number of sensitive topics including: death of loved ones (on page), grief, guilt, PTSD, and toxic relationships.

ONE

Cass

Who brings a hot date to a three-year-old's birthday party?

At this point in my acquaintance with Sam Killian, nothing should surprise me. This is the guy who mooned the guests at his brother's wedding. Who duct taped a harmonica to the grill of his sister-in-law's car. Who changed the auto-correct in his mom's phone so every time she texted "bye" it changed to "penis." You know, all the frat boy classics.

The man is twenty-seven with the mental age of a fourteen-year-old boy, and that's generous. No one brings a date to a kid's party, not when the date is dressed like she thinks this is a night club. But then this is Sam, who I've known and happily avoided to the best of my ability for the last six years, ever since his brother and my sister tied the knot.

"How did he think this was a good venue to introduce his latest fling?"

My sister, Anastasia—Annie to everyone—giggles as she cuts the crusts off a PB&J sandwich, or more accurately cashew butter and fig jam. It's that kind of children's party. Spencer, the birthday boy, won't eat them any other way.

"I think the 'fling' label is somewhat of a stretch."

True. That implies some sort of longevity, more than a one and done.

"But here. Really?" An hour ago, I came across the happy couple upstairs, coming out of the guest bathroom. She had a blissed-out look on her face and he was pulling up his zipper.

"He brought someone else to his parents' anniversary party last month." Smiling, she touches my arm. "I know he pisses you off but maybe don't think about it so much."

"I don't! I just find it fascinating that this same man is responsible for saving lives."

Sam's a firefighter, though God knows why he bothers. The guy doesn't need a job because both the Killian boys inherited pots of money from their late grandfather. Annie's husband, Jake, the eldest Killian son, is a software developer, because he loves tech and wants to be a useful member of society.

As for Sam? I've no doubt he's contributing as a first responder, but I suspect it's just as likely another prop in his playboy persona, a tool to attract women like the redhead with a skirt so short I can tell the color of her thong.

Purple.

"He loves his job," Annie says indulgently. That tone is typical around Sam. Peter Pan would never grow up so why not let him do his thing?

"Good for him!" I say cheerfully, as I drag my gaze away from—oh my God, is he feeling up his date near the bouncy castle? Surely, they've already mauled each other enough in private.

Ignore him. So he bugs the hell out of me, but I only have to see him a couple of times a year on my rare visits to Chicago from New York. This is precious time I need to be devoting to my sister and her babies.

"Hey, Spence, what's your favorite present?" I hunker down to my nephew's level.

He scrunches up his face as he thinks really, really hard. "Fire truck!"

"Oh, yeah?" I don't need three guesses to know who gave him that.

"He loves that fire truck," Annie says with a twinkle in her eye. She gets a kick out of my antipathy toward her brother-in-law as long as it doesn't affect the kids. "Sam got special decals for it to reflect his new squad."

"Course he did."

The air changes because guess who's decided to grace us with his presence? I stand and turn to face the favorite uncle himself.

He's handsome, I'll give him that, in a rugged, carved from unyielding granite kind of way. Not my type at all, but I can see the appeal. If I didn't know he came from money, I would think he's a blue-collar guy who works with his hands. They look rough, calloused. Capable.

I prefer smoother, office-appropriate men, who don't look like they might break me in half or put me over their knee because they'd assume I like it. I'm sure he works out— excessively. No one's neck is naturally that thick. Maybe he pulls Cadillacs with it while he calls out to his fuck-de-jour, "Look at me, babe!"

Today he's wearing what could best be described as a muscle shirt, though the early October air is a little cool for short sleeves. There's something almost obscene about the way his T-shirt's sleeves mold to his biceps, like they're imprinted onto the fabric. He would probably tell you he runs hot, the kind of statement a man like him would use as a chat up line. *I run hot, babe, therefore I am hot.* Or, *I run hot, babe, but it makes stripping so much easier.*

To be fair, I've never heard him speak like this. The Sam Killian alter ego I've created in my imagination just happens to also be a jerk.

"Cassie," he says, though it's not my name. I go by Cassandra in my professional life and Cass to my family and friends. Sam knows this. "You're looking well."

The taunt in his tone is unmistakable. He doesn't approve of my floral dress with a full skirt (too old-fashioned) or the way I've done my hair (a braided updo because it's generally unmanageable otherwise). Sam likely tells his dates how to wear their hair (long, flowing, all the better for him to hold onto while he ... *bleh*) or which outfits work best for children's birthday parties.

He's a good foot taller than me, and as my neck strains to meet his gaze, I pin on my most diplomatic smile. In my job as a financial planner, it's the smile I give a client who thinks he can afford a champagne retirement on a beer bottle pocket.

"Sam, I hear you have a new job."

He puffs up, the cock of the walk. "Rescue Squad. I'm pretty excited about it."

"Yes, all those people depending on you."

He smirks at the dig I can't help giving. "Don't worry, I'm a total pro when I'm wearing the uniform." Implying that's the only time he keeps it professional.

He scoops up the birthday boy. "Hey, Spence!"

"No kissing!"

"What? But I love kissing." Is it my imagination or does he flick a sly look my way?

Annie whispers to me, "Spence suddenly hates kissing. He thinks it's girly. Not sure where he got that from."

Sam grins at his nephew. "Have you had any cake yet?"

"Cake!" Spence yells, so excited about everything.

"I think he's going to have a sandwich first."

The bane of my existence rolls right over my suggestion. "So this cake of yours—is it chocolate or strawberry or mayonnaise or maybe cactus flavored?"

Spence giggles. "Cactus," though he pronounces it "Cackass."

"Cactus cake—yum! I bet it's ... spiky! Like your face!"

That sends Spencer into a torrent of giggles again. I love his laugh even when it's earned by Sam Killian.

"Sammie," a breathy voice cuts through the little boy's joy. Purple Thong is standing behind him. "Where's the little girl's room?"

"Hey, Candy, have you met everyone? This is my sis, Annie, my sister-in-law, Cassie. And this little monster is Spencer the Cactus Boy."

"I'm not a cack-ass boy!" But he loves it all the same, especially as everyone is laughing, and Spence adores being the center of attention.

Annie, in hostess mode, smiles at Candy. "Let me show you to the restroom."

"Oh, I thought ..." Candy sends a significant look at Sam. She knows where *one* of the restrooms is and had evidently hoped to explore the tile further with dear old Sammie.

"Thanks, Annie," Sam says obliviously as he helps himself to one of the sandwiches intended for Spence. He crushes it in a single bite.

"Me too!" Spencer squirms a little and Sam puts him down.

"Okay, I guess we're doing a bathroom field trip!" Annie takes her son's hand and walks into the house with a hip-swaying Candy, who sends a forlorn look over her shoulder at Sam. He completely ignores her.

Instead, his attention is completely focused on me. For a

moment, this gives me an odd thrill until I realize what it means: I have to talk to him.

There's an awkward pause while we size each other up. Usually, we have other people as a buffer, but in the rare moments when we're alone, the air seems to be extra-charged.

"You know, I'm not actually your sister-in-law." He called Annie his sister, which registered a small pinch of envy in me at their closeness.

His lips twitch. "Aren't you?"

"No, you and I are not related."

"And this bothers you because ..." His mouth curves as a light bulb goes off in the dim room that passes for his brain. "It'd be weird if we *were* related, I guess."

I don't ask *what* would be weird because I know exactly what he's alluding to.

"I just like the details to be correct."

But Sam's already moved on because details are unimportant to him. He doesn't care that I'm annoyed, or maybe he prefers when I am. It gives him a perverse pleasure.

"Kind of surprised you're here," he says.

"Oh?"

"You made a special trip from New York for a kid's birthday party?"

"Spencer means the world to me. And I like spending time with my sister and Jake." *But not you.*

His smile says he understands completely. We've always seen eye to eye on our mutual dislike.

"Where's the boyfriend?"

"Derek is in the middle of an important merger right now. He's heading to London the day after tomorrow for a couple of weeks and there's a lot of prep for the trip." I would have liked him to come with me to Chicago, but he's usually far too busy for personal events like this.

Sam holds my gaze, and I wait impatiently for whatever drivel trips off his tongue next.

"How long have you two been together?" Because he loves the sound of his own voice, he answers his own question, "Since just after Jake's wedding, right? That's, what, six years?"

Has it really been that long? It's easy to forget when you're busy with work and the routine. Derek's job as the lead associate in McKenzie Clark's Mergers & Acquisitions division requires long hours, especially in the weeks leading up to a deal. I don't usually begrudge his commitment to his work, though it would be nice if he could make time for the things and people I care about.

We had a fight about it before I left. He asked me to get a gift for his parents' 40th wedding anniversary because "you have time for that sort of thing" and he doesn't. Like I'm his personal assistant. It devolved into an argument about our priorities and how misaligned they are of late.

Things have been stale for a while, and when he gets back from the London trip, I'm going to push for couples' counseling. Anything to get us out of our rut.

Sam is waiting for me to comment on my lengthy relationship without a ring on it. As I've yet to weigh in, he adds, "Guess he's not rushing to complete *that* merger."

This guy is the worst. "It's really none of your business. But if you must know, we don't think a piece of paper is necessary to declare our feelings for each other." It comes out sounding prim and ridiculous, my standard tone around Sam Killian.

Now he's looking at me intently, like he can see the need inside me. To have a life like my baby sister's, with kids and birthday parties and a noisy extended family. But I'm also a busy professional, as is Derek, so our current relationship status suits us. We are perfect for each other, even if some nights I let my mind run away with wishing for things I can't have.

Because Sam's remaining unusually silent, but typically judgmental, I'm unnerved and come out with the first thing that pops into my head.

"What happened to the dancer you brought to the Christmas party last year?" I've no doubt he's plowed through several women since.

"Oh, you know me, Cassie—"

"It's Cassandra."

"It is?" Like this is news to him. "Well, I'm not like you, the serious-about-life-and-love type. Much prefer to have my fun while I can."

I smile thinly. "Before your looks fade?"

He leans in, and God help me, he smells incredible. Sandalwood with top notes of something citrusy. "Probably gonna be a while before that happens. I mean, look at me."

I do, taking in that strong jaw, aquiline nose, the cobalt-blue eyes, the sensual lips. He also has great hair because of course he does. Wavy, the kind that's perfect for the threading of fingers. More annoying than the jaw and nose and eyes and hair is that he's right. Looks like his won't fade, they'll merely mature into distinction, though a part of me hopes his party-hard lifestyle will eventually have some negative effect. Such as leprosy of the dick.

I've spent too long without returning a verbal volley, which puts this silence firmly in the Sam Killian win column.

Finally I manage, "So, you're pretty. Good for you, *Sammie.*"

"Now, I don't mind that at all. Lots of my friends call me that. Lots of my dates, too." Moaning that name in the throes is the unspoken part. The man is so obvious. "You're not really a nicknames kind of girl, are you?"

"I'm not a girl. And a little less condescension if you don't mind."

His eyebrows go up. "*I'm* the condescending one?"

"You think *I* am?"

He chuckles, but it's kind of mirthless for once, or maybe I'm just more in tune with his feelings. We have this much in common, both annoyed to have to talk to each other, yet neither of us willing to be the one to end it.

"For the last six years, you've acted like I'm no better than something on the bottom of your high-heeled shoe."

"The night before Jake and Annie's wedding, you placed a fake snake on my chair—"

"Now I apologized for that. That was supposed to be Jake's chair."

"And you assumed I was Annie's mom. I'm only five years older than her." At thirty-two, I'm also five years older than Sam, and feeling more ancient with every passing second.

Another lazy, incorrigible grin. I want to punch his teeth in.

"You know I didn't really assume that. It was a little joke, Cassie—*Andra*. Besides you practically raised her. Did a great job, too."

This compliment shocks me into speechlessness.

It's true—at least the part about me raising Annie. Our sperm donor was never in the picture and our mom, Aileen, was a flaky mess, always running after any guy who paid her the slightest bit of attention. Once Annie turned thirteen, Mom thought she was old enough to be alone. But really she thought *I* was old enough at eighteen to look after her.

Bye bye, college plans. And don't even think *about dating.*

No one knew I'd already secured a place at the School of the Art Institute, that I was planning to move to Chicago in the next six months. No one would ever know.

I spent the next five years making sure that Annie was

raised right, made it to Cornell, and had the best possible start to her adult life. I eventually started college myself, though later than everyone else, and in a more practical field. I didn't mind because Annie was my number one priority. Still is.

"She's all the family I have." The moment the words leave my mouth, I feel raw and foolish. I'm just giving him more ammunition.

"You have us, the dreaded in-laws," he says blithely. "But I can see why you're not in a hurry to claim me."

This is more like it. Though I sense his humor is a bid to cover my unfortunate display of vulnerability.

"Never a truer word." There's my prissiness again, only this time I'm playing into it because ... Sam likes that about me.

Why did I think that?

An age-old memory digs its sensuous claws into my psyche. *Tell me how much you hate me with that smart mouth, Cassie.*

"So back to the 'we're not related' thing, huh?" He shuffles closer, sending out another whiff of clean body scent that makes me slightly woozy. "I think maybe you like me more than you're letting on."

I hear it clearly, the barely masked threat of the past. There was a time when I almost let my guard down. Almost let him in. But common sense ruled, and I told him it would never happen. All these years later, I should feel victorious, secure in the knowledge I didn't make a stupid blunder.

Yet each time we meet, he acts like I should be grateful he once graced me with his attention. And I'm left wondering if maybe I *did* miss out.

Ladies and gentlemen, the Sam Killian playbook in action.

"That's where you're mistaken," I say, trying to sound reasonable instead of ... whatever I think Sam Killian might get a kick out of. "You and I are never going to get along, which is fine. We don't have to. We see each other a few times a year, and I imagine that'll be even less as the kids get older. There's no need to cry over it."

"Understood." His gaze is level and direct, the word almost strained through his perfectly straight white teeth. Sam's ego can't stand it when a woman won't kowtow to his charm.

"I'm going to get another drink before we cut the cake," I say, moving away. "Enjoy the rest of the party."

"Sure. You, too."

Two

Sam

Cassie—or should I say, *Cassandra*—Ferguson really knows how to piss me off.

She thinks *I'm* condescending? The woman has never spoken a word to me that doesn't drip in her own special brand of superiority.

So maybe I'm a little immature—or was. At twenty-one, I had my head up my ass when I met her the first time. I'd just returned from six months of traveling the world after graduation and thought I knew everything. It took me a while to settle and figure out my place, but now I know where I'm meant to be. A firefighter, someone who makes a difference.

Not that Miz Ferguson would ever see that. To her, I'm just the manwhore trust fund kid with a job that allows me to indulge my thrill-seeking tendencies and get me any woman I want. What the fuck is wrong with that? You'd swear I'd crushed her toes during our dance at Jakey's wedding—I didn't because I'm also a smooth-as-shit two-stepper.

Cass hated that.

Just like she hates that Spence and Maya adore their uncle Sammie. I could enumerate the million other reasons why the woman can't stand to be in the same room or backyard patio as me, but we'd be here all day and I have places to be.

"Are you talking to yourself?" Jake passes over the beer I left near the grill.

Maybe my lips were moving, replaying that conversation with Ms. Stick Up Her Fine Ass and wondering if I could have come up with more cutting responses.

"No, just—" I sigh. "How do you do it, Jakey?"

"What? Look this good in a linen jacket?"

"It's crumpled, and all you're missing is your croquet mallet." Though he is wearing the new pair of Comme des Garcons X Nike sneakers I bought for him. We're both sneakerheads and I love surprising him with new ones. "I mean, how do you put up with her?"

He knows exactly who I'm talking about. This is not the first time I've asked this burning question about my blister-in-law.

"She's pretty cool if you give her a chance."

Bet she is. Pity she won't give *me* a chance; I'm imprinted on her brain like some dinosaur fossil. But there was a time she might have considered me as more than a hard-on with two legs. We came close ... Now that moment is lost to the past, and we're locked into fighting positions.

"How come D-Bag never comes to visit?"

Jake doesn't correct me. He's not a fan, either. "Derek is a very busy guy, which I guess suits them both because she's busy, too."

"But too busy to create a life together? You'd think they'd be married by now."

My brother eyes me suspiciously. "Since when is creating a life with someone of interest to you?"

"It's not. Got all I need right here." I get the benefits of a ready-made family of incredible cuteness without the hassle of responsibility. "But it's just weird that they seem so separate. Not like you and Annie, or even Mom and Dad."

That's our cue to look toward Sylvia and Kenny. My dad had a stroke last year and while he's much improved, it's still tough to see the usually virile guy at less than a hundred percent. Mom's fussing about, making sure he has a plate of food and beer with a straw.

"Dad doin' okay?" I ask, though I know he is. I spent all day with him yesterday, binging half a season of *Better Call Saul*. He was in good form, but I still defer to Jake's opinion when it comes to his health. They're on the same wavelength.

"Yeah, he is, getting stronger every day. So get this. Mom was asking whatever happened to whatshername, the gal in PR? Madison?" He grins. "You brought her to two Killian shindigs in a row and got your poor mother's hopes up."

Madison Maitland. What can I say? I liked her but she was at least ten years older than me and took me as seriously as I take myself. (Meaning, not very.) When a woman is in a different place in her life and looking for something you can't give her, it's hard to close the gap.

"Don't worry. I won't do anything that pulls focus from you, little prince."

"Shut up."

Jake can grumble all he wants but that's the dynamic, clear and simple. He's the Killian golden boy and nothing I do will change Mom's mind on that.

At the grand old age of thirty, my brother is three years older than me. But it may as well be three hundred in terms of our mindset. He married Annie at twenty-five, a couple of years after Maya was born (one-night stand, out of wedlock, the horror!), then along came Spencer five years later. My brother is the living-and-breathing poster boy for responsibility-in-the-burbs while I'm—not. I'm still sowing my oats, as they say, enjoying the carefree life of a single firefighter with a healthy sex drive and an enviable sneaker collection.

"Another thing Miz Ferguson doesn't approve of," I mutter, because I'm still unreasonably caught up in her dislike of me.

"She's never gotten over the snake-on-the-chair intro."

Or my B material joke about her being Annie's mother. Of course I knew she wasn't when I met her but until then, I'd heard nothing but amazing things about St. Cassandra. I got it, she was a paragon of sister-slash-motherhood, and I was to treat her with the respect such nobility warranted.

"You put a snake on Aunt Cass's chair?" In typical sneaky kid style, my eight-year-old niece Maya has appeared out of nowhere, looking horrified. She's kind of a rule-follower, like her aunt.

I share a quick look with Jake, who grins and grabs his daughter in a fatherly hug. "He was kidding, sweet stuff. You know your uncle Sammie is a bit of a joker."

"Hey, bug, how's my favorite niece?"

She's wearing a Taylor Swift hoodie—which I gave her for Christmas—and gives me the evil eye coupled with a nose twitch. More St. Cassandra vibes. "I'm your only niece."

"True, true. How are those sneakers treating ya?"

My brother shakes his head. "You didn't have to do that."

"Yeah, I did! It might be Spence's big day but everyone should get gifts, right?"

"Cass thinks so, too," Jake says. "*She* got Taylor Swift tickets for February."

Huh, I should have thought of that. Score one to Cassie.

Maya hugs me, kind of unexpectedly because she's not one for sentiment. "Thanks, Uncle Sam. It was nice of you to think of me. When can I take a ride with you on the Ducati?"

The audacity. "When your dad says it's okay."

Jake mouths "fucker" over his daughter's head.

"Dad, can I?"

"Need to wait another few years, M."

A sad-eyed Maya walks off to talk to her aunt, whose face lights up in the presence of her niece. I will say this for the woman: she might be a pill to me, but she's never anything short of amazing with the kids.

My brother is jabbering on, yanking me out of a daydream where I'm pulling on Cassie's braids while I …

"You *could* make more effort with her."

"Who, Maya?"

"No, Cass. Annie and I would like the people we love most in the world to get along. For the kids' sake."

"The kids' sake?" I sound like a parrot, uncomprehending but determined to keep the conversation going.

"And mine. But mostly the kids. As they get older, they're going to pick up on the vibe between you two. It'd be good if you were a bit nicer to each other."

"I'm plenty nice. She's the one who thinks I'm a jerk."

Jake remains silent.

"Shut up. I can't help it. But I promise to make more effort." Whatever Jakey needs to hear.

Of course, that would require Ms. Can-Do-No-Wrong to meet me halfway.

Which I do *not* see happening at all.

THREE

Sam

It's my first day at Engine 6. So this is not where I was assigned after graduating from the Academy. No, that would be Engine 70, though Six was my first choice—the place is legendary after all. A couple of my academy buds, Abby Sullivan and Jude Torres, ended up here, though, so I already have connections and I've made more over the last year. I bided my time and put in for a transfer, and now I'm here to take up my spot on Rescue Squad.

It's rare for a relative newbie to get a place on Squad. Competition is fierce, but I've been making a name for myself this last year. The Peyton Hotel incident? Yeah, that was me, the guy who rescued the kid who fell down the elevator shaft. It should have been one of the squad on call, but I was on site first and time was of the essence. Little Jenny's parents sent me the nicest Christmas card and a crate of pears this past December.

Then there was the motorcycle crash of the mayor's daughter. I held Sienna's hand all the way to the ER and was available to talk to Mayor Robbins before the doctors had a chance to tell her Sienna would be fine.

So a couple of high-profile rescues. Not to say I haven't put in my time on the bread-and-butter of a regular engine's work: medical emergencies, cats in trees, plenty of fires. I'm a hard worker, and while people think I jumped the line to get my rescue squad spot—or used my newfound fame to butter up CFD's Media Affairs division—I don't care. I'm meant to be here where my talents can be best utilized.

Parking the Ducati in the Engine 6 lot, I'm about to head in to meet my new crew when I get a text from Jake.

First day? Did you bring your lunch box,
little bro?

ME

Couldn't find my Hello Kitty collectible, but I
made do with the BlackPink one. Thanks
for that.

JAKE

Least I could do on such an important
morning! Maya is excited for you as well.

A photo comes through of my niece wearing a firefighter helmet and carrying what looks like a garden hose. She's told me many times that she wants to be me when she grows up, which I'm happy to rub in my brother's face.

ME

Very cute. I can't wait to bring her to work
one day so she can be proud of at least one
male adult in the family.

JAKE

Funny. Lately she's been talking about
being a gamer like her dad so you can
forget about that role model shit. Keep it for
your own kid.

I almost choke on the thought.

ME

Don't even joke about it. Godfather and
uncle is more than enough responsibility.

JAKE

You say that now but sometimes the little
swimmers make the call.

ME

Double-bagging my dick going forward.

Jake lucked out with Annie, but if I was tied to the likes of
Candy for life, I'd be miserable.

JAKE

Loving the imagery. Did I tell you my son
threw up all over my linen jacket after the
party?

He sends another pic, this time of Spence stuffing his face
with not-cactus cake at his party. There I am, giving him all
the encouragement, secure in the knowledge that I will *not* be
on hand later when it all goes south. The perks of uncledom.

Cassie is in the photo, too, looking on with an expression
close to ... I want to say disapproval, but that's not right. It's

softer, like yearning. Weird, that, and even weirder is how it makes me feel.

ME

You're really selling this parenting gig. I'll get right on it.

JAKE

I wouldn't change a thing.

I know he wouldn't, toddler puke and all. The man was born to be a dad. I'm so happy for him.

JAKE

All the same, thank God for date night. Me and the missus are heading to the city for a fancy meal this evening.

ME

Sounds like you're gonna get lucky!

JAKE

Already am, bro. One day you'll understand.

If he says so.

ME

About to head into work. See you for the game this weekend?

I have tickets to a Chicago Rebels hockey game, courtesy of my friend Jude, who's dating right-winger Hudson Grey. It's nice to have connections—and especially nice not to have to concern myself with finding a babysitter.

JAKE

Can't wait. Take care out there, little bro. No unnecessary risks.

ME

Never ;)

Walking into Engine 6, I'm greeted with an empty bay. It's 7:45 in the morning, so there should be a few people sitting out here like old farts at the park, playing cards or pretending to understand chess. At least that's how it is at my former house. With no one to see me get sappy, I take a moment to breathe it in. There's something special about the firehouse at Six that gets me absolutely stoked. Only the best work here and several of the firefighters who got their wings at this house are legends.

For a moment, I question if I'm in the right place—and not just location-wise.

I've always been the joker in the pack, the kind of teen who drives a car into a mailbox (twice) or hosts a forbidden party my senior year in high school that trashes the house. I was a C student who rarely attended classes at Northwestern but somehow managed to eke out a degree, biding my time until my trust fund kicked in when I turned twenty-one. My grandfather left a sizeable chunk to Jake and me, enough to ensure I never needed to work a day in my life.

I enjoyed myself for a while—travel, booze, women—and then one day on a trip to a topless beach in the south of France, I saved a woman from drowning in the clear blue waters of the Mediterranean.

It gave me a thrill that I tried to find again with base jumping, paragliding, snowboarding, bungee, every extreme sport or adventure available. But nothing could replicate the feeling, so I turned to saving lives for a living, first as an EMT. Then I realized that firefighters get more attention of the female variety, so I moved onto that. Turns out I happen to be very good at this job.

I need to stop second-guessing my presence on Squad and recognize that I'm where I'm meant to be, even if there's no one here to greet me at this ghost house.

Heading inside past a couple of offices, the Wall of the Fallen, and toward the lounge, I push open the door and hear what sound like party poppers going off.

"Surprise, asshole!"

That's more like it. Abby and Jude rush forward and hug me, while over their shoulders I spot Lieutenant Luke Almeida, my squad leader, and Captain Wyatt Fox, the chief at Six. I've spent plenty of beer-soaked nights drinking in the bar the LT owns with his family. His oldest brother, the cap, is a hard-ass, but he runs a tight ship—totally necessary with this crew of reprobates.

"Thought you might have forgotten I was coming," I say to Abby and Jude.

"You kidding?" Jude's face lights up with a grin. "Seeing as you haven't shut up about it for a month, that does not compute."

Abby shakes my shoulders. "We got you cake!"

"Cake for breakfast. Awesome."

And it is. A classic Costco chocolate sheet with "Welcome to Squad, Hollywood!" iced on it. Since my high-profile saves, I've earned a nickname which I'd hoped to leave behind. Still, if that's the worst they can come up with, I'm doing okay.

Because I hang with Abby and Jude on the regular, I know most of the crew on the various shifts at Engine 6. Rescue Squad is divided into similar platoons and my shift will run at the same time as Jude's, which means Abby is just finishing up her overnight and about to head out. She waited around to welcome me, which doesn't surprise me because she's absolute quality.

Jude and I live in the same building in Lincoln Park. I'd expected to catch a ride with him this morning, but he said he had errands to run, and now I know why.

"So, this is how we're doing it, Garland," I say to him, using his nickname. "Starting off with lies."

"Apparently I had to be here to lift the fucking cake out of the fridge, man." He grins, all blue-eyed sparkle. These last few months have been eventful for him. He recently moved in with his guy and he's happier than I've ever seen him.

I'm seated, shooting the shit with my new crew, stuffing my face with cake, when Abby comes up behind me and kisses the top of my head.

"You out, Sullivan?"

"I am." She's heading home to see her man, Roman Rossi, formerly my LT at 70. We're an incestuous lot at CFD.

"Say hi to RoRo for me. Tell him I miss him."

"Sure you do, liar." She squeezes my shoulders. "You made it to Six, Sammie. Proud of ya."

I'm proud of myself. I can't wait to prove that this is where I belong.

My first morning on Squad is quiet, which gives me time to settle and get to know the quirks of my new crew. Team Leader, Luke, is de facto head of the Dempseys, a family of firefighters who've all worked at Engine 6 in some capacity or another over the last ten years. Their foster dad, Sean, has a prime place on the Wall of the Fallen, along with their eldest brother, Logan. I can't imagine working at the firehouse where my dad and brother died, but the Dempseys feel a special connection to this place that's tied them spiritually to the bricks-and-mortar of it for years.

Also on Squad is Tyler Brooks, a hardworking farm boy

straight from the prairie. Rounding out the crew is Alexandra Dempsey, one of the only women in CFD and the only woman on Rescue Squad. She's another Dempsey, a mom of two, and a total badass.

We spend the morning checking equipment, running ladder drills, and cooking. I'm not on the food roster this week but I reckon I will be soon enough, so I hang with Luke in the kitchen and get a feel for what kind of food is popular with this shift. Apparently, it's more gourmet on Abby's shift as she works with Gage Simpson—another Dempsey, you can't turn without stepping on one—who's married to a five-star chef and is himself a whizz at the stove. Luke's more meat and potatoes, which is fine by me.

None of the morning calls need Squad, but every time the siren goes off, I'm on my feet, ready to fling myself aboard the truck.

After the third time Luke looks up from his poker hand and shakes his head. "Killian, you're gonna throw your back out with all this jumping up and down."

"Just ready to go."

He nods, takes a sip of his water. "Pretty excited about imminent disaster, huh?"

"Of course, I don't want anyone hurt, but if it happens, I want to be the one on site. In case you haven't heard, I'm a whizz at this."

He gives me that world-weary look, the one these older guys in the business seem to have carved into their faces. Not that he's old, but he must be close to forty. A family man, like most of the guys here.

"You'll get your shot, Hollywood."

It's another ten hours before we get a call-out that needs our special skills, a road traffic accident just after seven on Fullerton with a reported crush of a minivan under the cab of a truck. Someone's probably going to get cited, but first we need to be heroes.

The ambulance is already on site when we get there. We arrived the same time as the engine, so Jude and his crew get busy trying to winch the truck off the minivan, which has been pancaked.

"We think someone's alive under that?" I mutter to Luke.

"Not looking good," he says. "Alex, we need you to get in there. Looks tight."

"On it."

The truck is hauled back enough for Alex to slide in underneath. "Male driver, female passenger." After a moment, she adds, "He's not viable. But she might—Ma'am, can you hear me?"

The next minute or so is taken up with Alex trying to communicate with the female vic while Luke outlines the extraction strategy. I'm trying to take in all the details, looking for ways I can be of use. It's one of those family vans, the ones that have decals with mom, dad, two kids, and a dog. My brother has one of those on his car and I'm always giving him shit for it. *You may as well add me to that*, I've told him. *I spend enough time with you guys.*

That's when I get the shiver, with every hair on my skin standing on edge. In this business, you learn to recognize these weird little signals, messages from the universe, like *Final Destination* portents of bad mojo. It's happening here, I suppose, because this car is the same color as Jake's, a silver Toyota Sienna. But there are a million of these vehicles in Chicago.

Luke's pulling out the Hurst tool, also known as the Jaws of Life, while Alex is still speaking soothing words to the trapped woman. I can't help myself: I'm circling the car, looking for the plate.

It's crushed, but I can make out the dealer information.

Evanston Toyota.

My brain's alarm is clanging. That has to be a coincidence. Fucking has to be.

"Killian, you with me?" Luke must have been speaking, but the siren in my head is blaring so loud I can barely hear what he's saying.

"Yeah, I'm—" Breaking off, I hunker down beside Alex. "Is she blond?" I'm trying to look past her, my heart rioting in my chest. There's a set of green fuzzy dice on the dash, and I know. I fucking know.

I gave those to Jake.

Alex squints at me. "Yeah, she is."

"Are there kids in the car?"

"Kids? Did you see something?" Alex cranes her neck, trying to get a handle on the part of the van that's already destroyed. The back of the minivan is crushed, but the kids wouldn't be here. They're with my mom because it's date night.

"No. No, I didn't." I sound like I haven't a clue what I'm doing, making dumbass assumptions, exactly the kind of amateur shit you do not want at the site of a major RTA. "I just—fuck. I think I know them. I think that's my sister-in-law."

Someone puts a hand on my shoulder and draws me back. There's shouting and some sort of commotion, and then suddenly I'm no longer at the scene. I'm behind the truck with Wyatt Fox, my new captain, and Jude, standing in front of me. Guarding me, really, because evidently, I already tried to bolt. Not away, but back to the crash. To make sure.

The shouting was coming from me.

"Can you call Jake?" This is from Jude, who sounds so reasonable, like he's the expert at the site of horrific fatality-causing accidents. That's supposed to be me.

I refocus on what he's saying. Call Jake? But he's ... *there*.

Fucking Jude, trying to give me hope.

"I don't have my phone." I usually leave it in my locker because it might get damaged during a call-out.

"You know the number?" Wyatt is holding his phone, too much of a pro to let a run interfere with his communication needs.

I nod, and he hands it to me. Jude places a hand on my shoulder, which could be supportive, restrictive, or both, while I punch the screen of my boss's phone with panic-clumsy fingers. It takes a couple of tries, but the call goes straight to voice mail.

"That might not mean anything," I say, trying to keep the desperation out of my voice. "He won't recognize the cap's number."

Jude nods, but it's a sad *whatever-gets-you-through-idiot* kind of nod.

"Can I see?" I ask.

Wyatt shakes his head as he takes back his phone. "Let's give it a couple of minutes."

"Please. If that's my sister-in-law, she needs to hear me."

Male driver. Not viable. That's what Alex said. That was my brother she was talking about. But how could she be so sure?

She's a pro, been doing this for years. That's how.

"Cap, please." I've never sounded so pathetic.

Wyatt gives me a long hard look, shares a glance with Jude, then a quick nod back at me. Fighting the instinct to run, I walk briskly around the truck, back to the car. Alex is still hunkered down, talking, telling the woman—*Annie, fuck, it's Annie*—she's in good hands. It's true. We're Squad, the best of the best.

"Alex," I say.

She looks up and past me to Wyatt, her eldest brother. Whatever she sees on his face has her moving aside.

"She's not conscious but she's still with us."

"And … the driver?"

She shakes her head.

I bend down and lean in, taking Annie's hand. The last vestiges of hope that this is someone else's tragedy vanish, replaced with a need to pull myself together. *Be strong, man. For Jake. For Annie.*

"Hey, baby mama, it's your favorite Killian." That's a joke we have, about how she should be with me instead of Jake because we're the same age. She always tells me I'm her favorite.

There's a gash on her head. Blood streams down the side of her face. I take off my glove and run a thumb across the blood, so it doesn't trickle into her eyes.

"It's okay, baby mama." My voice sounds all quivery, not like me at all. Where's the ice in my veins, the badassery that got me to this coveted spot? "I'm here. I'm not goin' anywhere."

I sneak a look past her, though really that's the last place my gaze should be straying. I need to know, to see for myself. The airbag deployed and now covers most of Jake's face, but I see enough to know it's not good.

To know it'll never be good again.

Someone squeezes my shoulder. It must be Jude because it's his voice that says, "Luke needs to open her up with the Hurst, Sammie." He adds, "the car," because that might have sounded like he was referring to Annie.

I stand back to let them split open the car's roof. The paramedics jump into action: a collar for Annie; removing her with quick, efficient care to a waiting gurney; wiping away the blood and applying an oxygen mask.

While this is going on, Luke appears at my side, and I manage to find the words that feel all wrong in my mouth. "The driver—is he gone?" I need to be told again, apparently.

My squad leader puts an arm around me, sheltering me from the crush of metal and death behind him. "He didn't make it. I'm sorry, Sam."

I snatch a breath, but all I can taste is the tang of blood in the air and the scent of diesel.

"The truck driver?"

"CPD are interviewing him now and ..." The rest is lost because Annie's eyes have fluttered open, moss-green, their usual sparkle dulled by pain and fear. I step forward and feel for her hand. Still warm, and she squeezes back.

"Annie, it's me. It's Sam."

I wait for her to say something. Ask about Jake.

The coward in me prays she doesn't.

Maura, one of the EMTs, places a hand on my arm. "We have to move her. Do you want to ride with us?"

Of course I do. I hold Annie's gaze and try to assure her, though I suspect she's not going to make it. She's too damaged. And in a way, I can't imagine her without Jake. They're a package deal and now ...

This is the end of my family as I know it ... and the start of a life I'm not sure I'm ready for.

Four

Cass

"With the way the markets are holding firm, everything is looking good, but we can't assume that'll always be the case." I smile at the nice, well-dressed couple in their mid fifties, seated on the sofa in my office. "But that's why we've diversified—bonds, Treasury bills, a cash buffer. At this point anything more than 50% in equities is too risky."

Bella Regan lets out a breath and shares a smile with her husband, Tom. "It's such a relief having you on our team, Cassandra. Selling up and retiring to France seems like such a crazy thing to do at our age, but it's been our dream for so long. Knowing the money is as safe as it can be is one less thing to worry about."

As a financial planner with Beacon, a boutique investing and retirement company in New York, I love working with people and eliminating their concerns. Of course, they can never be completely absent, but I'm on hand to help people get to a position where they feel the future is solid. No shocks, a steady road. After years of uncertainty during my teens because of my mother's flightiness, it shouldn't be a complete surprise that I'd lean into a job like this. Not especially sexy, but I'm helping people live their dreams one mutual fund at a time.

Tom clasps his hands, a signal that he's ready to get going. "We're having a going-away party before we leave the States, this Friday night. Perhaps you and your fiancé would like to come?"

Not my fiancé. I don't correct them, though. After six years together, it's an easy assumption to make.

A sudden flash of Sam Killian's smirk nicks at my good vibe. *Ugh.*

"I'd love to stop by. Make sure you're not spending the nest egg before you skip town!"

They laugh dutifully, and then we're shaking hands and I'm walking them to the door. I have about ten minutes before my next meeting, a Zoom call with a guy who wants to surf Bondi Beach after he retires from his city planner job. That gives me a chance to look at the photos Annie sent me yesterday from last weekend. It usually takes multiple nagging messages from me to get her to give me the goods.

"Tea, coffee, me?"

My friend and co-worker, Gina Diaz, is standing at the door with two cups in her hand.

"Okay if I pick coffee over you?"

"Fuck yeah it is." She shoots a quick glance over her shoulder to check no one heard her. Beacon is a pretty stuffy workplace.

She places the cup on the coffee table and takes a seat on the sofa my clients just vacated. Gina's a senior associate at Beacon, who took me under her wing when I started working here three years ago. Whenever I feel like I have no clue what I'm doing—which is about 90% of the time—Gina's on hand to tell me I've got this.

"What are we looking at?" She gestures to my phone.

"My nephew's birthday party."

God, Spence is so adorable. I love his little face so much. Of course, he wasn't quite so adorable when he was hurling his guts out after too much cake and ice cream. Uncle Sam's influence, no doubt.

"Oh, the hot EMT bro-in-law." Gina grabs the phone and fans herself with it. I never said he was hot; Gina worked that one out all by herself. And there's the Devil himself in far too many photos. The camera certainly loves all those muscles, the clear sky blues, that heartbreaker of a smile.

I take the phone back. "He's a firefighter now. Probably wasn't getting enough attention while he was bringing heart attack victims back to life."

One of the photos is of Sam standing behind me while I chat with Sylvia, his mom. He had just brought a slice of cake for us both, which was kind of sweet of him. Though maybe it was because it would have appeared odd to give something to his mom and leave me out.

At the time, I'd assumed it was another of his usual jibes. *Birthday cake for the party pooper.* (So he didn't say that, but I know he was thinking it.) I'm not a party pooper. I just want to ensure everyone has fun in a safe, appropriate way.

"He could bring me back to life any time," Gina says, practically drooling.

"He banged his date in the bathroom during a child's birthday party. The man has no shame."

Gina shrugs. "I love the no-shame ones. Be honest, if you were single ..."

"Nope. A himbo like Sam Killian would be the last man I'd be with. Sex isn't the be-all and end-all, G."

"Says the woman who's getting some on a regular basis."

Not as regular as I'd like, though I'd never share that. Gina's a single mom, divorced for two years, and is finding it hard to "get back out there," as they say. Things might not be perfect with Derek, but having someone to come home to, even if the sex is infrequent or indifferent, is better than the wilderness of single life in your thirties.

"Hey, I need to get ready for my next appointment."

"Ooh, got it. Meet for lunch at the elevators?"

"It's a date."

Gina heads to the door of my office, just as someone steps inside.

Sam.

There's a weird moment while my brain flips over, struggling with the cognitive dissonance. How a man who exists in one part of my life is now suddenly in this other part, my everyday reality. We were just talking about him, too, and for the briefest second, I wonder if I rubbed some internal magic lamp and conjured him like a genie.

That flash of whimsy dissipates as quickly as it appeared. Sam's here in New York at my place of work. Is he in the city for his job and decided to look me up? But that can't be right unless it's a firefighter safety conference or something like that. He'd never seek me out of his own free will, either, unless Annie or Jake sent him.

I'm clearly grasping at straws, my mind desperate not to go to more unsettling places. Sam's here because something is wrong.

Gina shares an amused look with me, then back at Sam, who looks like a hulk in the doorway. "You're Sam, right?"

With a curt nod, he passes over her to me. I've never seen him so grave.

"What's happened?"

"Could I come in?" Though he's already in. Invading my space. My city. My peace of mind.

Gina's picked up on the vibe, her expression shifting to concern.

"It's okay," I say to her, lying through my teeth. "Sam is ..." I don't know what he is. "Could you give us a minute?"

"Sure," she says uncertainly.

Sam comes in as Gina walks out, closing the door behind him. I stand to meet him, my heart racing, gearing up for horror.

"Is it one of the kids?" But if it was, Annie would have called me.

"I think you should sit down, Cassandra."

Cassandra. He didn't even sound sarcastic.

"Just tell me."

He inhales sharply. "A car accident last night on Fullerton. The kids are fine—they weren't there. But Annie and Jake are gone."

My knees crumple, and then I feel strong arms around me and the sofa's leather, cool to the back of my thighs. My vision blurs fast and I swipe at my eyes because I can't lose it. Not yet.

"Both of them?" He said so, but I need to hear it again. I need it drilled into me because this can't be real.

He nods. "A truck lost control. It happened fast, no chance for either of them."

Perhaps he's used to giving out bad news. People must die in his presence all the time, but maybe they have special people in the fire department to handle this. He's good at it, though. Much better than I would have expected, with that calm demeanor, direct gaze, and hand-holding.

What was it I said about those hands? Rough, calloused. Capable. I should pull away, but I need capable right now.

"Do the kids know?"

"Maya does. Spence ..." He blows out a breath, a whole world of hurt in it. "They're with my parents right now, but I'll have to get back today."

With his dad's bad health, his mom is usually run off her

feet. Maya is quiet and studious, but Spence has a ton of energy. He would need constant vigilance.

"Why didn't you call?" I can't believe he got on a plane to deliver this news. "When did it happen?"

"Last night about seven. They were headed to a restaurant for dinner. For date night."

That's one of the things I love about my sister and her husband, how they always make time for each other. It's tough with the kids, but they do weekly date nights, carving out space just for them.

Or they did.

"You should have told me the minute you found out."

"I thought—" He pauses, restarts. "You said Derek was headed to London."

Oh. No need to say another word because I get it.

He didn't want me to be alone when I got the news.

I have friends and co-workers. I could have called anyone, but I wouldn't have. I'm not sure I would've told Derek immediately if he wasn't in the same room as me.

Sam somehow understands.

The moment I recognize this, the sheer kindness of it, I break. People use the term "floodgates" and that seems to be what's happening. I'm liquid grief, a mass of quivering emotion. My sobs must be outrageous. I get the sense of a door opening, some murmured words from Sam, and the door closing again. Gina must have popped her head in to see what's wrong.

Only everything.

Next, I feel a solid weight—those strong arms again, only now I'm curled into his body, my head against his chest. He's wearing a blue-striped button-down shirt. Vaguely, I recall that it's the first time I've seen him in a collared shirt since the wedding. Did he dress up to deliver the news?

I'm conscious of getting his shirt wet, of ruining it after he went to all this effort to look nice. I'm also conscious that this is awful for him, too. He and Jake are so close, as close as Annie and me.

I inhale a bunch of snot and wipe my eyes. I must look a mess.

"Sorry," I murmur, scrabbling for some purchase on reality as embarrassment sets in.

"It's okay." His hand is still on my back, soothing in concentric circles.

"I mean, for your loss."

He nods, a quiet strength to him I would never have expected.

"Your parents must be devastated. I-I should call them."

"No rush on that. Plenty of time to comfort each other." He holds my gaze with red-rimmed eyes. He must have cried before he came to see me. "Is Derek still out of town?"

"He's due back in a few days."

"Maybe he could come back sooner?"

Maybe. Right now, I can't even think about Derek. I'm destroyed but that has to be set aside. "The kids, Sam. They're too young for this."

"I know. But we're going to get them through it." There's a determination in his voice I don't think I've ever heard before. This version of Sam seems so together, so in control. A force to be reckoned with.

We're going to need that strength for the kids—and I'm going to have to match it in the weeks and months ahead.

It's my second visit in as many weeks to Chicago and I've moved from devastated to numb.

Annie's gone.

The light of my life, my touchstone in the dark. I've never

gone a day without talking to her, checking in, texting. And now ... nothing. There's a void where my heart should be.

I still can't believe it. Last week at Spence's birthday party, she was so happy. So full of life. And she had the perfect one, too, with Jake and her babies.

Now the kids are alone. Not for much longer, though. I'm here to take care of them, to do whatever it takes.

Sylvia's a mess, which is understandable. Jake was her bright, blue-eyed boy, and she's had a rough year with Kenny's health problems. She's been keeping an eye on the kids but there's no way that can last. She has far too much on her plate.

Thankfully, Jake and Annie made a will. I encouraged Annie to take that step when Maya was born. No one wants to think of the worst, but I'm a planner, and when she asked if I'd be the kids' guardian in the case of disaster, I came back with a wholehearted "yes." Now they have no one else, or no one with full capacity to take them under their wing. I'll do it because I love them, and I love my sister.

The lawyer's receptionist shows me into his office, in a ten-story building in downtown Evanston, just north of Chicago and a few miles from where Jake and Annie lived with the kids in Winnetka.

Sam is there before me.

We haven't spoken much since I returned to Chicago two days after he came to see me in New York. A boomerang visit, he called it, because he couldn't leave the kids for too long with his mom. I wanted to return with him but thought it better to wait until Derek was back from London.

By the time I arrived in Chicago, all the funeral arrangements had been made. Sylvia, I assumed. I held Maya's hand through the service. We didn't bring Spence, instead leaving him with friends of Sam.

That was three hours ago. The rest of the afternoon was spent at Sylvia and Kenny's in Lake Forest, in a daze of *thank yous* and *what a tragedy*. Now I'm waiting for confirmation of what happens next. Derek went back to the hotel to catch up on his calls to the team in London.

"Why are you here?" I ask Sam, a touch brusquely.

He narrows his eyes, the ones that have lost their sparkle. He didn't bring a date to the funeral, which I suppose is a small mercy, but he did look good. No one should clean up this well. He's wearing a designer suit that shapes his broad shoulders to perfection. The tie is a lovely cornflower blue that highlights his hot cobalt gaze, though right now they look a little tired—both the tie and his eyes.

"Same as you."

That doesn't really answer my question, so I turn to the lawyer, Mr. Sommers.

"Do you know how long it'll take for the paperwork? The guardianship details." I assume the kids have been well provided for, with Jake's trust fund going to their care and education.

Mr. Sommers coughs slightly. "That's what we're going to discuss, Ms. Ferguson. Typically, these things take a few months, but in this case, we recognize that an emergency order of guardianship needs to be put in place. I understand that you're based in New York—"

"Yes. But I can stay for a few days and wrap things up. I've already started investigating schools for Maya. And there's a preschool near where I live. Of course, it has a waiting list a mile long, but I know one of the board members—she's a client of mine—so I think we can fast-track it."

Mr. Sommers looks slightly bemused. That's when I feel it, the heated stare of the other person in the room.

I turn, feeling like my head is in a stop-motion jerk. I know it's tough for him—it's tough for us all—but I'm not sure I deserve such disdain.

"What? I'm just being organized."

"Sure you are," Sam says. "But if you'd take a second to listen, you'll realize that John here has something to say."

I blink, not liking his tone but reluctant to get into it with a witness. We usually keep the animosity on the down low.

"Of course. Go ahead, Mr. Som—uh, John." They're on a first names' basis? I've evidently missed something.

"Joint guardianship can be tricky, especially when the guardians are not based in the same city," the lawyer continues. "Or state."

"Wait a second. Did you say joint guardianship?" I slide a look at Sam. "But Sylvia has too much going on with her husband's ill health. She can't look after two very active kids."

Sam taps the arm rest with his fingertips. There's impatience in the gesture. "And no one expects her to, Cassie."

"It's Cassandra."

Sam raises an eyebrow and shoots a look of *see what I'm dealing with* at the lawyer. When he came to New York to deliver the bad news, we were in sync, united in shock and grief. I can't imagine anyone ever holding me as securely as he did then. Now we're back to our usual dynamic.

Only there's something else going on. Some subtext I'm not understanding until Sam speaks again.

"Well, Cassandra." Attitude *fully* noted. "The joint guardianship is with me. You and I are going to be looking after Maya and Spence. And we'll be doing it in Chicago."

FIVE

That's impossible. My head is spinning at the sheer implausibility of it.

Annie wouldn't have done this, and if she did, she would have told me. She knows—*knew*—how I feel about her brother-in-law.

"Is there some legal reason for doing this?" I ask the lawyer because I refuse to believe that's an actual instruction in the will.

"The will is very clear," he says, dashing my hopes. "Both of you have been assigned as guardians to the children in the event of the incapacitation or death of their parents. This assumes, of course, that you're willing to take on this role. If one of you wishes to renege, there's a legal process for that."

"Not going to happen," Sam says at the same time I say, "No chance."

We glare at each other. Oh boy, this is going to be rough.

"But my life isn't in Chicago," I continue cautiously.

"The kids' lives are," Sam says, as if I don't already know that. "Along with the rest of their family."

The insinuation is that I'm not family, or not enough. "Yes, of course, but ..." I don't have a strong argument, not unless I insult the man before me. But surely, he can see—anyone can see—that he's not guardianship material. How would he fit it in between his daredevil job and his manwhoring extra-curriculars?

"I have a job in New York. An apartment. A fi—a boyfriend." Not a fiancé. Derek and I hadn't discussed the likely outcome of today's meeting, the outcome where I'm now the parent to two small, grieving children. I wasn't quite ready to have that conversation with him so I'd let him assume that the kids would be staying with their grandparents until I had the official word from the lawyer. Derek would be on board—I hope—once it's clear that these were my sister's wishes.

But a shared custody agreement? How would that even work?

Mr. Sommers looks mildly sympathetic. "This is a tough situation all around. One of you could initiate proceedings for full custody"—he says this with a certain distaste—"but no judge would grant it immediately. There would be an expectation that you try to work this out amongst yourselves or take it to mediation before getting the courts involved. And given the strong family ties to the Chicago area, the preference would likely be for the children to remain here, at least for the foreseeable future. Perhaps you should take a few days to think about next steps, Ms. Ferguson."

I'm not sure what the correct response is here. Initiate these custody proceedings? Give in to Sam? Is there some middle ground that works best for the kids? I need to talk to my own lawyer—which means I need to find one—not the guy who's clearly in the pocket of the Killians. I'm also very conscious that they're wealthy and have the resources to drag this out.

The lawyer pulls out an envelope. I recognize my name in Annie's loopy script.

"This is from your sister." He hands it over and I take it with shaky hands. "And there's one for you, Sam. From Jake."

The introduction of this personal touch from beyond the grave gives us both a moment to breathe and recall that everyone involved is hurting.

Sam's awfully quiet as he turns the envelope over in his hands. Pain rolls off him in waves.

I strive for a more conciliatory tone. "Is this what you want?"

"What I want is for my brother and his wife to still be with us. But that's not possible so we have to work with their wishes and what's best for the kids."

"But is this what *you* want? To be the parent to these kids?"

His eyes turn cool, picking up on the barely veiled criticism. I just can't hide it.

"Because you think I wouldn't want to step up? That I'm not a suitable guardian?"

"I-I don't know if you are. I've seen no evidence of responsibility from your end."

His nostrils flare. "Don't worry, Cassandra. I'm more than capable of taking care of those kids. After all, I'm just a big kid myself, right?"

"I've never said that. And that's not especially relevant here."

"No, it's not. What's relevant is what's best for Maya and Spence. We have to get them through the next few months— longer than that. We have to work together."

I'd never have expected such ... reasonableness from this man. Though likely it's a show for the lawyer, anything to make me look like the bad guy for wanting to whisk them away to a safe and secure home.

He's right about this one thing—we have to work together —but that doesn't mean he's going to get his way. This lawyer might think I have little chance of getting full custody anytime soon, but I'm going to need a second opinion. When I return to New York, my nephew and niece should be with me.

Because that's what's best.

Outside the lawyer's office, I ask about a bathroom. I need to be alone to see what Annie wrote, an explanation for what she's just unloaded on me. The receptionist points toward a door along the corridor and I head there quickly, lumbering like a drunken toddler. I think I hear Sam calling my name —*Cass*—but I'll break if I talk to him now.

I lock myself in the stall, though I don't sit down. It's nicer than the standard public restroom but that means jack in this day and age.

I have a couple of texts from Gina. She wanted to come to the funeral, but getting last-minute childcare for her kids was impossible.

GINA

I'm here when and if you need me.

An hour later she sent another.

Gunderson stunk up the microwave again with a salmon poke bowl. Freda made a sign.

A photo of the sign follows.

> The next person who puts fish in here will
> rue the day.

Someone, likely not Freda, who is the office hall monitor, doodled a comical old man shaking a fist. I sniff, half-heartedly smiling at life going on without me.

GINA

> Just a break in regular grief programming.
> Still here if you need me.

Carefully, I open the envelope the lawyer gave me. Just one page, which disappoints me. I don't think any of this can be explained in so few words.

Dear Cass,

I hope you never have to read this, but if you are reading, it means something awful has happened. The instruction is to give it to you in the case of Jake and me being out of the picture (I know, a euphemism you won't appreciate!). Sis, you're getting this letter because we need your help.

When Mom left us, you stepped up. You put your life on hold, and if this is happening, you're going to have to do it again. Luckily there'll be enough money to take care of everyone, including you (these people have pots of it!). I know you have a career and a life you love, but I'm hoping that you'll be able to balance that with Maya and Spence. You'll also have Sam. I can't imagine what the poor guy is thinking, especially as this will have a major impact on his sex life :) But Jake and I truly believe you guys would make a great team as co-guardians of our babies. What that looks like is up to you. I only ask that you give him a chance and think through how it will work.

I know I've disappointed you, Cass. First off, I'm guessing you saw this single page and muttered, "for fuck's sake" because I couldn't write a tome explaining it all. But mostly I know you had plans for me. You wanted more than an unplanned pregnancy and child-bride wedding (sure, I was 21 when we got hitched, but I know what you thought). You worked so hard to get me into college and I screwed it up my first time out of the city by thinking with my vaj! Sorry, sis. But also, not sorry because I wouldn't trade my life with Jake, Maya, and Spence for the world. I'm where I'm meant to be. (Though if you're reading this letter, I'm evidently meant to be somewhere else. God, I hope they have sour cream and onion Pringles in heaven. I hope I make it to heaven.) Don't worry about me, though I'll try to give you a sign about the Pringles.

All these things happen for a reason. And you taking care of my babies is meant to be as well.

I'm guessing, because Sam got his own letter, that he's in a bad place. Be kind to each other. That kindness will go a long way.

I love you, Cass.

Annie

I'm not sure how long I stay still, making myself smaller, clutching the paper and wishing I'd never had to read it at all.

Oh, Annie. How could you do this to me?

These days, I'm in a constant state of dehydration (tears) and rehydration (face splashing). I take the second step in this new skincare regimen, dry my hands, and open the door.

Sam is there. God, why can't he leave me alone?

"Yes?"

"Just checking in to see if you're okay."

My first instinct is to scream at him, some variation of "of course I'm not okay!" alternating with "how dare you assume I'm not?" But then I remember Annie's request.

Be kind to each other.

Is that what Jake told Sam in his letter?

"I'm fine. Just catching my breath."

"It's a lot to take in," he says neutrally.

"But nothing we can't handle." My cheer is forced, though I'm not sure I need to hide that from Sam. We've never really needed to fake it around each other. Rather than be prescriptive, I decide to keep things on an even keel. "What happens next?"

If he's surprised at my agreeable tone, he doesn't let on. I'll agree with him all the way to a custody hearing where I emerge victorious.

He tilts his head. "Let's talk about it."

I slip into the hotel room quietly, conscious that Derek is probably still on a conference call with his team in London. He's lying back on the bed, his finger positions on his phone indicating he's playing a game.

I don't expect him to be long faced while I'm gone, but it bothers me all the same.

"Calls all done?"

"Yeah, just a moment ago. There's resistance to the terms of the share option package." He moves off the bed and comes to greet me with his arms open. I fall into them, needing his solid warmth and soothing tone. "How did it go?"

My muscles re-tighten at his question. "Terrible. Annie and Jake picked Sam and me to be joint guardians."

I'm hoping that phrasing it like a worst-case scenario, where I'm forced to work with someone like Sam, will get Derek on my side quickly. Perhaps I should have prepared him more, but that can't be helped now.

He draws back with raised eyebrows. They're not that expressive, not like Sam Killian's which always seem to be telling me something I don't want to hear.

Two men have never been so different. Unlike muscle-bound Sam, my boyfriend is rangy and loose-limbed with what books would describe as "boyish good looks," including big brown eyes and sandy hair that doesn't encourage tousling or tunneling. It's too short for that, which is fine. Derek is very clean-cut, something I appreciate in a man.

Right now, his expression is carefully blank, and I almost wish I could read him better like I can Sam.

"I assumed the grandparents would be on the hook. How's that going to work?"

"I don't know. I thought I'd be here a few days to help wrap up things and then the kids would move with us back to New York."

Derek's demeanor changes—I can read this perfectly. "With us?"

"Sylvia doesn't have the energy to manage the kids, not with Kenny's health."

"Yeah, but Sam's on hand. And the kids' lives are here. Schools, friends, all that."

Whose side is he on? "But he's not qualified for this."

"And you are?"

"More than him. I raised my sister."

"Once she was a teen. Not quite the same thing." He must see my hurt because he quickly backtracks. "Of course, you're qualified, but is that what's best for them? They've just lost their parents. Is taking them away from everything they know the best way to help them grieve?"

He sounds so reasonable, just like Sam Killian an hour ago in the lawyer's office. Yet I can't help thinking that Derek's not really thinking of the kids' best interests, only his own.

We've never discussed children in any deep way. Or rather, I've brought it up and he usually changes the subject. I've not pushed back on that or demanded that he talk about it. Part of me assumed he's right—who wants kids when our lives are already perfect? No responsibilities, or at least none that involve the well-being of pliable little minds.

But now everything has changed. For all intents and purposes, I'm about to become a mom to two kids who need me. Derek doesn't seem to understand that my life has already changed irreparably and that means his life will change as well.

"We haven't covered the topic of kids much," I say, still

using my tiptoeing-on-eggshells voice. Even today of all days, I need to be careful. "For us."

He takes a seat on the bed, rubs his eyes. "We haven't. To be honest, I never thought we needed to, that we were on the same page. I remember when we met after your sister got married. You were disappointed that she dropped out of college to have a kid and get hitched. You thought she was too young."

I'm surprised he recalls that. "What's that got to do with kids?"

"You said at the time that kids just break your heart. You make all these sacrifices, and they throw it in your face."

Was I really that bitter? At the time, I was upset, worried that Annie was throwing her life away. I'd worked hard to get her through high school, to push her toward college, to future-proof her life. And one night of passion wiped all that effort away.

By the time she married Jake, I'd come around to them as a couple. As a family. But obviously I still had some residual resentment, which I'd shared with Derek. Interesting that he remembers and is so ready to produce it as evidence now.

"I was concerned about her, the unplanned pregnancy, the whirlwind relationship with Jake, giving up college. I might have expressed my concern in a way that sounded resentful, but my sister was happy." For too few years, but she and Jake built a wonderful life together. "I was happy for her, eventually. That doesn't mean *I* didn't want kids of my own. Or that I'm ready to give up on my nephew and niece because it's geographically inconvenient."

Derek studies me, like he's seeing me for the first time. Does he really have no idea who I am or what I want? Or have we coasted on our routines for so many years that these fundamental needs and values come as a surprise?

"You've got to do what you think is best," he says, all diplomacy.

I do. And it also means I need to start laying the groundwork for a custody case, the sooner the better.

I take a breath, glad to have a purpose to see me through the next few weeks. Only I suspect Derek's not going to like the sacrifice I'll have to make to move this forward.

"Let me tell you what I have in mind."

Six

Sam

"How did it go?"

My mom meets me at the front door of the house in Lake Forest where we grew up, drying her hands on a dish towel. She's still wearing the suit she wore to the funeral, likely because she hasn't had a moment to spare. She looks absolutely wrecked.

"Cassandra expected to get sole custody."

Mom bristles like an offended cat. "Those babies can't be taken away, not when they need their family around them. What would she do? She works." Said as if it's equivalent to cannibalism. My mom has never worked and neither did Annie.

"Lots of people work, Mom. I don't think she was thinking it through. She knows you have a lot going on—"

"Not so much I can't take care of those kids!"

I place my hand on her shoulder and kiss her forehead. "Jake and Annie drew up wills and appointed both me and Cassie as guardians."

Cue the Sylvia Killian mouth drop.

"I know. I've no idea how it's going to work either. But the lawyer was clear that the kids are staying here, at least for now." I've no doubt Cassie has her own lawyer on speed dial while she works out how to screw me over. And while John Sommers can advise on the broad brush strokes, his specialty is estate planning rather than family law. I'll need to consult with someone else to shore up my family's position.

Jake's letter is hot lava in my pocket. I haven't opened it yet. I'm not ready to have that conversation, which I imagine will be earnest encouragement and lots of "rah rah, you can do this!" I didn't even realize I was a choice, except now I recall a half-drunken conversation a couple of years back.

If anything happens, Sammie, you'll look after them for me. My family.

Course I will, bro. I got you. Now gimme another shot of that Laphroaig.

But, to put it in writing? To trust me, of all people, with the care of his most precious people? Clearly, he never expected to have to put that faith to the test.

My mom's still stunned but, in true Sylvia Killian style, manages to find the words to express what we are all feeling about this new development.

"How are you going to do this? You don't have any experience with kids."

In the last five years, I've channeled my worst impulses into being a professional do-gooder, but my parents haven't forgotten the Sammie of old. I don't make it easy with my frequent swapping out of bedmates and my disinclination to settle. Sure, there's my job, and while it makes them proud, they're still waiting for the punchline.

Bottom line: I'm the last person who should be in charge of impressionable young minds. I'm nothing like Jakey.

But there's no way St. Cassandra is taking those kids away from us.

"I'm a quick learner, Mom. And Cass will be helping."

"In what way?"

I grimace, remembering my parting words to her in the lawyers' office.

No point paying for a hotel. If you're going to be here for a few more days, you should stay at Jake and Annie's.

She'd looked surprised until the enormity of that offer dawned on her.

Where will you be?

In the room next door.

She hadn't liked that one bit. But if she wants to start establishing her case for being sole guardian, she needs to put in the work. She can't parent them from a thousand miles away. She also needs to know that I will be on her sweetheart-shaped ass every step of the way.

This reminds me that I need to broach a tricky subject with my mom.

"I'm thinking of taking the kids back home to the house, trying to get them back into a routine." I read this sage bit of advice online while I was waiting for Cassie at the lawyer's office. "Cass will be staying for a few days while we work out the logistics, and it would be easier if we set up a household of some sort."

"What's wrong with here? This is the best place for them."

"Mom, you're dead on your feet." I squeeze her arm, trying to soothe. We have a nurse come in every day for a few hours to help but of course, Mom wants to do everything herself. No one is ever good enough.

"Between Dad and the care you've provided for the kids these last few days"—not to mention second-guessing every decision I made for the funeral arrangements—"you need a rest. That's what I'm here for. What Cass is here for."

"But—they're not ready." *You're not ready.*

I might never be, but the sages of the Internet will provide. I have two weeks compassionate leave, enough time to arrange childcare, figure out routines, soothe a few sore hearts. Luckily money isn't an issue, and we can afford to hire a nanny if it comes to that. It likely would because Cassie isn't going to give up her job, either.

"We'll figure it out."

My mom looks skeptical, but even she must see that all these strong-willed adults under the same roof will not help the kids adjust to their lives going forward.

"If you think this is best." Said as if she knows better but the adrenaline is fading, and her tiredness is finally asserting itself.

"I know you don't think I can do this."

"No, that's not it. I'm just not sure it's fair on you."

Fair? Nothing about this is fair.

Mom hasn't asked me about the accident, about what I saw. A small part of me wonders if she blames me for not doing more. This is supposed to be my job, after all, but when it came down to the wire, I couldn't do a thing. I don't want to have to tell her the details, so I need to come up with a story that makes it clear it all happened quickly. That it was over before I even made it on site, even though I can still see Annie's green eyes as they fluttered open one last time. She couldn't speak but her eyes said it all.

Take care of my babies.

The kids are in the living room. Spence is playing with a Transformer toy while Maya is reading a book on her iPad. Abby looked after Spence during the funeral at Jake and Annie's house, but Maya came to the service, sitting between me and Cassie with a steely fortitude beyond her years.

I take a seat on the sofa beside my niece. "What's the book about?"

"A wizard." Before I can weigh in, she gives me a withering look. "Not that wizard. A girl wizard."

"Isn't that a witch?"

Maya raises green eyes to mine, her mom's eyes. Cassie's, too. I've never noticed it before—maybe I preferred not to— but Maya is the spitting image of her aunt. Blonde, fair, serious. Spence takes more after his dad, which means more like me.

"Not in this book."

Telling her that her parents were gone was the hardest thing I've ever done, even harder than telling Cassie, which was awful. Maya hasn't cried yet, at least not in my presence. I wonder if I need to get a therapist for her. For them both.

Spence knows something is up but as far as he's aware, his parents are on vacation. He thinks they're hanging with Mickey Mouse because Disneyland is the only vacation spot he knows.

"How would you feel about going back home?"

She winces at the mention of "home." It can never be the same for her. I wonder if it's a good or bad thing to take them back there.

"I don't know," she says, and I love her for her honesty.

Taking a leaf from her book, I come up with an immediate counter. "Or we could stay at my place in the city."

She thinks on that. "Like we're on vacation."

"Exactly. We'd need to pick up some stuff at your house, but you can give me a list. Your aunt Cass could do it."

I'm not sure if this is normal—asking an eight-year-old for input about where they'd prefer to live—but then nothing these days is normal. Jake and Annie should be here and I sure as hell should not be a dad when I have no fucking clue what I'm doing. Shouldas abound.

"Spence might be scared." She whispers this as she leans in closer to me, an invitation for me to hold her.

I put an arm around her and gather her close. "You mean if he's not in his usual bedroom."

She nods.

"But what would you prefer?" Because I think I can look after Spence. He can sleep with me if he's scared. Also, I can control the battlefield more if we're at my place.

Cassie's going to hate this idea. A petty, immature part of me enjoys that.

"I-I don't think I want to go home just yet. But I need some things."

Good. "Okay. Make a list on your iPad and send it to me. Do you know how to text from this thing?"

She gives me that imperious Cassandra look and says patiently, "Yes, Uncle Sam."

"Great. Hey, buddy," I call out to my nephew.

He looks up.

"C'mere, I want to run something by you."

He brings his toy over and stands before me. He's getting big, but not so big I can't still scoop him up and put him in my lap while giving him a sloppy kiss on the neck.

"No kissing!"

"Right, got it. So, Spence, your sister and I have this great idea. We're going to hang out at my place and watch movies for a while."

"Can we bring Waffles?" Waffles is the family's Irish setter, and I cannot leave him with my mom. Luckily my building is okay with pets, and if they weren't it wouldn't matter because fuck 'em.

"You betcha."

"And Mom and Dad will be home soon?"

I should be better at this. At the Firefighter Academy, we have communications training for dealing with the public and people who've suffered loss. But we don't usually have to work with kids—that's what social workers are for.

"One day. In a little while."

Now, to make another difficult call.

SEVEN

Cass

We've pulled up in a town car outside the apartment building in upscale Lincoln Park, but I'm taking my time. Dithering, Derek calls it.

We should be at Annie and Jake's house in Winnetka, but Sam said Maya wasn't ready to go back. Then he followed it up with a list of stuff I needed to pick up once I'd checked in for a key from the neighbor. I don't mind running errands, but I would have liked to be consulted about the living arrangements. Sam's taking charge, using his closeness to the kids, to assign me to a secondary role.

Derek turns to me. "Honey, I wish I could stay. You know I would if I wasn't so swamped with this deal."

"It's fine! I'm just glad you could come at all."

"Like I could leave you alone in all this."

But that's exactly what you're doing. Derek flew in with me yesterday, but he can't stay because of the Pilkington merger, which is still at a critical juncture. He's returning to London in a few hours.

"I'm not looking forward to spending any more time with Sam Killian than I have to."

It's one thing to be holed up in a five-bedroom mansion with more than adequate wandering room, quite another to be in a cramped condo in the city. I find it hard to believe there are places for all of us to sleep. Though maybe it's bigger than I imagine. The building is called the Gloucester, which is about as pretentious a name as I've ever heard.

Derek looks sympathetic. He knows my feelings here—I voice them often enough.

"It won't be long." Though he doesn't say how he knows this. "And maybe you'll find he's not the worst after all."

I start at that. "You're taking his side now? He's an absurd choice for a guardian!"

Derek gives a pained smile. He thinks Sam is just as ridiculous as I do, but he's being awfully nice about the man lately. Sam Killian might be King of the Hot Idiots, but apparently that doesn't disqualify him from being the kids' caregiver.

"Cass, you have to do what's best for the kids."

"You think they should stay here? With him?"

"No, no, not at all." But I know what I heard—and it's confirmed by his next words. "Are you ready to be a mom? It might put a stall in your career track."

"This is what Annie wanted." Plus plenty of women have children and succeed professionally. Gina, for one, though her divorce is recent. She had the support of a partner until she caught him cheating with her best friend.

"I know," he says, soothing, though on Derek it comes off as patronizing. "I just don't think you should dismiss Killian so quickly. He might have a better support network than you think."

That's what I'm afraid of. Annie was all I had and now I've never felt more alone, which is a strange feeling when you're in a long-term relationship with someone. A by-product of the grief, I suppose.

"You said you had the name of that lawyer, the one who specializes in family law."

"I'll call her and send the details to you." He squeezes my hand. "Let's not make any rash decisions. You're in a vulnerable state right now so I need you to take some time. Deep breaths."

If I breathe any deeper, I'll only use it to scream at him.

"I should go," I say before I lose my temper. "I'll grab the stuff from the trunk."

He gets out and helps, by leaving the suitcases on the sidewalk, one for me, and one filled with the items Sam asked me to pick up from the house. "Cass, I'm going to miss my flight. Otherwise, I'd ..." His voice notches an octave deeper, and it doesn't take long to figure out why. "Sam."

My new roommate must have been waiting inside the building's foyer, watching for me. Now here he is in a Chicago Fire Department T-shirt stretched tight across his pecs, like he has to convince the world of his good guy credentials. *We get it, you run into burning buildings.*

Okay, that's not fair. When will I stop feeling so angry?

"Where are the kids?"

"Upstairs."

"Alone?"

Sam's lips flutter, like he expected this. He's only too happy to provoke me. "My friend Hudson is with them."

A stranger? Perfect. I share a quick glance at Derek, but he's already leaning in, pumping Sam's hand and muttering something about loss and taking care. A quick kiss on my cheek, a promise to call, and then he's gone, all while Sam Killian watches—and judges.

As the car drives away, he says, "Let's get you inside."

In the lobby, a uniformed doorman comes forward with a luggage cart, like the kind you find in nicer hotels.

"This is Benji," Sam says. "He runs things around here. Benji, this is Ms. Ferguson."

"Cass," I say, not wanting to be overly formal. Derek's always calling me out for being too nice to doormen and servers, like it's a sign I'm not comfortable with wealth. And maybe I'm not. I wasn't born into it like the Killians.

"Why don't you go on up, Mr. Killian?" Benji says, and the notion of anyone calling Sam mister almost makes me laugh. "I'll follow with the luggage."

"Sounds good. Come on, Cassie."

I don't correct him. I won't be here long enough to let that bother me.

Stepping into the elevator, I'm suddenly conscious of the small space. Sam takes up a lot of it and I find myself inching away to the wall, anything to create more of a boundary between us.

"How are they?"

"Maya's putting on a brave face. Spence still doesn't know."

It's been five days. "Where does he think they are?"

"Disneyland."

I bite my lip. I can't criticize because I'm not sure I'd know how to handle it either. When I took over as parent for Annie, she was already a teenager. I never had to mother her when we were younger, so solutions for the three-year-old demo aren't in my wheelhouse.

The elevator stops and he gestures for me to leave before him. Once out, he leads the way.

"How many apartments are on each floor?"

"Just two. My neighbor's a party girl who sleeps all day. The walls are thick, so her nighttime activities won't bother you."

Huh, I'll be the judge of that.

He turns before we get to the door. "Thanks for going to the house and picking up what the kids need. I would have gone but it was better to get the kids out of my mom's as soon as possible."

"How's Sylvia holding up?"

"These last few days have been draining for her with looking out for the kids as well as my dad."

"It's a tough situation all around."

He opens the door and we're immediately greeted by a friendly beast. Waffles! I'm overwhelmed with memories. "I had no idea he'd be here."

"Couldn't leave him with my mom and as soon as I mentioned that we were staying here for a bit, Spence was all over the Waffles situation. I think he'll make a good distraction."

I don't mind. In fact, I'm psyched to see him. Waffles was my dog as a puppy, but I couldn't keep him in my apartment in New York.

"He used to be mine."

Sam looks surprised. "Yeah?"

"I had to give him up. Those trips to Chicago were just as much to see him."

I hunker down to give Waffles a hug, letting myself absorb his doggie warmth and strength.

A knock sounds at the door. Sam opens it to find Benji there with the luggage. I leave them to it while I take in the space, Waffles as my tour guide.

I'm not sure what I expected—a bachelor pad, perhaps, with emphasis on a 60" TV and an entertainment system. Maybe pictures of dogs playing poker, the floor littered with half-eaten wings and lacy thongs. Judging by the roomy entryway, this place is huge—about three times as big as my apartment in New York—but also strangely intimate.

That might have something to do with the gallery of photos on the wall. I know I need to see the kids, but I've stuck here, staring at photos of the Killian family. Informal shots at events I haven't attended because I live in a different city, and my outsider status is nowhere better encapsulated than by this wall.

Except there are a couple of me. One is with Annie, a candid of the two of us laughing, maybe taken at Thanksgiving? I've never seen it before and it's odd to see it now on a stranger's wall, like my own life is being lived without me.

Feeling discombobulated, I turn to the other one that features me, from Annie and Jake's wedding. I'm standing with my sister, Jake, and Sam, with Maya in my arms. She was almost two years old, and I spent most of the day carrying her around. I didn't need to do that, but I wanted to help. I wanted to—I don't know—be a part of the family that Annie was marrying into. This rambunctious bunch, who were surprisingly down to earth, considering their wealth.

The night before, at the rehearsal dinner, I'd encountered Sam for the first time. I'd met most of the Killians over the years except for the youngest son who was always away. College, living it up, spending his trust fund.

"Sam, this is Cass."

"Your mom."

Annie smiled. "My sister-mom. The best of both worlds."

I'd felt old in that moment. Annie was giving me my due, but she'd already distanced herself from me, embedding with the Killians and their home-made perfection. For over two years, Annie had been part of the Killian family unit in Chicago while I was slowly pushed to the edges.

Annie's "sister-mom" correction was meant to acknowledge me, the important role I'd played in her upbringing. For years, it had been the two of us and when she told me she was pregnant after a one-night stand, a girls' trip to Chicago, I'd vowed to take care of her. That we'd bring up the baby together.

But Jake stepped up, in true hero fashion, because he knew a good thing when he saw it. He'd fallen for Annie the moment he laid eyes on her, and her pregnancy was a sign that they were meant to be. The Killians and their charm sucked my sister in.

I won't be left out again.

My hand is nudged by a wet nose. Waffles is looking for attention, and it's enough to pull me out of my memory download.

Further in, we come to the living room. It's bright and airy with nice, comfortable furniture and modern art that's surprisingly not dog or poker themed. Maya has headphones on and doesn't notice me. But Spence does. His face lights up, then collapses in confusion.

He thought I was Annie.

We look alike, more a similarity in coloring than a close resemblance. I hate that the sight of me might have caused him a single drop of pain, but I know this is a minor cut compared to the hurt that lies ahead.

Another man is in the room, sitting with Spence. I recognize him instantly: Hudson Grey, forward with the Chicago Rebels hockey franchise. It's so strange to meet someone famous in this situation.

"Oh, hello. When Sam said Hudson, I didn't make the connection."

He smiles, a little diffidently, color flooding his fair skin. Then he turns serious again as he stands and reaches for my hand.

"So sorry for your loss and that I couldn't make the service." He murmurs it like he doesn't want the kids to hear.

I swallow. "Thank you. That's very kind."

He looks around, seeming unsure of next steps. "Maybe I should let you settle? We live in the building so give us a shout if you need anything."

"Okay. Thanks for watching them. I'm a big fan."

Gosh, what a stupid thing for me to say. I *am* a big fan, but now is probably not the time to gush like a silly schoolgirl.

He looks a little surprised as he mumbles his thanks. Smiling, he ruffles Spence's hair and inclines his head to Maya, touching her shoulder lightly. She looks up and nods, then blinks as he walks away, leaving me to think that I have no clear idea of Sam's relationship with the kids, of who else is in their life. The ties between uncle and niblings are likely much stronger than I realized.

Stronger than mine.

I sit between them, and Maya politely removes her headphones. I didn't notice before, but I see now that she has a sketchbook and has been doodling. Though doodling isn't an adequate descriptor.

"Wow, Maya, this is amazing." She's drawn several characters that look like fairies or vampires. Vampire fairies with wings and sharp teeth. Something lurches inside me, a call back to another time when I used to pour myself onto the page like this.

I place an arm around her. "How are you?"

"Okay. Did you get the stuff?"

"I did. Your uncle has your suitcase at the door."

Nodding, she puts the pad down and slips out of my grasp to go investigate. Fine, it gives her something else to focus on.

"Let me know if anything is missing."

"Okay," she calls back, a strange distance in her voice. Or maybe it's how cavernous the apartment feels.

I take a closer look at Spencer, who's playing a game on Maya's iPad.

"Hey, Spence."

He looks up, expectant, his little snub nose the cutest thing I've ever seen. I'm fighting tears at the yearning in his expression, yearning he doesn't know what to do with.

He crawls into my arms which is when Sam walks in.

"Hey," he says as he takes a seat beside us.

Spence is buried in my neck. He knows something is wrong, but he has no idea what or how to deal with it. I'm right there with him.

"I was going to order pizza," Sam says. "What do you like?"

"No olives or green peppers."

"Gotcha. Maya's in her room—well, she and Spence are sharing. I've put you in the bedroom at the back. Unfortunately, you have to share a bathroom with me."

"I'll manage." It emerges from my mouth stiffly. We're acting like strangers—which is what we are, I suppose. There's an underlying tension because we both want something the other can't have.

Full custody of the kids.

Or I assume that's what he wants. That he'd love to elbow me out of the picture. We haven't discussed it. I wonder if we might never discuss it, just let the lawyers have at it.

For now, we're forced to be careful. After the surprise of the will, we've been painfully polite to each other.

It won't last, but I won't be the first to break.

———

The pizza is thin-crust, Neapolitan style, and surprisingly good. (Us New Yorkers have high standards.) Before the delivery, I asked Maya if she needed help unpacking her suitcase, and she looked at me like I'd asked the most ridiculous question in the world.

"I'm not a baby."

"I know that. But we all need help sometimes."

She shook her head, pitying me. She suddenly looked older, which cracked something in my chest. It was a week for heartbreak, that was for sure.

We ate at the dining table, which looked like it rarely got any use. I suspect Sam doesn't cook much and probably exists on takeout when he's not working long shifts at the firehouse.

"When do you have to return to work?" I ask him.

"I've got a couple of weeks leave." There's challenge in his voice. In other words, I'd better not think I can use his not being around as fodder for my case. "How about you?"

"I can stay as long as I need to." It's not strictly true, but I can do most of my client meetings on Zoom and see how far I can push it. My boss Joanna has been very supportive so far.

"Can we watch *Toy Story*?" Maya asks. "It's Spence's favorite. Or one of them."

"Of course!" Sam and I say in unison, then share a weird moment of recognition combined with annoyance.

"Come on, Spence," Maya says, taking her brother's hand to lead him to the sofa. I'm about to ask if she knows how to use the TV—other people's TVs are always so needlessly complicated—but the opening scene of the movie is already on the screen before I can verbalize an offer of help. I'm guessing the kids have spent a lot of time here.

I close up the pizza boxes and head to the kitchen while Sam follows.

"Where should I ...?"

"Top of the stove is fine for now." I leave them on the counter because I don't like leaving things on a stovetop even if it is completely safe.

"If you need to go out," I start, "then don't mind me."

He pulls a beer from the fridge and holds it. I shake my head and he proceeds to uncap it.

"Why would I be going anywhere the day I buried my brother?"

I blink at his direct approach. I'm used to people talking around their feelings, the double-speak glibness of the business world and even Derek.

"I didn't mean tonight. I meant in a couple of days, if you're suffering from cabin fever."

He frowns. "Might be time to discuss how this is going to play out."

"Oh?"

"Yeah, oh." His mocking tone rankles. I might have been playing coy, but I don't need that attitude.

He seems to realize that because his next words are gentle. "Everyone's grieving here, Cass. You, me, the kids, my parents. This isn't the time to be looking for fissures. The people who matter most are Maya, Spence, and you, and I'm—"

"Wait, why are you including me in that group?"

He runs a hand through his hair. It's thick and lustrous and doesn't look like it has hair product in it, unlike Derek's which always feels stiff. Or used to. I don't touch him much anymore.

"Because you lost your sister. The one person who meant the most to you and now you must be feeling incredibly alone. Here in a strange city, trying to be brave for the kids. I'm saying that you don't have to do that. I can take the kids out if you need time for yourself, to scream, to … break."

My mouth has fallen open. I'm taken back to that moment in my office a few days ago when he held me close as I absorbed the news into my blood and bones. I hate that he saw that, that he was the one to hold me and I'm determined it will never happen again. One meltdown is more than enough.

"But this has happened to you as well." Unless he and Jake weren't as close as I thought.

"It has. But I have my family—my parents to lean on."

It sounds like they would have to lean on him. And if he's allowing me this grace, where does that leave him? When does he have the time to fall apart?

"I won't be breaking," I say. I have to be strong because it's my best chance of getting full custody. I need to project stability, security, and serenity. "I won't be doing anything that makes it worse for the kids."

"Okay. I'm just saying you have the option. It's going to take time for the kids to adjust, for us all to adjust. We need to make the best of it."

Yet again, his reasonableness puts my back up. I can't believe how different he sounds. How mature. It has to be an act, or a grief-induced personality change, because the Sam Killian I know is not ready for this responsibility.

"Yes, we do," I say. "I think I'll unpack and then watch the movie with the kids."

He nods, turning away as I leave.

EIGHT

Cass

I can't sleep.

It's a combination of things. Pain, grief, worry for the kids, out of my comfort zone. I'm *here*, in the same place as Sam Killian of all people.

That conversation after pizza was something else. Why the hell does he think I need time or space to break? It's bad enough he witnessed me losing my mind when he came to New York. Now he's trying to make out he's the strong one, that he has what it takes to be the rock for everyone: the kids, his parents. Me.

So he might have hit on a few obvious points—how alone I now feel without Annie, how out of my element I am in Chicago. True, he has his family, and probably a good support network. The funeral was like a firefighter wake with a huge complement of his co-workers. He has hotshot hockey player Hudson Grey available for babysitting. This place he's living in, a vintage three-bedroom condo in a pricey part of town, speaks volumes about the league I'm miles from. The

Killians have money, enough to win any court battle that might ensue.

And I have nothing. No Annie, my boyfriend in a hurry to leave with no assurance that I'm making the right call. The deck is stacked against me.

I sit up in the bed, instantly regretting my woe is me attitude. The kids are what's important, and I have an irresistible urge to check on them.

Activating the light on my phone, I use it to map my way to the kitchen, which takes forever because this place is huge. I help myself to a slice of pizza and some water, then head to the kids' room. The door's ajar and they're sleeping in the same bed for now; Sam said he had ordered another one to be delivered soon. Spence has kicked off the covers and is sprawled higgledy-piggledy. Maya is curled up like she's trying to protect herself from all that exists outside her frail little body.

Oh my heart. A few moments later, I'm out, worried my tears will wake them.

I take a moment to compose myself, my back to the wall, listening for the sounds of the kids' breathing, and my heart in a pitter-patter of distress. I pray the pain will eventually recede or turn into a different kind of ache. I can't imagine living with this for any length of time.

As I pass by Sam's room which is next to mine, I notice that his door is also open a few inches, probably so he can hear the kids if they wake. That warms me a touch, though it shouldn't. He just wants to be first up if they need him.

That's when I hear it: a moan.

At first, I think it's one of the kids, but it's closer than that. I stop and listen—no sound. But when I move away, I hear it again. Louder, agitated, and coming from Sam's room.

Pushing open the door, I peek inside, letting my phone create a pool of light near the end of the bed. Sam is tossing and turning, his head moving from side to side on the pillow. His chest is bare, the sheet twisted around his thighs, but thankfully he's wearing boxer briefs.

"No, don't ..." His voice is a distressed murmur. "Stay. Stay with me."

He sounds so forlorn, not like the Sam I know. But this is a sad and forlorn time for all of us. His dreams will reflect that.

I should leave him alone to his grief.

Yet I can't go. Immobile, I watch from the doorway, frozen as the lump of muscle in my chest. It beats. Barely.

I hate to see anyone's pain, even someone with whom I have "issues." When he moans again, his neck strains with the effort of trying to make whoever or whatever is in his dream cooperate. To stay. To not hurt him.

"Sam," I whisper, hoping that the introduction of my voice might disrupt the air's energy enough to throw his dream off course. "It's okay."

It's not, but we tell ourselves these lies all the time, don't we?

"Stay," he moans, a little louder than before.

I know this instruction is not for me, but I move forward all the same and place my phone on the nightstand, the light down. My eyes have adjusted to the dark, enough to make out his body as he moves around.

I want to touch him but I'm suddenly afraid. Not of Sam, but of the shifting dark, of being as alone as I feel. I want to be home in my own bed, away from all this strangeness. But the kids need me, and in this moment, so does this man. I sit on the bed and wait, looking for an opening to alleviate his distress.

"No, no, don't," he says, and now I touch my hand to his shoulder. As soon as I do, he says, "Annie."

Just one word. My sister's name.

My heart clatters hard.

He shifts against my hand, as if his body senses the intrusion. Next thing, he's turned and grasped my wrist. It's unexpected. A visceral blast of electricity barrels through me. I don't know if he's awake; I assume he's not. Does he think I'm Annie?

He's not letting go and the manacle of his hand is strangely soothing. I should be pulling away but something about his grip reassures me. Am I so starved for affection that a guy in the throes of a nightmare is looking like a viable option for comfort? Not to mention he's dreaming about my sister.

But he's no longer moaning or tossing. He appears to have calmed with his hand wrapped around my wrist. I should extricate myself, remove myself from this situation. It would be easy to do; yet I remain, drawn to his supreme physique. It's wrong to ogle, but I can't help my eyes which seem to be operating independently of my brain.

What a fine specimen of man he is. His chest is broad and smooth, his shoulders knitted with muscle. It takes every inch of willpower not to use my other hand to touch and verify how good he would feel under my fingertips.

I want to do the same to his rumpled hair, which looks soft and silky. His eyes are closed, the lashes casting half-moon shadows over his cheeks. In the graying dark, I can make out high cheekbones, that strong aquiline nose, those lips that look pillowy soft, though that might be because I know the contours of his face intimately.

I need to leave. Using my free hand, I squeeze his bicep. That's when I realize I've made a mistake because in a ninja-worthy instant, I'm in his arms, pinned by a half-sleeping player. Even unconscious, Sam Killian has all the moves.

If I didn't think I should leave before, I certainly do now. Before I can draw back, he moans again, and that sound goes straight to my core. It's just so ... sexual. That's how I've always thought of him: a supremely sexual being, good for one thing only. These last few days have revealed another side to him, but I'd prefer to return to before. When Annie and Jake were alive. When Maya and Spence still had their parents.

When Sam Killian was a too-sexy-good-for-nothing-else jerk.

One strong arm has circled my back. I'm notched into his chest, fitting perfectly there, and thinking that maybe I can stay for a little while. Slip out when he's calmer. His nightmare appears to have receded, and my presence might be helping.

I feel a change in his body language, the slumbering giant coming awake.

"Cassie?"

"Uh, yeah." I'm still in his arms and he's not recoiling.

"What's going on? Did you have a bad dream?"

Did *I* have a bad dream? I pull back and sit up, taking the opportunity to empty my lungs and turn my phone over to shine a light on the situation. The dark is far too dangerous.

"I was checking on the kids—"

"Are they okay?"

"Yes, but I heard you moaning. I think you were having a nightmare." *Or something was happening where you were asking my sister to stay.* I'm too embarrassed by the situation to probe for details.

Rubbing his mouth, he asks, "And you came to tuck me in?" His tone is tinged with amusement. Of course.

"I came in to see if you were okay. The minute I touched you—" Full-scale smirk now. What a relief to have my usual opinion of him rear to life. "To wake you from whatever terrible thing you were dreaming about—" The terribleness of which I'm not certain, given that my sister was involved. "You grabbed my wrist and pulled me in."

"Right." Elongated and as sarcastic as I've ever heard it.

Quickly I scramble to a stand, taking my phone with me. The light casts shadows about the room, but also highlights the muscle factory lying on the bed before me. That's when I notice something I didn't before, despite how close we were physically.

The man is erect.

"God, you're disgusting."

That makes him chuckle. "You're the one wandering into my room in the middle of the night and laying hands on me."

What an asshole. Sam Killian might be grieving, but underneath it all, he's still the same immature, horny little frat boy. I want to punch him in his damn erection.

"Next time I hear you screeching in your sleep, I'll put in my ear plugs."

"Now, Cass—"

But I'm already out of the room before he can utter any more nonsense.

Nine

Sam

I awake to a quiet apartment.

It shouldn't be. There are kids and a dog and *her*. Not that she makes much noise, but it's been less than twenty-four hours and I can hear her breathing from two rooms away, the awareness almost painful.

Last night, I had another nightmare about the accident. It started a couple of nights after, or I assume it did because one night I woke in tears and my body felt like it had run a marathon. I have no idea why it's affecting me this way. It's not as if I was present when it happened or bore any responsibility for how it all went down. I was too late to do anything.

Yet I obviously have something weighing on me if I'm dreaming about it. I can't recall the details, but something tells me they're different than the reality.

Waking up with a woman in my arms shocked the hell out of me. It took no more than a second to realize someone was there and that someone was Cassie Ferguson. She was holding on tight and for a second, I wondered what I'd done to deserve this amazing moment. But then it came to me.

She was there because she's a good person, willing to help someone she doesn't like all that much. And I'd repaid the favor by getting turned on.

Embarrassed—and no woman has the capacity to do that to me but her—I reverted to my usual manner in the presence of St. Cassandra. Make fun of the situation and get a rise out of her. Because it's a damn sight easier than the alternative.

It's after nine in the morning. I haven't slept past 6 a.m. in five years, so that says something for my state of mind. After a visit to the bathroom, I trudge to the kitchen and find a post-it note on the fridge.

We went out for a walk in the park with Waffles. Be back soon. – Cass

Not the full Cassandra. Major progress.

I should check the bedrooms, make sure she hasn't done a moonrise flit or a sunrise dash with the kids. But she's far too upstanding to pull a trick like that. She'll follow the rule of law, dot every *i* and cross every *t*, so there's no confusion about how she won.

Grabbing my phone, I shoot off a text. When I get a response, I head outside and down one floor in the elevator. The door to an apartment is open with Jude, my best friend, standing there, his arms crossed like he's annoyed I took so long.

"Jesus, it was less than sixty seconds, Garland."

"Whatever. You want coffee?"

"If it's going."

When I reach the door, he takes me in his arms and hugs me. Jude's a tactile kind of guy, which is good because I really need that comfort right now. Better I get it here than seek it out in all the wrong places.

"How's it going?"

"It's going. She's out with the kids and the dog at the park." I follow Jude into the kitchen. "No Hud?"

"Gym and practice." He pours coffee and moves the half-and-half my way so I can doctor it to my liking.

We take a seat at the kitchen table and let the moment rest. I'm wrecked, I feel it, and I know I must look it.

"How about breakfast?"

I don't object and he gets started while chattering about work, a recounting of an incident involving a man chained to a bed, which has me chuckling for the first time in a week.

I dig into scrambled eggs with chives, like I haven't eaten in forever. We don't talk much, but when I'm finished, the heaviness returns to my shoulders.

"How long is Cass staying?"

"Long enough to figure out a plan to steal the kids."

He frowns. "You really think that's her game?"

"Yep. She doesn't approve of me. Doesn't think I'm parent material. She's not going to move to Chicago so if we share, it's going to be disruptive for the kids. I have a better case because their grandparents are here." Not because of my own qualifications, which, frankly, are zero.

"She doesn't have parents or other relatives to help out?"

"Not that I know of. Jake said their father was out of the picture and their mother wasn't in their lives much. Cassie raised Annie in her later teen years. She's five years older, but it sounds like she had more of a mom role once their mother took off. Which is all to say that on paper, my situation looks better, but she's got experience and is going to do everything she can to win."

Jude assesses me. "It's about the kids, though, right?"

So the *win* comment might have sounded like this is a contest. I don't know how else to term it.

"Of course it is. But they're not leaving Chicago, Jude."

"Whatever I can do to help. Babysitting, bribery with

hockey game tickets, anything you can think of. Which reminds me ..." He checks under some papers and pulls out something that looks like a chart. "Hudson asked the Chicago Rebels nutritionist to draw up a healthy meal plan. You don't have to follow it to the letter, but it could give you some ideas."

One of the first things I said to Jude when I heard I would be in charge of the kids was: *I don't even know what to fucking feed them.* Annie and Jake were big on organic diets, while I'm big on pizza. A quick glance reveals recipes like turkey tacos and healthy mac n' cheese (is that even possible?).

"This is great. Thanks."

"And because that's a lot to deal with to start, we got you one of those meal planning subscriptions that includes kids' and adult meals. First delivery is today and should tide you over for a week. I told Benji to be on the lookout for it." He smiles at me. "You still have to cook, but it might be fun to involve the kids or Cass? Good way for you all to bond. Anyway, just some ideas to ease the transition."

Jesus, how lucky am I to have this kind of support? I place a heel to my eye, praying I won't lose it. "You're a good friend."

He shrugs. "You've been the best for me, especially this last year as I worked on getting my head out of my ass. You made me see the light with Hudson."

"I think Hudson made you see the light." Jude had a rough couple of years where he went on a bout of self-destruction while he figured some stuff out. He bunked with me at my place for a while to get back on his feet and we've been tight ever since. He's in a great place now, his mental health more secure, his career at CFD stable, his love life picture-perfect. "So how are things going with the Rebels hottest forward?"

"They're, uh, going."

That pulls me up short. If these two dummies are in trouble, I'm going to lose it. "What does that mean?"

"Nothing. How are your parents?"

Nope. "What's going on with you and Hudson? Is everything okay?"

"Yeah, it is. We're just …" After a slight pause, he mutters, "fuck it," quickly followed by, "we got engaged."

"Are you kidding? When did this happen?"

"Just before the accident. That night, actually."

Damn. And he's kept it to himself so as not to pull focus from my grief. "Garland, you could have told me."

"It just didn't seem like the time."

"Give me all the details."

He does, filling me in on how they were celebrating the anniversary of their initial hookup in the same hotel room where they first met, how they both had the same idea and brought rings, how they'll probably wait until after the hockey season to tie the knot.

"We even have a wedding planner. Charlie Love, you know her?"

"Penthouse Charlie?" She lives on the top floor of our building with her husband, Max Henderson. Her services are very high end.

"Hudson wants to go all out. Show the world how much this means to him." He sounds both embarrassed and proud, and I can't make fun of him no matter how much I want to.

"Where's the ring?"

He takes it out of his pocket. It's a black and titanium beveled band, very modern.

"You should be wearing it. Celebrate this amazing love you've found and cherish every fucking second."

Jude's eyes look a little wet. He slides the ring on, and we both admire it, giggling like fools. I step around the island and give him a hug. "Congrats, friend. I'm so happy for you."

"Thanks, Sammie." He sets me back and takes a good long look at me. "How are you? Really?" In other words, *you look like shit.*

I release a breath. "Jake was everything to me. I can't imagine a life without him, but I have to do exactly that because the kids need it. They need me to have a backbone through all this."

"But you have to think of yourself, too."

That'll have to wait. "It'd be easier if she wasn't here. She's watching my every move, filing it away."

"She's probably not even thinking of that. She's grieving, too."

I run a hand over my mouth, recalling last night and how good she felt in my arms. "Yeah, I know. I'm probably being too hard on her. But the first thing I thought when I woke up this morning is that she took them."

Jude grimaces. "You need to talk to her about that. Try to come to some sort of middle ground."

He's right, but I'm not sure I know how to play nice with someone who's threatening me and mine. The mention of Charlie the wedding planner reminds me of something.

"Max Henderson is a divorce lawyer, right?"

Jude gives me a sharp look. "Think I should have him on retainer?"

"No. But divorce law is family law. And divorce lawyers deal with custody disputes all the time."

"True."

I know Max well enough to chat with at the mailboxes. We've shared a few laughs about our trust fund baby status, though Max is one of those saintly types who gave his money away and lives off his lawyerly gains (*after* he bought the penthouse at the Gloucester, mind you). I'm holding onto every penny of mine so I can buy new sneakers and protect the people I love most in the world.

I haven't had a chance to ask the estate planning lawyer for a rec, but perhaps I won't need to.

"Maybe I should talk to him. I'm pretty sure Cassie's already lawyered up. I need to keep up with her for when she starts her campaign."

When I return to the apartment, everyone is back. Spence is holding an ice cream and immediately offers it to me. "Want some?"

"Not right now, buddy." I raise my gaze to Cassie.

She blushes and it's fucking adorable, which is the last adjective I would ever have applied to her. Usually, she wears boring suits or vintage fifties-style dresses, but today she's gone casual. Her fair hair is tied back and she's wearing a zipped running sweater with tight yoga pants. I'm unreasonably drawn to the shape of her, which is fine because when it comes to this woman, I'd rather think dirty thoughts than nice ones.

"I thought it would be okay. I know it's early but—"

"It's fine." Since when am I the one who needs to have a dessert-at-nine-am situation justified to me? "Ice cream for breakfast sounds awesome."

"Ice cream for breakfast!" Spence acts like this is a new idea, even though he's currently living the dream. He now offers his ice cream cone to everyone, even the dog, with the tag, "Ice cream for breakfast?"

Maya looks at him in disgust. "We already have some, dummy."

"Hey, don't call your brother a dummy," I say at the same time Cassie says, "Maya!"

"Well, he is. He doesn't know anything." She takes his ice cream cone and drops it, making a big splat on the floor. "And this ice cream isn't even that good."

Exit with maximum flouncing. Damn.

Spence starts to cry. Waffles, that furry opportunist, slurps at the ice cream offering, which saves us having to clean it up, I suppose.

Cassie opens her mouth, but I get there first. "You take care of Spence. I've got Maya."

She nods and immediately hunkers to Spence's level.

I find my niece in her new room. Her suitcase is upended, and she's rifling through it.

"Hey, bug." I enter and sit on the bed. "What are you looking for?"

"My coloring books. They're supposed to be here."

I don't remember that from the list, but it doesn't surprise me because Maya loves art. Cassie does, too, or she used to.

"Your aunt might have missed them. Not a problem because we can go get them anytime."

"I need them now." She throws a sweater on the floor. A pen soon follows.

"Hey, hey." I curl my hand around hers and bring her down to the bed beside me. "What's going on?"

She shrugs, a shit-ton of hurt in that gesture.

"It's okay to be sad. We all are."

"Spence doesn't even know. He keeps talking about Mom and Dad hanging with Mickey."

"I know. We need to figure out how to tell him but he's too small to understand." I worried that she didn't fully comprehend it either but now I realize that she does, all too well. She looks older than her eight years, and I hate that she's lost some of that innocence.

"Do I have to tell him I'm sorry?"

"About the ice cream?"

She nods.

"Probably. He likes ice cream so you can't really give him a hard time about it. And ice cream for breakfast *is* awesome, isn't it?"

Her eyes fill with tears. "It is."

I put an arm around her thin shoulders and gather her close. "How are things with Aunt Cass?"

"Fine. She keeps asking if I'm okay."

"Yeah, kind of a stupid question, but she just wants you to know she's there for you."

Another shrug. "I want to go back to school."

"Thought you'd like the break."

"I'm missing everything. I don't want to fall behind."

I'd assumed that pulling her out of school for the last week was for the best? Shows what I know. "When do you want to go back?"

"Tomorrow?" She peers up at me. "But will Spence be okay?"

"Your aunt and I will keep an eye on him. But for now, let's go out and tell him we're sorry you dropped his ice cream. And then we can figure out how to get your coloring books. Maybe your school stuff." I squint. "Do you have school stuff?"

"My backpack. My Taylor sweatshirt. The new shoes that Mom ..." She bites her lip and swipes at her eye.

"It's okay to cry, Maya."

"I know but if I do, then it means ..." A weary sigh.

"What, bug?"

"They're not coming back."

I think of the letter from Jake in my bedside drawer. I know exactly what she means. This fucking sucks.

"I get it. You never got to say goodbye. But it's okay to let it out." *Just not on your brother, please with a cherry on top.*

She sniffs and I wonder if maybe she might lose it, but she inhales deep like she needs to for my sake, not just hers. I'm surrounded by indefatigable women.

I kiss the top of her head. "Let's go see your brother."

TEN

I'm not sure how much longer I can keep all this emotion in. Taking the kids out to breakfast seemed like a good idea, a way to instill some normality. I don't even eat breakfast, so I had coffee and cut up Spence's pancakes. Maybe I should have included Sam, but he didn't sleep well and when I checked, he was dead to the world. Better he gets his rest while he can.

On the way back, Maya started acting out, but I let her snide comments to poor little Spence slide. She's hurting, and slapping her wrist seems like a bad idea. She feels the pressure of being in the know when her brother gets to live in a world where his parents are still alive. That's not fair on her.

After she blew up, I brought Spence into the living room and sat him on the sofa.

"Hey, little guy, did you want more ice cream?"

He sniffs and shakes his head. "Maya's mad at me."

"No, she's not. She's just upset, but not with you."

"I want Mom."

"I know you do."

Annie, I've never needed you more than I do this minute.

There's movement at the entrance to the living room. Sam's there, holding Maya's hand, and the sight of them together tugs at something in my chest.

I can almost feel the little squeeze he gives her hand. I'm envious of that connection, which makes me a rotten person.

Maya walks toward us, sits down, and puts an arm around her brother. "I'm sorry, Spence."

Spence leans into her, like she can fix everything, kind of like how Annie used to with me. *Mom's not coming back, is she?* Those were tough days, trying to be strong and brave when all I wanted was to collapse under the weight of disappointment in my mother and of my own dreams shattering. Now the sight of Maya and Spence, ports in each other's storms, has me close to tears. *Not here, not now.*

I shoot up. "I-I'll be back in a sec."

In the bathroom, I splash my face with water, desperate to restore some sense of normality to a situation that's far from normal. Sam obviously has a closer relationship with them. I shouldn't feel so isolated but I'm a stranger to the kids, only seeing them a few times a year because I was always so busy. Sometimes I felt bad wanting to travel without Derek so I put his needs ahead of mine. Neither did I think I should muscle in where I might not be wanted.

I open the door to find Sam there, which is becoming our usual dynamic—me behind a closed door, him waiting patiently for me to get over myself.

"You okay?"

"Of course! Where are the kids?"

"They're watching *Moana*. We should talk."

"Is Maya okay? She seemed a little subdued."

"Well, yeah. I think it's starting to sink in and she's likely feeling the burden of being the one who knows."

Just what I thought. So strange to have this guy on the same wavelength.

He inhales a deep breath. "About last night. I was kind of a jerk to you."

Not expecting that. Not even sure I want to talk about it.

"Yeah, you were. But you get a pass for a while. I think we both do."

His lips curl. "So I've got to cut you some slack for some as yet unnamed sin?"

It's said in a teasing manner but the moment his sensual mouth forms that last word—*sin*—I'm taken back to those close quarters in the dark.

To how good it felt to be held by him.

How amazing it felt to offer him some measure of comfort.

There's danger in finding common ground, especially for anything outside of the kids' care. But the alternative seems to be friction, which is fraught with a different kind of risk.

"I'm sure I'll do something you won't like. You'll have to give me some grace."

"You're pre-forgiven." He grins, and I can feel my mouth shaping a smile in response. *Don't flirt with him.*

But it's more than a surface flirtation. I want to ask about his dreams, or rather, his nightmares. I want to know why he called out Annie's name, something that might be better left in the secretive dark.

Thankfully I don't get a chance to make an idiot of myself because Sam turns the conversation back to safer territory: our joint mission.

"Maya wants to go back to school. Tomorrow."

I blink. "That sounds really soon."

"Maybe. But she's a worrier. And she's worried about falling behind, the usual FOMO with her friends. I think this would be good for her. Would give her structure."

He's probably right, but I'm not prepared to accede so quickly. Seems I need to assert myself, if only to establish a baseline going forward. "Shouldn't she stay home until she's had a chance to grieve?"

"That'll take months. She can't stay out of school for months so why not let her be with her friends and focus on something else?"

"But ... Spence will miss her. They need each other right now."

I'm trying to be reasonable, not override his decision-making purely because that's our usual pattern. I'd just like there to be *some* discussion.

He considers my argument, another thing that surprises me. He doesn't agree with me but at least he's not shutting me down immediately.

"They do need each other. But we also need to be careful about assuming each of us grieves in the same way. I don't want to force Maya to be the strong one just so we can get Spence through this. It's not fair on her. It would be different if we were forcing her back to school, but this is her choice. If it ends up being too soon—which we'll tell her is an option— then she can come home."

Home. To this place.

He reads my mind. "The home we're re-making for her. For both of them."

"It sounds like you've thought it through."

"Amazing what you can learn on YouTube." That makes me smile, and he gives a wry one back. "Surprised, huh?"

Big time. I'm waiting for the other shoe to drop. If I'm to succeed in my mission to obtain full custody, I need that shoe to plunge off a cliff.

"Not at all," I lie. "You're just thinking of what's best for Maya."

"I like to think so. So about dinner. Hudson and Jude

subscribed us to one of those meal delivery services so that'll keep us going for a while, and they also drew up some meal plans. Like the responsible adults they are."

"That sounds good." Jude must be Hudson's partner, who I may have met at the funeral? All these people so willing to help.

"But we need other supplies, snacks and the like, so I'll head to the store. Are you okay here with the little terrors?"

"I am." I watch him go, marveling that we've achieved this peace between us and wondering how long it'll last.

Not long at all.

The next morning, I drop Maya off at school—which is in the suburbs, a forty-five-minute drive in heavy traffic—and on the way back, I pull over to call Derek. It's almost 3 p.m. in London.

"Hey, I thought you were going to call last night."

He coughs. "Yeah, sorry. This time zone stuff is messing with my head, and we're still ironing out the details."

"I thought it would be all wrapped up by now."

"I wish. I meant to call sooner, but ..." I already know what's coming. "I won't be able to come see you this weekend, Cass. There's just too much to finish here."

Oh. "I was hoping that you could spend time with the kids."

A pause, then: "Have you had a chance to talk to Sarah Strauss?"

Sarah's the lawyer friend he recommended. "I have a Zoom call set up with her for tomorrow. And I've been talking to schools about whether Maya could start mid-year."

"What does Sam think of this?"

"Well, he doesn't know, does he? Not officially. Though he

has to suspect I'm not going to sit around and wait for them to get comfortable at his place."

"About that ... are you sure you should be living with him?"

"That's where the kids are. If I don't stay here, then it looks like I'm not serious."

He hums in disapproval. "Listen, could we talk about this later? I'm about to head into a meeting."

"Sure. I'm disappointed you can't come visit."

"Yeah, me too." There's a muffled sound and then he adds, "I'll check in with you later, okay?"

Before I can agree, the line goes dead.

He should be here with me, but his job is important. This merger is important. I get that. But I need him on my side while I figure out how to remove Sam from the equation.

It's in this troubling frame of mind that I get back to the apartment and find a note from Sam.

Gone to the park with Spence and Waffles. Join us!

That exclamation point sounds kind of fake. Or maybe I'm reading too much into everything. Sam has given the impression that he wants this co-guardianship arrangement to work. I'm just not seeing how it would if we're not in the same city.

This muddle of thoughts is swirling around my brain as I wait for the elevator. It opens to reveal a gorgeous blonde wearing a lovely floral print dress with a blue frock coat.

"Hi, there," she says with a smile as I step inside. She looks like a fifties-era movie star, Hitchcockian and mysterious.

"Hi." I hit the button for the ground floor, though it's already selected.

"Did you just move in?"

"Temporarily. I'm staying with Sam. With our nephew and niece as well."

Smile fading, she places a hand on my arm. "You must be Annie's sister. I'm so sorry about what happened."

"Thank you. Did you know her?"

"Not terribly well, just in passing when she and Jake came to visit. We usually get an invite to Sam's rooftop parties. He was close to his brother. Well, you know that."

The elevator doors open and we both step outside. "I'm Charlie, by the way. I live on the top floor with my husband, Max."

"I'm Cass. Cass Ferguson."

"Nice to meet you, Cass. Now, if you ever need a break, feel free to come visit. Maybe we should exchange numbers? Just for emergencies. It's always good to have a backup in the building."

Which is how I make my first friend in Chicago.

Trailing in the wake of Charlie's perfume as she rushes to meet with a client of her wedding planning business—"thankfully more bridechilla than bridezilla!"—I head over to Lincoln Park. The late October sky is blue, the air is crisp, and it's been one week since Annie and Jake left us.

I shouldn't phrase it that way, as if they're somehow to blame. They're not—the truck driver is and there will likely be some sort of settlement with the insurance company. But it's not fair that he walked away with hardly a scratch because he was in the bigger, tougher vehicle.

I'm getting angry again, and I struggle to repress it before I spend time with my nephew.

On reaching the park, I spot Spence on a swing. Sam is off to the side talking to a tall, built guy with longish hair, holding the leash of a golden Lab. He looks sort of familiar, maybe from the funeral? The guy says something, Sam laughs, and I'm struck by how gorgeous he is when he lets loose like that. He's never like that around me but then why would he be? I'm not looking to make Sam Killian laugh.

A part of me is annoyed that he can do that, now, so soon after what happened. That all it takes is a conversation with a friend.

As I approach, the friend steps away to answer a call, which would be my cue to wave or announce my presence except Sam is otherwise distracted—by a curvaceous blonde who's appeared in his path with a cute Pomeranian and a cuter smile for my co-guardian.

And boy oh boy does Sam Killian look like all his birthdays, Christmases, and snow days have come at once. He drags lightly on Waffles who's sniffing at the Pom, which is such an appropriate proxy for their owners that I almost laugh. These two, practically in heat, can't get enough of each other.

She smiles again.

He says something hilarious.

That earns a sultry giggle.

He leans in, and the result is another pretty tinkle.

Out come the phones. Numbers are exchanged. (Some sort of record, surely.)

Poor Sam. He's managed a week—I assume—without a woman to warm his bed, except for my unfortunate visit to soothe him during that nightmare. Good to see him getting back on that horse.

A scream pierces the air.

I switch my attention to Spence, who is on the ground. He must have fallen from the swing, which should not have happened, *would* not have happened if Sam wasn't so distracted. (Or if I wasn't so distracted by *him* being distracted.)

I rush over, but Sam gets there first. He already has Spence in his arms and the sight of this big lug soothing my nephew almost calms me.

Almost.

"You weren't even watching him!" I take Spence out of Sam's arms, and his shock at my accusation means he doesn't resist. "Spence, baby, are you okay?"

He holds up his palm. It's a little raw but no skin was broken. However, tears are streaming down his reddened face. Poor little guy.

"It's okay. Let's get you home." My gaze meets Sam's, which I like to think is guilty.

"It was an accident, Cassie."

"It's Cass. And it's not an accident if you're standing around flirting instead of keeping an eye on him. He's too young to be left unattended."

"He wasn't unattended. I dropped my guard for a second—"

"Exactly." Spence is wearing a tiny Chicago Rebels hockey jersey I haven't seen before. It's so damn cute that it makes me even more mad. "Where's his jacket?"

"Back at the house. It's 60 degrees." It's unusually warm but that's not the point.

"He could catch a chill."

"Cass—"

"Let's go, Spence." I'm anxious to make a quick exit. Sam and his friend follow at a safe-from-shrapnel distance with Waffles and the Lab. (I must have scared off the Pom owner with my screeching.) We head inside and wait at the elevator.

Sam looks bemused—or maybe amused. "This is Jude, by the way."

Now I know where I've seen him before. Not only was he at the funeral but he's Hudson Grey's boyfriend. He made the news a few months ago, something about his sketchy past.

I nod at him, feeling foolish that this is our formal introduction.

The elevator doors open, and I enter, with Sam

accompanying. Jude smiles at Sam, likely deciding it would be better not to be in a confined space with me.

"Later, Garland," Sam says to his friend, then to me as the doors close, "You okay?"

I bristle. "I'm fine."

"Because you seem sort of on edge."

"Anyone would be if they found their kid being neglected."

"Cass, I was not neglecting him. Kids fall down, get scrapes all the time." He holds Spence's hand. "You're okay, right, buddy?"

A wet-eyed Spence nods because what else is he going to do?

"Stop getting him to agree with you. He'd do anything you say."

"He's agreeing because he wasn't hurt. Just got a fright when he fell. Perfectly normal."

On the sixth floor, we exit. "What would you know about perfectly normal? There you were planning your sex life instead of watching your nephew." In case that sounds like I care about who he screws, I quickly move on to my next grievance. "And I can't believe that guy is your friend."

We're at the door to the apartment now. Sam has his key at the ready but isn't using it.

"Why can't you believe it?" There's a quality to his tone that skitters a flurry of *uh oh* down my spine.

"He went viral on social media last year. Something about his drug-binging past."

"Malicious gossip."

"Sure. Of course, it shouldn't surprise me that you hang with unsavory characters."

"Unsavory characters? What is this, Jane Freakin' Austen?" His expression is positively stormy. "Of course you're going to think my poor decision-making extends to my choice of friends."

"Well, I don't know anything about you or your friends, Sam. The kids need stable influences. Good influences." I gesture impatiently at the door because he's taking his sweet time.

Scowling, he opens it and I push through to the bathroom, where I wash Spence's hands gently. The rawness appears to be dissipating, so maybe it wasn't such a big deal after all.

Sam follows and leans against the door while I soothe Spence, though really, I'm soothing myself. I'm not sure what's wrong with me. Perhaps I'm moody because of my frustrating talk with Derek.

"You okay, Spence?" I ask again, anxious to avoid Sam's penetrating stare.

"Can I have ice cream?"

Definitely okay. "Maybe later. How about playing with your transformer?"

He nods, and a minute later I have him set up in the living room. By common assent, Sam and I head into the kitchen.

He opens his mouth, but I get there first. "I might have overreacted."

"You think?"

I ignore his sarcasm. "I just went into crazy Mama Bear mode. I know I'm not his mom, but it feels that way."

He pauses, evidently recalibrating what he was about to say. "You're the closest to a mom he has right now. Of course you're going to be worried. And I should have been paying better attention, but I wouldn't let him on a low-hanging swing if I didn't think it was safe. I'm a first responder. I'm not terrible at this despite what you think."

"I-I don't think that. I'm just protective of them. If anything was to happen, I don't think I'd forgive myself."

His face scrunches in surprise at that statement which sounded somewhat overblown, but he doesn't question it. We've both lost so much, and I suspect he understands how tight I need to hold onto what's left of Annie.

"You're wrong about Jude. He's one of the best people I know. He's always been here for me when I need him."

Discomfort slithers down my spine. "I shouldn't have said that. I don't know anything about him except what was on the gossip sites."

"It was blown out of proportion. He's a great guy. He and Hudson are solid, and yeah, he made a few mistakes when he was younger but that's not him anymore. I'd trust him with my life. And I'd trust him with the kids any day of the week."

There's challenge in his voice.

"Okay, another overreaction on my part."

He's obviously suspicious about my contrition. "Is everything okay?"

I shift uncomfortably. "I'm just a little disappointed that Derek can't visit this weekend. He's still in the middle of a business thing."

"You can say 'merger'. I know what that is."

I feel a smile touching my lips. "I just wasn't sure how detailed I should get. He's busy, so that's that."

"It's kind of a big change for him, too."

"What does that mean?"

He shrugs those gigantic hero shoulders. "His girlfriend is suddenly a mom. That's going to interfere with his life in a major way."

"Interfere? You make it sound like he thinks having the kids around is a bad thing." *Get out of my head, Sam Killian.*

"So, what *does* he think?"

"He—we haven't had time to discuss it properly. But he wants what's best for the kids, just like I do."

"Uh huh."

"Don't *uh huh* me."

That makes him laugh, which for some reason makes me laugh. I should be angry with him for all his assumptions about Derek, never mind what just happened in the playground with Spence, but instead I'm feeling strangely seen. Again.

Until he ruins it by speaking. "How did you end up with that guy anyway?"

"We met at an alumni mixer for NYU and hit it off."

"Makes sense, I suppose. You seemed to have a certain kind of guy in mind."

"What does that mean?"

"Back when we met at the wedding, you made it clear I wasn't your type."

True, because he wasn't. Isn't. And it was clear that Sam Killian was only interested in one thing: scoring a conquest against the uptight sister of the bride. "That was a long time ago."

"Sure. We were different people."

"Well, I was."

Another upturn of his lips. "You still think I'm that fun-loving kid with too much money and too little sense."

"You were always the ultimate playboy. And at Spence's birthday party, I didn't see much evidence that anything has changed. That was less than two weeks ago."

"And people can't change?"

"In a matter of days? I just saw you flirting with someone in the park!"

"Flirting? Come on, we were chatting about the dogs."

Like I didn't see them exchanging numbers. "Never mind. We just have very different ways of viewing this guardianship."

He shakes his head in pity, though I can't tell if it's for me or for him. "You've never wanted to see me as anything but a guy who thinks with his dick. I happen to be able to put that part of myself aside to deal with what's important. It's never affected my job—which I happen to be very good at—and I know what it means to be responsible. But you'd rather think I'm frozen in time, the guy you dismissed because you were worried you might enjoy yourself a little too much."

Of course he would think that. "That's not why nothing ever happened between us. Is it so crazy that there's a woman on this earth who won't fall for your charms?"

"Kind of." He leans in, and the scent of him curls into my lungs, like a sensory validation that *yes, it was crazy that I turned you down.* "I think you wanted to kick off your heels and let go that night, Cassie. I think you were this close"—he holds his thumb and forefinger together—"but you couldn't get over your disapproval of me."

I wish it was that simple. Yes, I thought he was a wastrel playboy, who was good for one thing—and my mental well-being was not it. But that wasn't why I turned him down.

I knew it would be good, but I also knew I'd lose some part of myself if I gave in to him. I'd already lost enough to the Killians.

A month after the wedding, I met Derek. He seemed to be everything Sam Killian wasn't: steady, established, ready for real.

"Since when do you care so much for my opinion, Sam?"

He huffs. "I don't."

But I see I've wounded him. He does care—or his bruised ego can't move on from that initial rejection, which has simmered between us over the years.

Every time I saw Sam since, I was confronted with how close I'd come to making a fool of myself that night. Sleeping with a younger man—okay, only by five years, but mentally, so immature. A man who I'd have to meet at family gatherings for the rest of our lives. I'd dodged a bullet, but he never let me forget it.

The smirks. The knowing looks. Then when I wouldn't respond to his flirting, the barely concealed antagonism. And now we're in this position where we are forced to work together as a team.

"The past isn't important," I say as cheerfully as I can. "All that matters is how we deal with the present and these kids' futures."

"Agreed." Spoken far too quickly.

But then I'm always suspicious when he falls into line.

Eleven

Sam

After the Spence playground incident, Cassie and I appear to have reached an uneasy truce. We sat and watched *Moana* together—my nephew is obsessed with *Moana*—ate lunch, and then I kept a close eye on Spence while she picked up Maya. (I'm guilt-racked about Spence's fall and my part in it, but I sure as hell won't be telling that to Cassie.) My niece was quiet about her first day back to school, and by mutual assent, we're giving her space.

After dinner, I tell Cass that I have to check in with Jude on something.

I suit up in a pair of classic Air Jordans and head to the elevator. While I'm waiting a text comes in from Candy. She wanted to come to the funeral, bless her heart, but I nixed that idea immediately while telling her I'd need space for a while.

CANDY

How's my guy? I'm here if you need me.

Followed by a photo of her amazing tits. It looks like she

might have slathered baby oil on them, too, yet I'm strangely unmoved. Sex holds no interest for me right now. I wasn't even flirting—much—with Pom Girl; I was giving her a rec for a vet, though really it's Jude's rec because he and Hudson have one for their dog, Crosby. Not that St. Cassandra would care for the details, so I chose not to share them.

The elevator arrives, but instead of going down to Jude's place, I head up to the penthouse.

Max Henderson opens the door, his hand wrapped around a cut crystal glass filled with expensive Scotch, no doubt. He's such a tool. This morning after I dropped off Maya, I called him at his office. He told me to stop at his place at any time, and after what happened at the playground, the time has come.

"Samuel," he says. "Welcome."

"Charlie not here?"

"She's out with a friend. Need a drink?"

Hell yeah I do. "Better not."

He invites me to the sofa, and I take a seat. I gave him the broad strokes earlier. "So I need to know what my options are."

"Well, you're in a good position. The kids' lives are here with extended family and one of their guardians, who was chosen by the parents. That's you. To take them out of state or to another location, even in state, Ms. Ferguson would have to prove you're not fit. Any negatives that might sway a judge against you?"

"I've screwed around. A lot."

Max gives me a look of *haven't we all*? "As long as it's not something the kids witness or affects your ability to care for them, you should be fine."

"I've kept it in my pants for a couple of weeks now. And I will continue to do so as long as the Eye of Sauron is on me."

Tit-pics notwithstanding. Though I'm not sure a risqué

photo from the woman I most recently slept with is a threat to my current state of celibacy. You know what is? Whining about being rejected by a woman six years ago. What the hell possessed me to even go there—and worse, *out loud*—with the woman herself?

Max's voice calls me back. "How's it going? Living with the enemy?"

"It's ... frustrating. Like I said, I'm being a very good boy and she's the best-looking thing in a ten-mile radius." I can admit my surface attraction to her. That's all there is to it.

Max grins. "Okay, whatever you do, do not fuck your co-guardian."

I already know the answer, but I wouldn't mind someone with the inside track framing it in legalese that might dampen the chattiness of my dick.

"That would be bad because ..."

"Because sex has a way of complicating everything. If you guys are going to come to an agreement, ideally one that has you taking the lead as the guardian, then you don't want to piss her off. You guys sleep together, indulge in something casual, then she sees you with a new woman? You think she's just going to let that slide, or is she more likely to use it as ammunition that you're indiscriminate with your affections? Do not give her the weaponry to bury you."

No doubt she already has a file going. Spence's tumble in the playground, the friends she doesn't approve of, every woman she's seen me with. I've never been good enough for her, not even for a steamy one-nighter. She threw it in my face back there, and I can't imagine she's going to change her mind about my suitability to parent any time soon.

No, I won't be banging Cassie Ferguson.

"She's got a boyfriend back in New York. And she and I happen to hate each other's guts."

Max looks alarmed. "Like that's ever stopped anyone.

Indifference would be better. Do not let your dick take charge here, Sam. Another thing you might want to consider is childcare. If you can get something settled, then that shows you're making strides to establish good routines for the kids."

We spend a few more minutes talking about the right time to make any legal moves. I'm reluctant to be the first to strike because any sign of aggression might provoke her into bringing out the big guns. Better to use my charm.

I head back up to the apartment and help Maya with her homework, something about multiplication tables, which is about my speed. (Though I would think the financial planner in the family should be working on the math problems!) By 9 p.m., both kids are in bed. Spence wants a story, so we spend a few minutes on *The Day the Crayons Quit*, which has him giggling before his little eyelids flutter closed.

I sit beside Maya and whisper, "Sorry you have to share with this little stinker." I have a bed on order. If Cassie wasn't here, Maya could have the other bedroom. Make it her own. As much as I hate to talk about it, I don't think they'll be living in their old house again. Too many memories, and as a City of Chicago employee, I can't live outside the city limits. If necessary, I'll find a bigger house in Chicago, one with a yard for the kids and Waffles, but all that can wait.

"It's okay," she whispers back. "He likes that I'm here when he wakes up."

I think she likes that, too, but Maya's too serious to admit something so sentimental.

"How did the day go?"

"Okay. Ginny Costigan hugged me."

"Hmm. What do we think of Ginny Costigan?"

"She has lots of friends."

Sounds like Maya and Ginny aren't besties. "What about your friends? Who do you hang with?"

"Priya and Alicia. They said sorry and then they told me what I missed in school."

Good old Priya and Alicia, keeping it real. Note to self: Reach out to their parents.

"If you want to hang with them after school, we could probably arrange that."

"I think I should be here for Spence."

God, that's so sweet. "Don't worry about Spence. Your aunt and I will take care of him. I just want you to feel you have everything you need."

Damn, that was insensitive. What she needs are her parents.

"Sorry, bug." I kiss her forehead. "Don't stay up too late reading, okay?" She has an e-reader that she's been sneak-reading for long past her bedtime. I'm not going to deny her that one small pleasure.

"Okay."

Outside the bedroom, I run a hand over my mouth trying to wipe away the tiredness. Trying to ensure Cassie doesn't see me failing at anything. Expression set to neutral, I head into the kitchen to unload the dishwasher but she's already there, putting the last of the dishes away.

"You didn't have to do that. You're a guest."

She doesn't like that, but she needs to know this is temporary.

"I'm happy to pull my weight. I should cook something tomorrow, if you're willing to risk it." We have a week's worth of meals from the delivery service Jude and Hudson gifted us. It's hard to fuck them up.

"Are you telling me there's something you're not good at?"

She opens her mouth, closes it with a lip bite that does something to me. "I'm not great, but I want to try."

Are we still talking about cooking?

"Sure. Sounds great." The bottle of wine I opened at

dinner is still on the counter. "Another glass?" She looks hesitant so I add, "Might make conversation with me more bearable?"

"When you put it like that."

I take two glasses of red out to the living room and put them on the coffee table. She sits on the sofa a couple of feet away from me, stretching to reach the glass rather than sit closer.

She's more wary of me since our conversation earlier, probably wondering if I'm going to keep reminding her that I was once attracted to her. That it's clear I still am.

But right this minute, I need to focus on the kids.

"We should get in touch with Maya's friends' parents."

"Why? Did something happen?"

"No, but she mentioned their names today, Priya and—"

"Alicia," she finishes. Of course.

"You already know them?"

"Yeah, Maya told me about them this morning when I dropped her off. And I introduced myself to their parents at the school."

Just when I think we're figuring out our baton pass-offs, Cassie is working out ways to steal it and race to the finish line. "You could have said something."

"The whole playground thing happened and then it left my brain. I'm not trying to one-up you."

I raise an eyebrow. "No?"

"Of course not. The opportunity presented itself, so I took the shot. That's it."

Fair enough. But we need to start digging into the nitty-gritty. "We should talk about the future."

She takes a sip of her wine. "What did you have in mind?"

"Realism. We both have to return to work at some point, so I reckon we need to look into hiring a nanny."

Her eyes go wide. "A nanny? They just lost their parents,

and you want to bring a stranger in?"

"It'll be an adjustment but it's necessary."

She squirms. "But a nanny? We can do this ourselves, can't we?"

She raised Annie during her teen years by herself. She's used to going it alone but I'm not. While we have options, I don't see why we should ignore the resources available to us.

"We have the means to make this easier, so why don't we draw on this support network?"

"I'm not used to throwing money at my problems." She meets my gaze. "I know that's not what you're saying, but I've always had to figure this stuff out by myself."

That sounds like a lonely existence. "Not anymore. We're in this together."

She looks uncomfortable, maybe even a touch vulnerable. While we're being so honest, I decide to poke a little.

"What does your lawyer say?"

"I haven't had a chance to connect with anyone yet."

That surprises me. I thought she'd be all over it and now I feel guilty that I've made the first move with Max. Maybe we can handle this without getting lawyers involved.

"You know I'm not going to let the kids leave Chicago. Their grandparents are here, everything they know is here. School, friends."

"Everything but me. But I suppose that doesn't matter because I only see them twice a year."

For fuck's sake. "I'm not trying to cut you out. I'm trying to let you know that moving them is a non-starter. So given that, let's figure out a plan for their care. Money's not an issue so it's just a matter of finding someone we can both be happy with."

It's tough to be talking about these things when we're both still in such messed-up headspace. But we need to put that aside in deference to the kids' needs.

"You're probably right, we can't bury our heads in the sand."

I marvel at my powers of persuasion. "How are things with your job?"

"They're being very understanding. And I can do a lot of it remotely, so there isn't really a rush to get back. Except for Derek."

Right. Derek. I've never liked him, though I've only met him three times. He came out for Spence's christening and a Thanksgiving one year. Then the funeral.

"What's that look for?"

I sniff, as if that can somehow wipe my expression. "No look."

"Surprise, surprise, you don't like Derek."

I shouldn't have an opinion. Like that's ever stopped me.

"He's not my kind of guy."

"No tattoos, not a big macho jerk, came by his fortune through hard work—you mean that kind of guy?"

No gentle peeling off of the gloves with our Cassie. Fair enough. Let's do this.

"He seems kind of"—I search for the right word— "precious. And he's not coming out this weekend to support you, so how much of a stand-up, self-made, Mr. Sensitive Guy can he be?"

"His deal is at a critical juncture," she says, though it sounds rote. How many dinners has Derek missed? How many trips postponed? Plans upended?

"Sure. He was kind of in a hurry to leave Chicago after the funeral."

"We're not doing this, Killian."

"Hey, you brought him up. That's what's known as opening the door in a court of law."

She chuckles, a very pretty sound that takes me back to

that simpler time when we first met, and I thought I had a chance with her.

"We're not talking about Derek."

"Because you can't defend his behavior?"

"There's nothing to defend. He's there for me when I need him."

Rubbing my chin, I nod slowly.

"Oh, shut it."

"You seemed upset earlier when you heard he wasn't coming."

"It's a difficult time for everyone and I'd rather he was here —is that so strange?"

"What's strange is that he's not dropping everything to be with you."

That came out more vehemently than intended. Like I think she's the kind of woman worth dropping everything for.

"Is that what you'd do for your girlfriend if, say, her goldfish died? What was her name—Candy?"

"Candy's just a casual acquaintance." I think casually about her oiled-up tits and congratulate myself on not getting a stiffie.

"Like so many of your acquaintances."

I shake my head. "You really can't see me any other way, can you?"

"A hedonistic playboy who enjoys playing roulette with his dick?"

I can't help my laugh. "Wow, didn't expect my dick to enter the conversation so quickly."

Her color is high, and she seems a touch flustered. At the mention of my dick? Interesting.

"What I meant is that being so casual brings risk."

"I know, I could so easily get my heart broken." At her skeptical look, I chuckle. "Oh, right, we're still talking about my dick."

That makes her laugh, though she's still blushing. I love that flush on her.

I'm starting to crave it.

"So you never went for casual relationships pre-Derek?"

"I didn't have time for that. After Mom bailed, I had to take care of Annie, make sure she got into college, that she was set up."

"But you went to college as well."

"Later. And I was a bit older than the other students, so I wasn't there to party or have the typical experience. My class load was too heavy."

She graduated in three years, Jake said. A real overachiever. But I understand her mindset. She was raising her sister, trying to see her right.

"And then Annie met Jake."

"I didn't think that would work out, but it did. I wished she'd finished her degree, but once she had Maya there was no question of what her future looked like. She was born to be a mom."

"Yeah, I remember the night Jake met her. Or the day after anyway. He called to say he was going to marry this amazing girl—and that was before she got pregnant. Once she told him, it was like a message from the universe. These two were meant to be."

And now they're no longer here.

We're both thinking the same thing and the sadness is a dark abyss I can feel myself falling into. But when I look up, I see a crack of light.

I see her.

"It's not right," she murmurs.

"No, it's not."

She takes the bottle and adds more to her glass, then prompts me. I nod my assent. For once we are on the same page and I find myself wanting to stay on this chapter forever.

Twelve

"Oh my God, Annie loved elephants. Did you know that?"

An hour has passed, and the strangest thing is happening: the atmosphere has turned convivial. We've opened a second bottle, though we're only sipping now, conscious of the need to retain some semblance of sobriety while the kids are under our wing. Or maybe conscious of the need to not let any chink show in our respective armors.

"She had that stuffed toy on the shelf in the living room."

"I gave her that. Years ago. I remember the first time we saw an elephant at the Bronx Zoo—I was ten, I think, which would've made Annie five. She said, 'look, Mom, he has five legs!'"

"Five legs?"

"Yeah, because of his giant elephant penis."

"Gotcha."

She bursts into laughter at the memory, and Jesus, that is fucking sunshine in my chest. In the thirty minutes since we've been exchanging stories about Jake and Annie, we've moved closer to each other on the sofa.

"And Mom was all, oh no, that's not—uh, let's go see something else. She couldn't handle it, which is strange considering how man-obsessed she was. It was hilarious."

"Bet you got it."

"I had an idea. I was a precocious child, with my nose in every book, learning as much as I could because Mom didn't take us to school half the time. We needed to fend for ourselves." She passes over that quickly. "I was quite up to date on elephant anatomy. I used to draw pictures of them."

"Do you still do that? Draw?"

Her nose twitches. "No, I don't have the time."

"You were so good. Everyone loved that drawing you did of Maya when she was a toddler." By everyone, I mean *me*.

Her breath hitches. "I'd forgotten that."

"It's in their bedroom."

She nods slowly, like the mention of it brings up a slew of memories, all of them painful. "Maya likes to draw. She's very talented."

"Runs in the family. She's like you in other ways, too."

She blinks in surprise. "She is?"

"Yep. Serious, studious, even with the artistic temperament, which is an unusual combination."

"You think all artists should be head-in-the-clouds types who don't understand how the world works?"

"No. But I guess that's the stereotype."

Her brow beetles. "Some of us have to come down to earth. Put away childish things and accept responsibility."

Ah. "And that's you and not ... me?"

She gives one of those if-you-can't-say-something-nice shrugs. My no-responsibility rich kid past sticks to me like skunk stink, never mind my assignment to Squad. Maybe I need to start leaving press clippings lying around.

"You think I don't have it in me to accept this responsibility."

She bites her lip and damn, there's something super sexy about that. She's even hotter now than the night I met her, and I was fucking bowled over then. Part of it is the friction that exists between us, but most of it is how much I admire her for the sacrifices she made for Annie. Hell, I've always admired her even when she bugs the balls out of me.

"This situation is going to require a different skillset than you're used to," she says, the perfect buzzkill to my happy thoughts about her hotness. "It's every day, managing these kids' lives, not just a couple of weeks. I'm not even sure you should be riding that motorcycle."

"What's that got to do with it?"

She flaps a hand. "What if something happened? What if you got into an accident?"

"So I can't interest you in a ride on my Ducati, baby?"

A shake of her head. "You will *never* get me on that thing."

A sudden image of her thighs wrapped around my hips, her arms snuggling under my shirt as we speed down Lake Shore gives me a pleasant frisson.

"Never say never. Maybe you have more experience than me because you had to take over as parent for Annie. But that doesn't mean you're the only one qualified to do this. I can ignore the elephant penis in the room when called upon to do my duty."

She laughs, enjoying that reference.

"I was like a mom to Annie at one point, but she was older. Thirteen." A conciliatory gesture.

"So, ten times more difficult than our kids." I can do conciliation, too.

Her face registers brief surprise she can't hide at the mention of "our kids."

"The moods were something else. Especially as Mom

wasn't dead, she just may as well have been for all the interest she took in us. Annie was really hurt that she bailed."

"Where's your mom now?" She didn't show at the funeral.

"Oh, with some guy on a houseboat in Florida. Or that was the last I heard. I tried to get in touch with her, to tell her about Annie, but she's not at the last number I have for her. She was never one for standing still."

That's cold. What a piece of work this woman must be, cutting herself off from her daughters like that, leaving her eldest to raise her youngest. It would explain why Cassie craves stability. That's somehow translated to a life with Dull-as-Dishwater Derek.

"You did a good job with Annie."

She blushes again and tries to shrug off my compliment.

"Don't know about that. But we made it work, even if money was tight and our Christmases were of the Charlie Brown sad-little-tree variety. I wish I could have done more for her at the holidays or on birthdays. I did worry that I'd ..." She pauses.

"That you what?"

"Failed her. By pushing too hard to get her into college, to prove I could succeed where my mother hadn't."

How could she think that after the amazing human Annie became? "You were there for her, stepping up when she needed you. Don't ever think you failed."

She searches my face, like she actually cares for my opinion for once. "I thought maybe she was rebelling against the life I wanted for her. That's why she got knocked up and dropped out of college."

"That was her life. Her choice. She took a leap of faith, and it worked out."

"They were happy, weren't they?" Her voice sounds

desolate, almost childlike. "She said they were, but not being here, I couldn't always tell."

"Jake was crazy about her and the kids, and anytime I spent a moment with her, it was obvious. They were relationship goals, Cassie."

She nods, while tears well in her eyes. Shit. I move closer and take her hand.

"I'm sorry, that was thoughtless."

"No, you're right. They were, and it should be okay to talk about them. We need to get used to that because of—"

"The kids."

Another nod. Managing the heartbreak is key because our little ones need us. But talking about the people we lost is important because *we* need it.

I'm still holding her hand and she hasn't pulled away. Instead, she's looking at our joined palms, like this is a strange turn of events. And I suppose it is.

"I'm sorry for freaking out earlier at the playground. I'd just spoken with Derek, and I think it had me on edge."

At the mention of Derek, she removes her hand from mine. Which is probably for the best because I think I could have held onto it all night. I must be losing my mind.

Max appears, the angel on my shoulder. *Do not bang your co-guardian.* I mentally brush him off like dandruff.

"It's okay. You wish he was here." The words are broken glass in my mouth.

"I—I thought I did. But now I realize that maybe I'm a bit relieved? Because I would have to be looking after him when my bandwidth is limited."

That makes no sense. "Why would you be looking after him?"

"He's not used to sitting around or relaxing. A support role doesn't really suit him."

Sounds like she's making excuses for the fact he can't be bothered showing his face.

I'm itching to say something negative about him, make myself out to be the stand-up guy he's not. But what would be the point? Derek and I are not in competition. He's already won.

Brakes screech. Not sure where that came from. I'm not and have never been in comp—okay, that would make me a liar.

I met this girl at my brother's wedding and wished like hell she hadn't turned me down. Instead, I was labeled the idiot little brother and she was the sensible older sister who chose not to make a terrible mistake.

With me.

I don't want to be anyone's mistake. I can't afford to be one now, not when the stakes are so high.

"Plenty of time for him to come around." I sure as hell hope not because his lack of support can only help my case.

"I suppose." She clearly wants this situation resolved sooner. She wants Derek to get with the program, her grief to dissolve, and for me to get the fuck out of her way.

"You know, you can't make this go faster. It'll happen the way it's supposed to."

She rolls her eyes. "Sure thing, Yoda."

"Now you're getting it."

"Oh, yeah?"

"I'm wise beyond my years. About time you acknowledged it."

She snorts, then immediately covers her nose. Another flush overtakes her cheeks.

She's embarrassed about that adorable little noise, which meant someone made fun of her in the past. Derek perhaps? I have no idea if he did the crime, but it definitely suits my narrative thinking he's the asshole here.

"Love that sexy snort," I murmur, testing. Probing for weaknesses.

I'm such a dick.

"It is *not* sexy," she says, this time with a sultry giggle that does something to me in the groin area. She's leaning in, her eyes fixed on me in a way that makes it impossible to look away. "About earlier ..."

"The playground?"

"No, later. That talk about what happened at the wedding. When I turned you down."

"I shouldn't have brought it up. You had every right to say no. I was just annoyed to be on the other end of it." Still am, apparently.

She bites down on her lip. "But you ... were really interested? That night?"

Is she kidding? I make a weird sound in my throat. "Cassie, of course I was." My hand cups her jaw—I can't help myself—and draws her close.

The skin at the nape of her neck is so soft and I rub my calloused fingers there. I want to kiss her. I want to feel those snarky lips surrender to my claim.

"Sam." It's a quiet murmur, one that tells me I'm affecting her but she's too much of a good girl to let her hormones dictate the play.

Good girl, bad idea. Max just got through telling me what a spectacularly bad idea it is.

Don't give her the weapons to destroy you.

But her lips. They look plump and pink and when they part, I have to call on every ounce of willpower I possess not to dive in and love the hell out of that mouth.

Okay, how about this? Another part of me queries, the boring, sensible part. *She belongs to someone else.*

I can't move in on another man's woman. At least, not any more than I already have.

That does the trick. Barely.

I slide my hand off her neck and take a deep breath to calm my pulse. It doesn't work but I'm not a quitter. I will breathe away this crazy lust I have for my sister-in-law.

She touches a finger to her lips, the lips I almost ravaged. Wishing I'd taken them hostage or relieved I let her—and myself—off the hook?

My phone buzzes on the coffee table. We both look to it, like a lifeline pulling us ashore from the sea of tension.

A pair of glossy tits, belonging to the ever-supportive Candy, light up the screen.

Cassie's expression hardens. "Ah."

"It's not ... anything."

"Of course not." She picks up her glass and stands at the same time, a lovely, fluid movement I'd be admiring the hell out of if it wasn't taking her away from me. "I'm going to run a bath. That okay?"

"Sure, I'll hold down the fort."

With a curt nod, she heads out of the room, while my gaze looks anywhere but at her ass. I take another slug of wine, wishing I could drink away these feelings.

Knowing that I can't—and that I've probably just made it worse.

Thirteen

Cass

"Waffles, don't eat that!"

I drag on his leash, pulling him away from some suspiciously chunky content in Lincoln Park before refocusing on my phone. I've finally connected with Sarah Strauss, the lawyer Derek recommended.

"Sorry about that. My dog's very curious. So you were saying something about background checks?"

"Yes, that would be one of our first avenues. We're looking for anything that can help our case. Behavior that's potentially troubling or damaging to the kids' well-being."

Would a photo of Candy's tits help?

"My co-guardian is a playboy type. Sleeps around a lot. Different woman every week, that kind of thing."

"Hmm, okay. But does he flaunt it in front of the kids?"

No, just me.

"Nothing I've seen yet." This conversation is making me uncomfortable because Sam *is* trying. He wants this to work.

Or at least, he wants the kids to stay here and for me to work around that.

"Okay. I'll start on the check and if you have anything to share—anything concrete—send it along."

We end the call, and I wonder why I don't feel better about it. I'm finally making progress, though deep down I'm not sure this is the right move. I was so sure a few days ago, but now I'm a mass of indecision.

Is it because we almost kissed last night? If anything, that should be buttressing my resolve to get out of here as quickly as possible. We're both so desperate for comfort right now that we're letting this chemistry between us override common sense.

This morning over breakfast, there was no mention of it, or of the fact he's sexting with Candy (and God knows who else. Maybe Pom Gal is in the rotation). I shouldn't care about the guy's sex life, except when he tries to involve me in it. Besides, I have Derek, who admittedly has been incommunicado over the last few days. We've done a couple of check-in texts, but we can't seem to connect. And I don't mean just by phone or FaceTime.

An attraction to my roommate, who also happens to be my competition *and* the enemy, while I'm trying to work things out with my long-term boyfriend is very inconvenient.

———

Later that afternoon, my mind is chock-full of these troubling thoughts as we pull into the driveway of Sam's parents' house in Lake Forest, an affluent suburb along the lake front north of Chicago. The house has a gazebo, which is further proof that the Killians' wealth hovers like a cloud over my future with the kids.

Sylvia greets us at the door, wearing an apron. Given her resources, I would consider this ironic if I didn't know that she loves to bake. She pulls the kids into a hug, her eyes tearing over before she recovers.

"It's about time you came to visit! We've missed you so much."

"Is Granddad in the den?" Maya asks.

"He sure is. He's watching a football game, a replay of something or other. Go say hi to him." Maya skips off while Sylvia turns to Spence. "How about a cookie? Fresh out of the oven."

"Chockit-chip?" Spence can't say "chocolate."

"Yep, your favorite." She leans in to kiss me on the cheek and gathers me in a hug that I return. I don't know Sylvia all that well, but I've always liked her. She acts like a mother should, meaning she's present in her kids' lives.

"Don't overload him with cookies, Mom," Sam says, which seems like something I'd come up with.

"Let him have all he wants," I respond. "We'll worry about the puking later."

I shoot him a glance, his lips quirk, and I can't help my answering grin. I really need to rein it in because I sure as hell do not need to be enjoying the vibes with this man.

So we almost kissed. Big whoop. It's not like it would have gone further. If his lips had touched mine, I would have pulled back, all affront, and taken my leave in a cloud of disapproval. Like I did, anyway, because he has someone else to take care of his needs.

Thanks, Candy, he's all yours.

With great solemnity, Spence accepts his cookie and heads into the living room, where Sylvia has set up a play area with toys and gadgets worthy of a kindergarten.

"Where did all this come from?"

Sylvia moves cookies from a cooling rack to a plate. "I brought them from the house. I want the kids to feel like this is their home away from home."

There's a slight dig in there, as if what Sam and I are doing is temporary and not quite good enough.

"Have a cookie, Cassandra. How's Derek?"

"Mom," Sam warns.

"What? I'm just wondering how he's reacting to all this change. It can put a lot of pressure on a relationship."

Sam makes a noise of discontent and grabs a cookie.

Rather than answer, I pick up one and take a bite. It's soft, chewy, delicious, and gives me time to form a response. Why isn't Derek calling me back? I know his work is important but what's happening here is important, too.

"He's very busy with work right now, but he's fully on board with whatever we decide."

Sylvia nods thoughtfully and I wait for her next prong of attack. It doesn't take long. "How long have you been together?"

"Six years."

"Oh, okay."

"Don't mind my mother," Sam says around his cookie-munching. He already has another one on deck in his hand, and I marvel at how he remains in such peak physical condition. "She's projecting her disappointment that I'm not hitched onto you."

Sylvia's eyes go wide. "I am not, Sam Matthew Killian. I'm just curious about who's going to be in my grandkids' lives."

She has a point. I want Derek to be involved but he's not been exactly effusive in his support. I need that support because it's me against this tight-knit family.

"I want the best for them, Sylvia. And I'm not going to let anyone be in their lives if they don't want that. I'm not sure how we're going to work it out, but I trust that we can all come to an arrangement that's best for the kids."

She nods at my vague response. I know what she wants to say. *Don't take them away. Don't let me lose more than I already have.*

Meanwhile, I'm working with a lawyer to do exactly that. Am I the villain here?

Sam jumps in to divert any potential blow-up over the kids' future. "Hey, Mom, maybe you should spend some time with your grandson. He's big on *Moana* this week."

"This year, you mean!" Sylvia says, her voice stridently cheerful.

I sneak a look at Sam, then back to Sylvia. "These cookies are amazing. I'd love the recipe."

Sam snorts at my transparent efforts to suck up to his mother, which has me shooting a glance of faux outrage his way.

Sylvia divides a strange look between us. Maybe she'd rather Sam and I didn't get along? "I'd be very happy to do that. Though Annie was always taking my recipes and then telling me she could never get them right."

"That was her ADHD. She had a hard time focusing on the details."

Sylvia looks a little tearful again. Sam makes a move, but because I'm closer I get there first and place my arm around her. She sinks into me for a moment.

"Hey, I'd love to see what toys you brought over for the kids. And maybe you can give me some advice on how to keep them entertained in ways that don't involve screens."

Looking up, I catch Sam with a strange expression, like he never would have expected this kind of empathy of me. In his eyes, I'm still the stiff, no-nonsense automaton.

Sylvia smiles tearily at me. "Thank God one of you is

thinking of these children's brains! Sam spends so much time playing video games that he thinks it's perfectly okay for these children to do the same."

That's harsh on Sam, who has been actively involved with the kids—playing puzzles, telling stories, letting them help while he cooks. I'm the one who defers to screens far too much. I open my mouth to say something, but Sam speaks up.

"I'll check on Dad and Maya."

He heads off, leaving me wondering, but not for long because Sylvia immediately lowers her voice. "So how are you, Cass? Really?"

I draw a deep breath. "Not great. This is the hardest thing I've had to endure. But you know what that's like. It's awful for you as well."

"It is. But we can pull together to make this work." She sends an indulgent look toward Spence who's playing with a set of puzzle blocks. "It's just …"

"What?" I dread hearing her beg me not to make any sudden moves in the custodial arena.

"I'm worried about Sam."

"In what way?"

She sighs. "Well, responsibility and Sam have never existed in the same sentence. The number of times his father and I had to pick him up from some rover party. He's always been such a wild boy."

I think she means a rave. Though no one calls them that anymore.

"Years ago, though."

"He's never been one to settle, and I worry this is all too much for him. That he might make mistakes."

And that I'll use those mistakes to my advantage.

"We're both going to make mistakes, Sylvia." Sam and I have agreed to give each other grace during this time. Yet here I am, looking for ways to get ahead.

I touch her arm. I want to tell her that it'll be okay, that I won't do anything rash. I can't just yet, but I'm beginning to realize that moving the kids away from Chicago isn't as clear-cut a decision as it once seemed.

Fourteen

Sam

I could stick around and chaperone the hell out of this situation, but I think Cassie can handle my mother. They need to get along because there will be plenty of these meet-ups in the future.

Thinking about the future has me revisiting events of the past. Specifically last night when I came this close to pushing Cassie down on the sofa and banging her brains out. Her lips were so inviting, her eyes almost pleading, so good thing I called a halt to it. (Before Candy's tits made a guest appearance, as if I need further confirmation that I'm not in this woman's league. St. Cassandra would never.)

Neither would she have let me get any further than a messy pass. Besides, I would just be taking advantage of a slightly tipsy, lonely, grieving woman with a bad boyfriend. I'm not that much of a jerk, no matter how blue my balls are.

My dad has a great den setup, which he's availed of more in the last year since his stroke. He used to spend more time outdoors, playing tennis and golf, but he gets tired easily these days. Luckily this indoor-with-TV business works for hangs with his grandkids.

On heading down, I find Maya curled up beside him as Dad watches a replay of a Bears game from the previous weekend.

"Hey, son."

Fuck, that gets me. It's a heavy weight to be the only one left. "Hey, Dad, what's the score?"

"Third quarter, Bears 15, Packers 12."

My dad and I have always been close, but he had a special connection with Jake, who molded his life in Dad's image, the family man, the guy with the plan. I took a while to find my place in the world, and my father has been understandably wary of my adulting credentials. Mom, too, as that dig about my video-game playing can attest.

"So, bug, how are things in the city?" Dad asks Maya.

"Okay. Waffles is farting a lot. And he puked the other day."

"You gotta take the dog to the vet," Dad says to me.

I had no idea the farting was a vet-necessary problem, and the puking is news to me. Jakey would have known this. Yet again, further evidence I'm not cut out for this domestic gig.

"What about school?" Dad drills Maya. "I heard you're back."

"Yeah." She launches into a chatty overview of what she's learning while my dad listens with one eye on the TV.

I need to talk with him, see how he's coping. "You know you're missing out on chocolate chip cookies, bug."

Maya narrows her gaze. "Do you want one, Granddad?"

"Nah, got to watch my figure."

She kisses him on the cheek and skips by me.

"I don't want one either," I comment.

She smiles serenely. "I know you don't. You're just trying to get rid of me."

"So smart."

Once she's out of sight, I take a seat beside my dad. He turns to me, his eyes a little shiny.

"How are you holding up, Dad?"

He lets loose a sigh. "It wasn't supposed to happen like this. I miss my boy."

Tell me about it.

He goes on. "I'm worried about your mother. She's not as strong as she pretends to be."

"I know. I've been trying to give her space, so she doesn't feel she has to take on so much."

"She loves seeing the kids. It helps more than it doesn't, so don't be a stranger."

Okay, I had that wrong. But then there's so much I don't know. "I should take the dog to the vet, huh?"

We chat about Waffles' apparently well-known digestive issues, and I listen, absorbing the wisdom of a man who raised a family of two spirited boys, three dogs, a parakeet, several hamsters, and countless goldfish. Maybe it helps him feel useful; it certainly helps me feel less foolish.

After a while, he asks, "How's it going with Cass?"

"Better than expected."

My father's lips twitch, which is usually a result of the ravages the stroke did on his body, but not this time. I know the difference.

"What?" I manage a smile. "We're both on our best behavior."

"Tough on you, though."

"I can do this," I say, trying to keep the frustration out of my voice. "I might not be a natural like Jake, but I can learn."

"I know you can. I meant that it's tough because you miss him *and* you have to team up with Cass in such close quarters. That's a lot to deal with. Makes everything more raw."

He's not wrong. I'm a powder keg ready to blow. I'm

pissed at Cassie, my mom, everyone who's put me in this position and thinks I can't hack it.

Mostly I'm pissed at Jake. "I'm not sure why he asked me to do this."

My father smiles. "He probably expected it would be the making of you, Sam."

Why does everyone think I need to be remade, forged in some crucible of suffering to become a better man? "But with Cassie? He knew how I felt about her."

"That you had such a crush on her when you first met her at the wedding? Yep."

Wasn't expecting that. "Nah. That was just the usual lusting after what I couldn't have."

He looks at me squarely. "Not just the woman, but the life. I know you've said being settled wasn't your thing, but don't think I never saw you looking a bit wistful at the cookouts and family gatherings. Now's your chance."

People will twist all manner of situations to justify their way of thinking. I don't think "wistful" is, or has ever been, in my repertoire.

"Dad, I'm going to do my best to raise Jake's kids, but I'm not sure domesticity is the life for me." Maybe Cassie would do a better job without me making a mess of it. "And there won't be time for dating or finding them a new mom. I'm barely holding on."

A direct look, straight into my soul. "Lucky you've got someone on deck."

I roll my eyes. Let him have his silly fantasy about Cassie and me. Maybe he needs to convince himself she's not the devil and won't take the kids away.

I, on the other hand, do not need convincing.

I finish watching the game with Dad, though I already knew the Packers made a late comeback and a miracle of a touchdown to beat the hometown boys. By the time it's done, he's dozing off in his EZ chair, so I pull the throw blanket over him, kiss his forehead, and go upstairs. We've been told it's okay to leave him alone for brief periods.

I could head to the kitchen and make sure war hasn't broken out, but I can hear laughter—Maya and my mom—which makes me think they're okay. Leaving them to it, I head upstairs, past my old room and into another.

Jake's.

Time travel might not be a thing yet, but who needs tech like that in the Killian household? Mom refuses to redecorate our old bedrooms *(what if you need to come home?)* and I'm torn between thinking this is a beautiful thing and a downright horror. Jake moved out over twelve years ago when he went to MIT, so this place is a perfect capsule of his teenaged self. A framed Bren St. James Chicago Rebels jersey (from when the team sucked), posters of *The Walking Dead* (from when it didn't suck), Katy Perry and Rihanna. An iMac that looks like a museum relic, books on coding, a PS2, his favorite game, *Grand Theft Auto*—all these bits and pieces that made up his life at this one pure point in time.

I take a seat on the bed and inhale. It doesn't smell musty, probably because Mom has her cleaning person include this room on the rotation. But it does smell of ... I check the closet and sniff one of his shirts. There it is, the scent of Axe Phoenix. He practically bathed in the stuff from the ages of fourteen to eighteen. It's faint, like the memories of that time, but I hold onto it because my brother is no longer here. If he was, I'd be razzing the fuck out of him for his personal grooming choices.

The ladies love it, Sammie.

*It leaves 'em dazed and confused, Jakey. Only way you can
score, I suppose.*

Grief sucker punches me in the throat for a second, and
my best, most articulate response is "Fuck!" I yell into the
closet, conscious that I don't want to involve anyone else in my
pity party.

A movement rustles at the door, and there she is: St.
Cassandra. The woman who seems to know when Sam
Killian's Worst Performance is on the card and appears with
perfect timing for a ringside view.

"Hey, I came to check on you. You weren't with your
dad." There's no accusation there, just a statement of fact. Her
gaze arcs over the room's walls. "Wow, this is fun."

Wordlessly, I close the closet door and take a seat on the
bed, opposite the writing desk. Woody from *Toy Story* is
propped against the keyboard.

She's still standing at the door. "Is there another time
capsule of little Sammie's teen years on this floor?"

"Sure is. Next door on the left. We told Mom to clean
them out, but she thinks we need a backup in case of some
disaster that only a mother can handle." Part of me wishes I
could come home again, shirk all these new adult
responsibilities.

Remaining silent, Cassie hovers at the threshold, one toe
in, and I find myself anxious about that. Like it's a metaphor
for our situation. "I'll have to come in and clean this room
out, I suppose," I say.

That bare admission brings her inside. She stands in front
of the bookcase, her finger coasting along the spines.

"We'll have to do the house as well." She turns, her
expression troubled. "I'm sorry. I intruded on a private
moment."

"No, it's okay. Seems like I have a knack for trapping you
in my web of trauma."

Her nose twitches. "I don't feel trapped. I'm here if you need me."

I think she means it, though she probably has no idea what her offer does to me. How all I can think of is touching her in a way that will free us both from this nightmare, if only for a while.

Lust-suppression activate. "Sorry to leave you with my mom."

"What? Oh no, that's fine."

I raise an eyebrow.

She chuckles. "I like your mom. She's practical and no-nonsense, just like I imagine a mom should be. Mine was so flighty."

"How so?"

"Cereal for dinner, no clean clothes, leaving us for days at a time, usually for some guy." She gives a small head shake, shrugging off some perceived self-pity, perhaps. "We survived, of course. It's just kind of nice when a mom takes charge."

"That's my mom. It's been a rough few days for her, though. Jakey made them so proud."

She sits on the bed beside me. "Don't tell me the rescue squad firefighter, Mr. Hollywood in bunker pants, the man the mayor has on speed dial, can't get no respect from his momma?"

That earns a much-needed laugh and surprise that she's got the goods on me. "Sure, she's proud, but Jake was another story. It's the family thing—she loved that he settled down. She was crazy about Annie and her grandkids. I'm a poor substitute."

"I'm sure she doesn't think that."

"Maybe I'm being too hard on her. I'm going to do my best but I'm not sure it's enough."

"It's a wrench in the life plan, for sure. For all of us. But we've got this—and your family will be stronger as a result."

I take a closer look at her, and all that earnest sincerity shining off her. "This is your family, too. Maybe not how you imagined getting your membership card, but you're in it now. No takebacks."

She swallows, her slender neck bulging slightly. I need to kiss that neck. I need to lay lips on her throat. I need to—

Get a hold of myself. I can't turn every single encounter with this woman into something sexual. Hauling myself out of the sensual quicksand, I say, "Mr. Hollywood in bunker pants? Been doing your research on me, I see."

"No need. On the weekly Zoom calls with Annie, I heard all about the amazing Sam Killian. Rescuing kittens from trees, damsels in distress, kids in bear traps."

"Wait a second."

She grins, and fuck if my heart doesn't do a loop-the-loop. "Okay, no bear traps, but Jake never shut up about you. He was so proud of his little brother." As if realizing that's going to set me off, she takes my hand. Soft against my rough, it feels a little too perfect in my possessive grip. Because, yeah, that's what it turns into when I squeeze back, thinking about my brother singing my praises to the woman who hates me.

"Bet you loved that. The check-ins tainted with your worst nightmare's shenanigans."

"I could have done with a little less of you." Another smart-ass grin. I'm starting to live for these bursts of sun.

While we're on such good terms, this might be a good opportunity to tell her something important.

"I'm thinking of going back to work." CFD has been understanding, not hurrying my return, but it needs to happen sometime. It's probably too soon but I worked hard to get that spot on Rescue Squad, and I can't risk them assigning someone else. If Cassie wants to use that as ammunition, let her. "I have feelers out for childcare, but you'll have to take on more of that burden during my shifts until we hire someone."

I'm testing the waters. Will this push her in?

"It's okay. I'm not going anywhere for now."

Neither of us have said anything about the legal situation. As far as I'm concerned, she can stay as long as she wants because the longer she stays the more secure my position becomes.

Or, that's what I'm telling myself.

Her gaze slides to the desk as her hand slips from mine. "Your brother liked Woody? The kids love *Toy Story* as well."

"I should give this to Spence." I pick up the figure and wiggle it in the charged air between us.

"And you know Maya would love that Rebels hockey jersey."

My niece is a huge hockey fan. "It's pretty old school from when the Rebels were one of the worst teams in the league. She'd get a kick out of it because her dad owned it." I take a breath, marveling that this tentative peace between us feels so damn good. I thought I preferred the sensual friction, but this is good, too. "I'd better check on Dad."

"No, you stay here for a little longer." She stands, squeezes my shoulder. "I can look in on Kenny. And then I promised your mom and Maya I'd help bake a cake, which is probably going to go terribly."

"Give yourself some credit."

"Oh, loved my burned taco meat the other night, did you?"

It was terrible, but I took over and managed to salvage it. We both chuckle, and with that moment of simpatico, I watch her leave, feeling better than when I walked in here ten minutes ago.

Feeling a little less alone.

Fifteen

Cass

It's been a week since I moved in with the kids, and we've settled into a rhythm, taking turns to drop Maya off at school and watching over Spence. Sam takes charge for a couple of hours while I make calls and run Zoom meetings with my clients. If I need to set up an appointment in the afternoon, he's there as well. He usually picks Maya up from school and runs errands on the way back.

He's also a good cook, though he's not cocky about it (unlike everything else). He says the meal-planning kits do all the work, even though I still mess them up. It's a good thing the kids aren't relying on me for sustenance.

I'm usually up first though, and I can muddle my way through Eggo waffles and Fruit Loops. Sam disapproves of my coffee-only approach to the first meal of the day, but it gives me more time to tend to the kids.

Most evenings after dinner, I catch up on work emails while Sam makes sure Maya's homework is done and Spence is tired out before bed. Because the morning goes by in such a rush, I usually wait until the evening to take a shower. But tonight, it's later than usual and I don't want to wake the kids —Spence gets upset by the sound of the pitter-patter of water —so I use Sam's ensuite.

For some reason, I had thought he was in the living room watching TV; it's on and I can hear what sounds like *The Mandalorian*. But Waffles must be watching Grogu and co alone because I walk in on Sam emerging from the shower.

He's dropped his towel and is now using it for its intended purpose—drying off. With his back to me, I have the perfect view of his ass, which is about as amazing as an ass can get. Next-level butt musculature. So nice I can almost feel my hands grasping it.

I've always known he had wide shoulders, but seeing all that golden skin is a revelation. He's more built than he was six years ago when I first met him, but it's not outrageous. They're the kind of muscles that would feel wonderful wrapped around you.

That do.

I blink at the thought. Save for a comforting hug from Derek when I broke the news of my sister and brother-in-law's death, I haven't had much affection lately. At the funeral I doled out perfunctory hugs to the Killian family and accepted quick ones from everyone who wanted to give them. My body didn't feel ready for that level of closeness.

But now something has toggled in me, a switch of my libido. It might have something to do with the nearness we've indulged in over the last week, whether it's letting myself be caged by his body during a bad dream or holding his hand as he remembered his brother in his childhood bedroom. There have been less obvious connections, too. His palm on the small of my back as we switch places in the kitchen. Our fingers brushing as we pass off backpacks, keys, shoes, the building blocks of this household we've strung together.

That almost-kiss …

It's all innocent, with no agenda (except for the kiss, but even that felt more of a cry for comfort than something sexual). Yet here I am, my body flushing, my nipples tightening, my mind abruptly overwhelmed by the man's in-your-face physicality.

This is the worst reaction I could have, and the knowledge of it has me taking a step back. The noise alerts Sam to my presence. He turns, his towel moving to cover, likely because there are kids in the house now.

But on seeing me, his expression changes from surprise to … not surprise. Like he expected this to eventually happen.

Like he welcomes it.

"Cassie," he murmurs, and just the way he says my name does something to me. Low, deep, and dangerous.

"Sorry, I was going to take a shower and didn't realize you …" I wave the rest.

"Sure, go ahead."

This should be my cue to leave and come back later. He's at the dresser now, pulling out ultra-thin sweatpants and then without warning, he drops the towel and hunches slightly to pull the pants on.

There's no missing his cock.

It's glorious.

It shouldn't be. He just exited a shower after all, but I can tell it's half-erect. Knowing Sam Killian, he walks around in a perfect state of arousal, ready to deliver on all the promise of that wicked smile. Penis potential. I should not be standing here, but he's almost issued a challenge.

One I'm apparently up to meeting.

So I remain, in as casual a stance as I can make it, as if this is perfectly normal behavior because we're just roommates after all, watching as he pulls on his sweats. Covers up his cock. And walks toward me with all that swagger I used to despise and now realize that I ... don't. It's more complicated than that. It always has been where Sam's concerned.

"Sorry to interrupt," I say into the awkward silence.

"No apology necessary. Mi casa and all that. Bathroom's yours."

I scurry in there like a frightened mouse and behind the closed door, take a deep breath. So I'm attracted to Sam—he's an attractive guy. He was when he was twenty-one, feckless and cocky, and he still is at the age of twenty-seven with years of experience, an important job, and a chin dimple I want to lick.

None of that should matter. We're adults and I have Derek, not that I need a boyfriend in another city to keep me faithful and out of Sam Killian's bed. Even if there was no Derek, Sam would not be on my radar in that way. We have a job to do, and we don't like each other.

At least, I don't think we like each other. Not in that way. Or maybe *only* in that way, and not in any way that might be threatening.

I need to talk to Derek.

Usually, I would text him before calling but not today. He was due to fly back to New York yesterday to finalize the deal. My call goes to voice mail after one ring.

"Derek, I'd love to hear your voice right now. Give me a call."

I wait a couple of minutes, but nothing. In the shower, I wash my hair quickly and give a fly-by scrub of my body just in case I miss Derek.

He should be here, in Chicago, but he's not, and I'm finding that this is the perfect statement of our relationship. I'm doing all the work and getting precious little in return. I quickly dress, dry my hair, and go to my room—I even put my head out the door to check the coast is clear, which is pathetic—just as Derek calls.

"Hey."

"Sorry I missed you. We were celebrating the conclusion of the deal." I hear the clink of glassware and the low murmur of conversation.

"Congrats! You must be so pleased."

"I am. So what's up?"

"I'm just feeling a bit overwhelmed."

He breathes out. "Of course, you are. You've got so much on your plate and it's good that you've figured it out before it goes too far."

Alarm bells clang, unease swelling that we've jumped right into the thick of it with little preamble. "Before what goes too far?"

He sighs. "Cass, you've done your duty. Now it's time to come home."

"Done my duty? It's been less than two weeks!"

"I get that. But you're just digging yourself a hole by getting into this custody thing with the Killians. They're not going to let them go, so where does that leave you?"

"It leaves me in the same position I'm in now. Those kids are my responsibility."

"But I'm not sure that's good for us."

My pulse flutters. "For us?"

"Yeah." There's a resignation in his voice. "Kids are fine when you can hand them off. Hell, I love my nieces and nephews, but I sure as hell don't want them living with me."

"What if something happened to their parents? Would you abandon them because it's not good for you?" My voice is brittle.

"That's a hypothetical. But there's always another way. You have the Killians and the kids would be better off with them. You can't use them as a do-over because you didn't get it perfect with Annie."

I can't believe he said that. "I am not using them as a do-over. These kids need me."

"I've no doubt they do—in the short-term. But you can be a good aunt without doing the mom bit. You already did it with Annie and she turned out fine, even if it's not what you wanted for her. And I'll be honest—I never thought kids were in our future. This isn't what I signed on for."

There it is, finally, in the black-and-white neither of us has been willing to print. "Right."

He clicks his tongue. "Just think about it realistically. If you do somehow manage to win custody and bring them to New York, you're going to need childcare because you also need a job." The implication is that I'll get no help from him. "Your whole life, and theirs, will be uprooted and upended."

"That's already happened!"

He sighs. "I didn't bring this up before but now's probably as good a time as any. How come you never told me Annie wanted you to be guardian? I'm assuming you knew this in advance."

"Because until it becomes a reality, it's only a hypothetical." *Remember those, Derek?* "Why bring it up if it would never happen?"

He's silent for a moment, and when he speaks again, it's measured. "I think it's something you should have told me because it would've given me a heads-up on how you feel about kids, family, the whole lot. It might be a hypothetical, but it speaks to a desire you've had that you never discussed with me. Something that's in opposition to my own wants."

He sounds so analytical, but that's how Derek sees the world. As binary problems to be solved. He's right about one thing: I could have brought up Annie's request with him sooner, but I didn't because I knew any discussion of it would be difficult. Derek would have viewed me as broody and might have started drifting away. After so long together, I couldn't imagine being out there again, alone.

But I'm imagining it quite easily now, probably because I *have* been alone even in the middle of this relationship.

"Are you giving me some sort of ultimatum, Derek? Me or the kids?"

"Kind of dramatic, Cass."

"But that's what's happening, isn't it? You don't see kids in your future, not even these ones I'm tasked with caring for."

"When you put it like that."

I swallow past the burn in my throat. "So that's it."

"I guess it is." He's not even trying to reason with me, probably because he knows that at the end of the day I'm beyond reason. My mind's already made up.

"I need to go."

"Okay, Cass. Take care." He hangs up first, the bastard.

I stare at the phone for God knows how long before I realize that after six years, Derek and I are history.

This would be the time to turn out the light and crawl under the covers to wallow. But I'm too angry for sleep. Instead, I head out to the living area where Sam is sitting on the sofa, in a too-tight tee and erotically-thin sweats that highlight his amazing thighs. Poking my wound with his hotness.

I take the beer bottle right out of his hand and chug enough to have foam leaking from the side of my mouth.

Sam stares, his expression one of shock. Nice to know that stick-in-the-mud, by-the-rules, St. Cassandra has the capacity to surprise him.

Let's keep that train rolling, shall we? "I'm going to need something stronger than this. I just broke up with my boyfriend."

Sixteen

Sam

I was not expecting *that*. If anything, I was expecting a pissed off Cassie because of what happened earlier in the evening.

I'd gotten more than a little thrill out of her walking in on me while I was naked, which is pretty immature, I know. She's so strait-laced I expected her to thumb her nose at my roughneck self and turn tail. Instead, she stayed, watching with something like hunger in her eyes.

I would have waited longer, but I could feel the beginnings of a chub situation and no way was I giving her the satisfaction of thinking I walk around with a permanent erection in her presence. Maybe that's half-true, but she sure as hell doesn't need the evidence against me.

So I kept it super casual as I walked to the dresser and found a pair of sweats.

And she kept it super casual as she let her gaze wander over my naked form, right up until the moment I covered up the dick that wants her.

I've been sitting out here, trying not to imagine her in my shower. She could use the kids' one, but along with kissing, Spence has a weird hang-up about the sound of water (*thanks, little wingman!*). Now I have all sorts of X-rated images swirling in my head. Cassie soaping herself up, her hands cupping those perfect tits, her fingertips delving between her legs getting herself clean in the dirtiest way possible.

My fantasies were tripping along nicely, minding their own business, when out she came, smelling of that pomegranate-coconut shampoo she uses, and helped herself to my beer—right out of my hand!

I immediately knew something was up. I'm smart like that.

"You okay?"

"Anything stronger?"

"There's liquor but maybe you should stick to wine. There's a bottle open from dinner."

I head into the kitchen and pull a glass off the shelf.

"You going to let me drink alone?"

"Well, I did have a beer but now I don't." I grab another beer, pour her a glass of red, and gesture to the island. "Sit."

She does, takes a slug of wine, and sets it back a couple of inches. She might be regretting opening the door here, so I figure a little encouragement is warranted.

"What happened?"

"You know Derek couldn't make it this past weekend."

"Right, the merger thing."

"Well, I called, needing to hear his voice ..." Her cheeks color with embarrassment, and we both know why. After running into a naked Sammie, she needed to call her boyfriend to remind herself that she had a fucking boyfriend.

I am positively giddy.

"And he said some things that made it clear he wasn't interested in being a father to the kids."

Ah. "This isn't something you guys have discussed before?"

"Not in concrete terms. I know he likes his life—our life—as it is. He's a work hard-play hard kind of guy and kids don't really figure into that. I assumed he'd come around or the circumstances would make him see sense."

"That's not really the way it works."

She glares at me. "How the hell do you know? Did you want to be a father before ten days ago?"

"Not exactly."

"Yet, here you are because circumstances have changed. I thought that would make Derek see the light."

I nod along. "But it didn't."

"No. And it was like this giant chasm had opened between us. We're on opposite sides, neither of us willing to step away from the cliff. But the difference is that I need to be here for these kids. I can't abandon them, so, if Derek wants to be with me, he needs to come around to my way of thinking."

The Cass way or the highway. "Is that what you told him?"

"I didn't get a chance to. He issued his own ultimatum before I got a chance to issue mine!"

She sounds so pissed at this gamesmanship that it makes me chuckle.

"It's not funny."

"It kind of is. So do you mind me asking something?"

She growls her assent.

"How come you guys aren't married?"

"We haven't been on the same page." She pauses, then starts again. "He said the piece of paper isn't that important. But I suspect it's because he thinks marriage is the kind of merger that requires financial arrangements."

Merger. She said it, not me. "Like a pre-nup?"

"Yes, which I'd be fine with signing. Derek makes a lot

more money than me. I felt as long as we were contributing equally to the household, my bona fides wouldn't be suspect—"

"Hold up there." I raise a hand. "You guys go fifty-fifty on the bills even though he earns more than you. How much more does he earn?"

"Mid six figures. So, five times as much as me. Maybe more than that." Again, she looks embarrassed, but she shouldn't. She got a late start on college because she was taking care of her sister. She's been in the post-graduation workforce for what? Six years? Seven? Of course she's not going to be earning top dollar yet.

"And I'm guessing you don't live in a hovel."

She frowns. "It's a nice two bed two bath on the Upper East side. The rent is exorbitant but that's New York." She straightens her spine. "I didn't want him to think I was taking advantage, so I offered to go half on everything. It's only fair."

"Is it? Because you guys have been together for six years and it sounds more like a business deal."

"You don't know the first thing about it. I didn't grow up with money so I'm not going to immediately latch onto the first guy I meet with cash and bleed him dry."

Peak-level defensiveness here. "Not saying you are. But after a few years of cohabitation, with a goal toward spending your lives together, he shouldn't be bleeding *you* dry. He earns five times as much but you're fifty-fifty? Fuck that." I move on quickly. "It sounds like you were more invested in this relationship than him. You wanted marriage and he wasn't willing to go that extra step. You wanted kids and he didn't. You're doing all the work here, and he's treating you like a roommate."

For a moment I wonder if I've said too much. No one likes to hear criticism of a venture they've invested years of their life in, especially when it's related to the heart. Then I realize the word I've used in my head to describe this is very apt: *venture*. A business arrangement. I can't believe this guy accepted the fifty-fifty expenses deal when they could have—should have—ratio'ed it out to something manageable. Hell, if I set up house with someone who had a lower income than me, which is likely because I'm very fucking wealthy, I sure as hell wouldn't be expecting equal contributions to the household.

She's turning it over in her head. "I can't analyze it now. All I know is that when it came to the most important thing—parenting my sister's kids—he told me that wasn't what he had in mind for his future. He said I should leave it to you and your family and go back to New York."

Back to our one true fight. Should I be thanking Derek?

"Which you have no intention of doing."

"Not a chance."

The challenge I hear should piss me off. But no, it only cheers me right the fuck up. Is it possible I want Cassie to stick around and help raise these kids? What does that even look like?

Because it couldn't look like this. Sitting in the kitchen, drinking wine and beer, chatting about the events of the day (even if the events involve her confiding in me about her useless boyfriend). As much as this connection appeals to me, it isn't real. It's borne of a mutual need to get through this soul-crushing time.

Right?

"Are you guys truly finished?" That's what she said when she walked in—and I'm strangely wishing it was true. But they've been together for a long time. One conversation shouldn't be enough to end it.

"I don't know." She rubs her eyes. "We probably should talk again. Maybe when we're not snapping at each other."

She takes a deep breath, like this is all it takes to psych

yourself up for a tough conversation. It shouldn't be so hard with someone you love, should it?

"Sleep on it, talk to him tomorrow. Though I find it hard to believe he's not calling you nonstop after your fight. I don't get this guy. If it was me—"

"Not everyone reacts like you, Sam. Some men prefer to let things settle."

I scoff. "Sounds like he's gonna settle himself right out of a relationship."

She stands and sighs. "Like I said, you don't know the first thing about it."

"I know enough. Derek is a fucking tool. All the times you've come out to visit, he's been here what? Three times?"

Her cheekbones are tagged with color. "He's very busy."

Still with the excuses, even now. This should be my cue to stay silent, but do you think that's likely? That would be a negative. I'm far too pleased at the opportunity to let loose on Derek's ass.

"If he wanted to be your partner, he should be making the effort. Supporting you here, never mind his stupid deal, and backing you completely. And he sure as hell should not be leaving you alone with another guy you have history with."

Her mouth drops open. "History? You think what happened—or *didn't* happen—between us is 'historical' in nature?"

I don't like her tone, but I'm already committed. "Did you tell him?"

"Tell him what?"

"Cassie."

"Don't you 'Cassie' me. I did not tell him that you once made a pass at me and I turned you down."

"And why is that?"

Her eyes fly wide in disbelief that I have to even ask. "Because it didn't matter, Sam. It was a blip, something I barely recall even when we're in the same room, never mind when you're out of sight. I didn't tell Derek because frankly, I forgot about it. When I do remember, it's so inconsequential that it's not even worth sharing. And if I did? Do you really think Derek would be threatened by you?" She tilts her head. "Or is that you projecting here?"

"Hardly." *Weak, Sammie. So weak.*

She waves a hand. "You certainly share your opinion of him often enough. All this stuff about him not supporting me, not having my back, our partnership being like a business deal—are you just trying to undermine our relationship for some nefarious reason that gets you a better angle on the kids' future?"

"Like I'd need to play games, Cassie."

"It's Cassandra."

"Sure thing, St. *Cassandra*." I'm closer to her now, or maybe she's closer to me. That gorgeous green gaze is alive with fury. "I don't need to chisel away at the foundations of what you have with Derek, sweetheart. It's already crumbling without my input."

She blinks. *Fuck.*

I am *such* an asshole. I rush in to fix it. "That wasn't fair."

She takes a breath, then another one, like she's trying to hold herself together.

"Hey." I cup her jaw and run my thumb over her trembling lip. She feels like a porcelain doll under my touch, though that imagery belies her strength. "It's okay. It's going to be okay."

"Is it?"

I don't know if she means her relationship or this pain that's gutting us both. I know what I want it to mean.

I want Derek out of her life.

I might say it's because no one that disinterested should

come anywhere near my nephew and niece, that everyone they encounter needs to love them unconditionally.

But that's not the reason.

I drop my hand. "It'll look better in the morning. You should talk to Derek again and figure it out."

Then I leave the kitchen as fast as I can.

Seventeen

Cass

There's a knock on the door. At least I think that's what wakes me up. A quick check of my phone and—oh, crud, it's 7:40 a.m.

I never sleep late but I finished that second glass of wine and that was enough to send me into a deep slumber. In my haze, I must have forgotten to set my alarm.

I sit up quickly just as the door opens. Sam puts his head around.

"You okay?"

"I overslept. You should have woken me."

He doesn't comment on that, which came out more critically than I intended. He's not my keeper. "I'll take Maya to school if you watch Spence."

"Of course. I'll be right there."

Grabbing a robe, I realize that the tank top I sleep in is gaping and I gave a top-notch view of the girls to my roommate. Fabulous.

Last night I sent a couple of text messages to Derek. It

shouldn't be over after one conversation. Sam Killian is wrong about so much but not about that.

> Hi, can we talk?

> I know it's late but I'm up.

Now I check my phone. Something came in after midnight, but I missed it.

DEREK

> Sorry, just seeing this. Call me when you wake up.

Something else happened last night. Sam and I got into that argument about Derek's support of me, but more interestingly about how Derek should feel threatened by a hot virile firefighter in my immediate orbit (not that Sam described himself as such or that I think of him that way or ... *never mind*). As if I can't be trusted and need my relationship with another man as a buffer.

Which made me think about whether Sam thinks we need a buffer. So there was that almost-kiss but I've done a great job of minimizing it. The alternative is too dangerous to consider.

Doesn't stop my tricky brain from straying down that path. Is there actually potential for something to happen here —something that would need my boyfriend as a cock-blocker?

Except he might no longer be my boyfriend. As much as I hate to admit it, Sam's comments about my relationship with Derek might be on point. Things have been broken between us for a while now, and Derek's accusation that I kept Annie's guardianship request under wraps instead of discussing the possibility, even after the accident when I knew it was more likely than not, is telling.

I wanted to present it as a fait accompli, to force Derek to accept the inevitable. Which is no way to communicate with the man I've been expecting to spend the rest of my life with.

Out in the kitchen, there's no sign of Maya but Sam is serving up pancakes to Spence who's waiting with his knife and fork at the ready. Wearing his Spider-Man PJs, he looks so adorable I want to gobble him up.

"Hey, little guy." I smooth his hair and kiss the top of his head—and get the usual "no kissing!" response—as I head to the coffee pot. A mug, a carton of skim, and an already-torn Splenda packet are waiting. For me? That's so considerate.

I sneak a quick glance at Sam, but he's busy with the pancakes. Perhaps sensing my scrutiny, he looks up, his expression unreadable. "You're eating breakfast this morning."

"I don't need more than coffee."

"Yes, you do. You've got to keep up your strength." He sets a plate of pancakes in the spot next to Spence, who is already cutting into his. "Help Spence with the butter and syrup and then eat your own."

"I've already said I don't—"

"Cassie. Sit." His tone is more resigned than bossy.

I do as I'm told. The pancakes do look delicious—round and soft, waiting for the perfect mix of butter and syrup. Poor Spence is struggling so I take the bottle from him and pour some on his plate.

"More," he says.

A little more comes out of the bottle.

"More."

"That's enough, Spence."

His face scrunches up, like he's going to cry, and I suddenly have no idea what to do. I feel hot and weird in my skin, making a mess of everything, exposed as a fraud. Derek, Sam, the kids. Panicked, I look up at Sam, who immediately comes to my rescue.

"Hey, buddy, what's going on?"

"More syrup!"

"You know something," Sam says, an ocean of calm. "How about we cut up this pancake and you dip it in the syrup? See if you have enough? I think your aunt Cassie would love to cut it up for you."

"Yep, Spence, let's do that." I make a few cuts, then cover one piece in a crazy amount of syrup before handing it off. "Here you go."

He sniffs his disapproval but takes it and plops it in his mouth. His eyes light up because, hey, pancakes and syrup.

Sam nods approvingly. "Pretty good, huh? Now, let your aunt eat her breakfast." Another pointed look tells me it's time to set a good example.

Maya appears at the entrance to the kitchen, already dressed in her school uniform. "I'm going to be late."

"Yep, got it." Sam flicks a glance my way. "Can you ..." He gestures to the mess he's made. One more reason I don't eat cooked breakfasts, but I appreciate that he's taking care of the kids.

"Got it. You guys head out. Spence and I are going to finish our pancakes."

Sam sends me a look of gratitude that makes me oddly warm. I should be annoyed at his bout of truth telling last night, not to mention that when he touched me, I wanted so badly to sink into him and take the comfort on offer.

Yet I can't seem to muster the appropriate outrage.

I'm cleaning syrup off Spence's hands and thinking about my to-do list—finding childcare for the kids is high on it—when I get a call from Sam. He should be on his way back from dropping off Maya.

I hit the speaker button. "Hey, what's up?"

"First off, everything's fine. Maya's at the hospital."

"What?"

"She got into a fight at school when someone pushed her, and she hit her head. We're at Lake Forest Memorial and the doctor's checking her for a concussion."

My pulse speeds up. "How did this happen? Were you there?"

"No. I'd just left when the school called me, and I had to go back. They'd already called an ambulance, but I thought it would be quicker for me to take her. That's where we are."

"I'll come over."

"You don't have to—"

"I'll be there as soon as I get Spence dressed." Spence. I'm not sure it's a good idea to take him to the hospital, especially if we have to wait around. "I can't bring him with me."

"Let me call Jude. He can watch him."

"I don't know if that's such a good idea."

"Okay, bring him along and witness the world end. Or stay there until I have more news."

Neither option appeals. I guess Door No. 3 is the winner.

"Could you call him?"

"On it."

A minute later, he sends a text confirming that Jude would be able to watch Spence. After quickly dressing him and myself, I bring him down to Jude's apartment, one floor below Sam's. He's already waiting at the door with Hudson behind him.

"Hey, Spencigan!" Crouching down, Jude puts out his arms and Spencer runs into them, whooping as the handsome firefighter picks him up. Gosh, I don't think he's ever been that excited to see me.

"Thanks so much for doing this." I nod at Hudson, who's viewing the Jude-Spence reunion with a soft expression. "I'm guessing this is not what you expected on your day off. Either of you."

Hudson breaks out into a grin. "Are you kidding? We're going to have a blast. We've got floor hockey set up and I think it's time Spencer learned how to play."

Floor hockey? That sounds dangerous.

"It's perfectly safe," Jude says because obviously my expression tells its own tale. "Take a quick look."

I follow them in and see a net set up and baby-sized hockey sticks. The puck is spongy. It's all so cute and I'd love to stay and watch.

"This is adorable."

"We thought it might be fun for the kids if you ever want to let them visit outside of emergencies," Hudson says, his cheeks pinking. "I have twin nephews who've just turned five, so we have experience."

Jude rubs Hudson's back and sends him a look of pure love before turning back to face me. I get the impression they'd like to have kids of their own one day. "He's going to be fine, Cass."

"Okay. Thank you." I ruffle Spence's hair but he's barely noticing me at this point. Hudson has taken him from Jude's arms, completely at ease with my nephew who is now getting a tour of the mini-hockey arena and a re-introduction to one of the game's officials, their lovely golden Lab, Crosby.

Jude places a hand on my arm, then draws me into a hug. "Just be careful and drive safe, okay?"

I'm so surprised that for a moment I'm frozen. Then my body relents and softens in his arms. It feels so nice to be held without any conditions attached.

He steps back and smiles. God, he is handsome. They both are. And so kind.

"I forgot about Waffles. He needs to be taken out and—"

"I'll take care of him. I have a key."

Thank God. "I'll let you know—well, Sam probably will —what's going on."

"Please do," Hudson calls out.

Thirty minutes later I walk into the ER at Lake Forest Memorial and spot Sam in the waiting area.

"Is she okay?"

He grasps my hand and pulls me down to the chair beside him. "She's getting a CT scan. Just went in."

"A CT scan?"

"The doc thinks she's probably fine, but I insisted."

"Oh. Okay." I didn't know that was a thing you could insist upon. "You're allowed to get bossy like that?"

"I know some of the medical personnel here. They're more apt to listen to me because of my work."

Okay, then. "What happened?"

"She got into a fight with someone called Jane Flaherty."

"Never heard of her."

He raises a wry eyebrow. "Neither had I. Anyway, the upshot is that they shoved each other around and our girl ended up hitting her head against a wall. She apparently blacked out for a few seconds, so out of an abundance of caution, we are here. How's Spence?"

"Learning how to play floor hockey with Jude and Hudson. They were so nice." I feel awful for judging Jude.

"They're good guys. The perfect guncles."

"Guncles?"

"Gay uncles. We need to be using them more. They keep offering and now's the perfect window to be taking advantage."

"Are you saying we should be using our grief to get free babysitting?" I cannot believe I'm joking about this.

"You said it first." He gives me an impish grin that makes me laugh.

"You're wicked, Sam Killian."

"So I've been told, but you never wanted to take advantage."

"I'm not really a 'take advantage' kind of girl."

"No. You're a straight shooter, Cassandra Ferguson."

That's what everyone thinks. Yet here I am with a crush on an unsuitable man—I can admit that much—while I'm still involved with another. Derek has left several text messages this morning, but events have overtaken me.

"I'm not some goody two shoes. I'm not a saint."

"That's not what I mean." He squeezes my hand. "You're a good and decent person. You gave up a lot to take care of Annie, and now you're doing the same all over again with these little horrors. Stuck here in a city you don't know with the enemy. I know it's tough."

Sam as the enemy? I open my mouth to disagree, but the nurse calls his name.

"You can go in and see her. Second door on the right."

I drop Sam's hand and race forward, with Sam walking quickly behind me. Inside the room, Maya is sitting on the bed, looking none the worse for wear. A white-coated woman is standing by her side.

"Ah, here we are." The doctor smiles professionally at me, but then her face bursts into animation at the sight of Sam. "Killian! Looking well."

"Hey, Jo, good to see you. Maya's my niece. What's the damage?"

"Minor concussion, so we'll follow the protocol. You know the drill there."

"I do."

I move toward Maya and take her hand, but she pulls away. "How are you doing?"

"It's not a big deal."

"The school thought it was." I don't want to get into it here. "We're just glad you're okay."

Sam and the doctor have moved to the side and are deep in conversation. Doc Jo places a hand on his arm, probably giving her condolences about his brother.

He looks appreciative, and after a minute or two, he kisses her on the cheek. My pulse rate has picked up, probably because I'm relieved that Maya is okay. I'd prefer to think that's what's going on and not that I don't like seeing Sam with someone else.

Sam finally drags himself away. "How's the head, bug?"

"Okay."

"Excellent. So I'm going to complete some paperwork while you get dressed." On his way out, he sends me a significant look, like I need to talk to her now. Or maybe he wants time to flirt with that doctor.

I can't believe I'm thinking of this.

"Let's get dressed. And maybe you can tell me what happened with this Jane girl." Her expression is mutinous. "Or not."

She pulls on her blouse and skirt while I grab her shoes.

"Maya, talk to me."

"Why? You're not staying."

I recoil as if hit. "What makes you think that?"

"I heard you and Uncle Sam talking. You want to go back to New York. Leave us."

"No, no, that's not it. I want to ..." I can't say what I really want, which is to separate the kids from everything they've ever known. I might think I'm best placed to care for them, but am I? If I can't even broach the subject with my niece, then something might be amiss with the plan as it stands.

"Nothing is decided yet."

A slight tilt of her chin, a light in her eyes, then the brief hope I instilled is tempered.

"She's not nice," she says after a moment's silence. "Jane."

"She said something mean?"

A slow nod.

"About ... your mom and dad?"

"That I'm lucky because I can get whatever I want this Christmas. Everyone will be sorry for me."

"Oh, honey. That's not nice. Not at all." I sit on the bed beside her. "Is she a friend of yours?"

"No. She's ugly."

I shake my head. "We don't need to call her names or say mean things about her." I'm guessing there's history here. "It might be good if you could forgive her."

"Why? She's all wrong!"

"Yeah, but maybe she's hurting as well. We don't always know what's going on in people's lives."

"Her parents are divorced. But her father is poor, so she doesn't get extra presents."

"I see. I'm guessing that made her sad and then she said something mean to you. Sad people do that, sometimes. How did it get to pushing and shoving?"

Maya looks ashamed. "I didn't mean to push so hard. But she pushed harder, and I hit my head."

I place an arm around her shoulder. "Okay, it sounds like you both made mistakes. We'll talk to the school and see what they have to say. You'll need to say sorry for pushing her—" She opens her mouth. "And she'll need to say sorry for whatever she did, too. We'll figure it out."

"You're not mad at me?"

"No. It's a tough time for you. I remember when your mom would get mad at people—she was kind of a hit first, talk later kind of girl. A bit like you."

Marianne to my Elinor.

Her eyes go wide. "I'm like Mom?"

"So like her."

"I miss her. And Dad. But mostly Mom."

"I know you do, honey. I miss her, too. And your dad. But mostly your mom."

She giggles because it's a funny way to phrase it. Of course, we miss her dad, but I want her to know it's okay to talk about them any time and in any manner she wants. There's no wrong way to grieve.

A knock on the door, and Sam puts his head in. I wonder if he got a date with the pretty doc, then decide that kind of thinking is beneath me.

"We ready?"

"Just getting our shoes on."

Eighteen

Sam

While Cassie takes Maya up to the apartment, I stop off to pick up Spence. Jude answers the door with a finger to his lips and invites me in.

Spence is fast asleep, snuggled up on the couch with Crosby. Hudson is sitting in an armchair, reading a book and keeping an eye on things. He gives me a small wave and goes back to his book.

Figuring I can let my nephew sleep for a few more minutes, I follow Jude into the kitchen.

"How was he?"

"Amazing. He's such a character, and Hudson really digs having kids around. How's Maya?"

I texted earlier to say she was fine, but I have an update on her mental state. "She was quiet on the way home and Cassie says it's because of this fight she had with some frenemy in her class. I'm guessing she's in a bad place. Might need counseling."

Jude nods. "It's a lot for a kid. It's a lot for all of you. How are you holding up?"

"Okay." *If I say it, it makes it true.* "I need to find a nanny."

"Cass not staying?"

"She says she is but she's not being realistic. Her job is in New York, the kids have to stay here, and I need to get back to work."

My friend is eyeing me closely. "Maybe Cass could stay longer." I must have made a face because Jude asks, "What?"

"The apartment isn't big enough."

"Seems plenty big to me." Then he raises both eyebrows. "I see."

"You see nothing."

"Thought you didn't get on."

"We don't. But we've come to an uneasy truce that's getting ... easier." *More like sexier.* "But that doesn't mean we should live together, not even for the kids. I'd never fuck again."

His smile is the smirkiest smirk known to man.

"Nothing's happened," I offer defensively. I'm the human embodiment of a medieval fortress these days, repelling all smirky accusations that besmirch my honor.

"Well, she's got a boyfriend."

"They sort of broke up."

Jude's eyes are as round as saucers. "They *sort of* broke up?"

"They had a fight over the kids. Derek's not on board and it's created a rift. If he has any sense, he'll say sorry and get with the program." I wonder if they've spoken since last night, but it's been a crazy day and maybe not.

My friend is watching me, all amusement. "If he has any sense ... you actually think they should be together?"

"Who else would have her?"

That makes Jude chortle—I think that's the word. It's kind of evilly gleeful and more exaggerated than a plain old chuckle.

"I know someone else who might have her," he offers because he's not already pissing me off enough.

My scowl has little effect on his joy. If anything, it makes him happier.

"So I'm attracted to her, but nothing will happen because that's a fuck-ton of complication I don't need. It would be better if she wasn't around—hence the need for the nanny."

The thing is, I would like Cassie to stick around. It's just easier with her. The kids like her, though she frets that they don't because her input in their lives so far has been at a distance. But they need a female presence and there's comfort in having one that resembles their mom. Confusing, but comforting.

But I don't want her near *me* while I have to be celibate. I suppose I could step out one day and take care of business, but that doesn't really appeal. I'm sexually frustrated but not willing to do anything about it.

"I can ask Hudson to check in with his teammates," Jude says, taking pity on me. "All of them have childcare arrangements befitting professional athletes and given your income level, that's the kind of thing you could afford, I suppose."

"That'd be great. Thanks."

Folding his arms and leaning against the kitchen counter, Jude smiles. "So you have the hots for your co-guardian."

For fuck's sake. "It's just a proximity thing. A we-don't-get-along thing. A two-weeks-without-banging thing."

"That's a lot of things."

"Shut up."

Walking back to the apartment, Spence wakes in my arms.

"Daddy?"

My chest goes tight. "No, buddy, it's your uncle Sammie. Did you have fun playing hockey?"

He nods, still sleepy, and burrows his face in my neck. Inside the apartment, I find Cassie and Maya on the sofa in their PJs, and something about the sight of them catches hard in my chest. Fucking Jude.

"Hey, are we having a slumber party?"

Cassie looks up, her face melting at the sight of Spence. It couldn't possibly be on seeing me. "We thought we'd have a movie day."

That wakes Spence up. "*Moana*!"

I sneak a glance at the girls who are mouthing "no, no, no."

"Maybe something else? Give your sister a chance. She's not feeling great."

"We were thinking about *Encanto*," Cassie says.

"Sounds great. But first, we should change into our PJs. Right, Spence?"

"PJs!"

I don't have any PJs, so I make do with sweats and a T-shirt, while Spence goes for classic Spider Man (Toby Maguire era). He climbs onto the sofa on the other side of his aunt, who's wearing sky-blue yoga pants and a matching V-necked tee—the fabric looks soft and her legs look amazing, even when covered. She doesn't have much skin on display, only her arms and collarbones and feet, but here I am, mesmerized by the sight of her toes. They're a sultry red.

Forgive me, Father, it's been two weeks since my last fuck.

It shouldn't be an issue, given my mood of late, but I'm used to a more regular outlet. What I'm not used to is having an attractive woman in my space with no possibility of anything good coming out of it.

Cassie pulls her knee up to her chest, which gives me an extra flash of calf, and somehow that does strange things to my body. Like this is Victorian era porn or something. Too late, I realize that my sweats are a little on the thin side. Time for a break in the kitchen.

"Movie day needs popcorn, people."

"Popcorn!" Spence repeats, snuggling into his aunt.

Cassie grins up at me, safe in her nest of love. "Guess you're on snack duty, Killian." A pretty flush suffuses her cheeks and I wonder if it's got anything to do with the fact my T-shirt isn't the loosest item of clothing in my closet. My guns and pecs have never looked better. Her gaze skitters down my body, which is when I recall I might be making my interest in her a little too obvious.

"Popcorn," I mutter and head into the kitchen to calm myself down.

I hope she breaks up with Derek officially.

Okay, I've admitted it. I want her and I don't want her boyfriend in the mix complicating it, because we don't have enough shit complicating it already.

Snack prep gives my dick time to simmer down, though my mind is still scrambled, thinking of the possibilities. When I come back out, I'm bearing M&Ms, popcorn, and sodas. This is a real treat for the kids because their parents usually kept them on super healthy and organic diets. We've been trying to do that, following the advice from Hudson's nutritionist, but I figure today is okay to stray outside the lines.

I take a seat beside my niece. "How we feelin', bug?"

"Kind of tired."

"Alright. It's okay to doze off if you want to."

Cassie catches my gaze. "We don't have to keep her awake?"

"No, that's the older protocol around concussions. These

days, it's better that kids get rest when they need it. We'll keep an eye on her." I turn to my niece. "Cool?"

"Cool," she says and lays her head on my shoulder.

I check over her head to find Cassie looking on, those beautiful green eyes trapping me in their depths. "Cool?" I murmur, feeling the absolute opposite.

"Cool," she murmurs right back before picking up the remote and starting the movie.

NINETEEN

Cass

The kids fall asleep not long after everyone has declared we don't talk about Bruno. I have a feeling we'll be playing this movie again before the day is through.

"You need something to eat?" Sam asks me over Maya's head. "Or have you loaded up on too many snacks?"

"A sandwich would be good, but I can make it." My phone buzzes with a call from Derek and my body recoils, which is not a good sign. "I should take this."

From the look Sam gives me, I'm guessing he knows who's calling. "Go ahead. I'll get lunch."

I move off to my room, answering as I go. "Derek?"

"Cass. I've been calling and texting all morning."

Irritation needles me. "Maya had an accident. We had to take her to the hospital."

"Is she okay?"

"Yes, it's a minor concussion but it was worrying all the same. We're keeping an eye on her while we watch movies."

A long pause while the weight of "we" hangs heavy in the fraught air between us.

He speaks first. "Yesterday, I might have been too hasty. Everything that's happened to you—Annie, the kids, all this upset—is going to make you feel raw. This is no time to be making life-changing decisions."

He's right, though I wonder which life-changing decisions he means.

"I don't want to rush anything," I offer, feeling my way into the conversation like a bomb disposal expert.

"Of course. You need to take care of the kids for now. Make sure they're safe before you come back to New York."

So, *that* decision.

"Okay." I'm still being careful about stepping on the landmine.

"And you can figure out some sort of support model that doesn't upend your entire life. You've already done the parenting bit with Annie."

I shutter my eyes as the bomb's tick-tick gets louder until finally, *Boom!*

"I think I'm starting to realize that this isn't going to work."

"I know it's hard to admit it," he says, a certain smugness in his voice. "But this is the best for everyone. Let the Killians take over—it's easiest all around."

"No, I don't think you understand, Derek. You and me." I take a shallow breath. "We're not going to work."

A few minutes later, I open the bedroom door. Sam is there with his back against the opposite wall, arms folded, biceps bulging. Not listening but waiting.

I shouldn't be so glad to see him.

"What's wrong?" I ask, listening for sounds of screaming or crying. All I hear is the TV, the song about the sister under pressure, which means they're on a re-watch.

"Nothing," he says. "The kids are awake again. How are things with—"

It takes but a fraction of a second to land me in his arms. Did I make the first move or did he just sense what I needed in this moment?

"Hey, hey, it's okay." His lips are soft against my hair, his arms the perfect cage around my body.

"It's official." My voice cracks slightly. "Derek and I are finished. I mean, we have been for a while, but it's taken me a couple of months to admit that it's broken." Longer than that. I hate giving up on anything, and there are so many sunk costs with a six-year-old relationship.

He nods, his jaw stubble deliciously rough against my temple. His hand is splayed over my lower back, supporting me in staying upright. Only I'm not feeling a little weak-kneed because of what just happened with Derek. It's all about Sam.

He draws back. "Is it because you're here?"

"He'll say that's the reason. That I want to change our lives too much and it's not what he signed on for. But I've known for years that Derek has a one-track way of viewing things. Everyone needs to get into his lane. I've been playing his tune for too long."

It's possible I'm overreacting but there's a curious feeling of relief coursing through me, loosening my bones. At least there was in the immediate aftermath of that phone call.

But now, in Sam's arms, I'm not feeling so loose. My body is registering all sorts of things: his body's unyielding hardness, its peak strength, his perfect grip. Also how good he smells. It might be a body wash or an aftershave, and I'm getting hints of leather, cinnamon, something citrusy. All divine.

I'm happy to have this conversation, but I'm not sure it

should be while wrapped in the embrace of a man as attractive as Sam. He's so overwhelming in his sensuality, always has been. Yet I can't find the will to pull away.

"So what comes next?" Sam's tone is low and rough.

"I'll move out of Derek's, find a place ..." Somewhere big enough for me and the kids, though I don't say that. We've reached a fragile peace that I don't want to upend just yet. "I can't really think about it right now. Derek will give me time to figure it out. It's all very ... amicable. Right now, I'm here for the kids."

His hand is moving over my back, a dizzying mix of comfort and eroticism.

"Well, we appreciate you here, keeping us in line."

I chuckle, and God it feels good. In the midst of the shittiest couple of weeks of my existence, I need a little positivity, even if it's in the form of a silly joke about me being the troop's sergeant-major.

"Did you just lump yourself in with Maya and Spence?"

"That's how you see me, right? No more mature than the little monsters in our care."

It's easier to agree than think about the alternatives. That Sam Killian has come a long way from the man-child I first met at Annie and Jake's wedding all those years ago.

"You're growing on me, Killian." And then I realize that he is, quite literally, doing that. There's no missing that bulge as it nudges my belly.

He takes an incremental, almost apologetic step back, very un-Sam-like, which only serves to emphasize the problem. Give it room.

But it's more than that. He's also staring, burning holes into my soul, his gaze in a two-step between my eyes and my lips. And I realize that I want this. Whatever's happening, I need it.

Kiss me. Please, Sam, just kiss me.

He doesn't.

Instead, he teases me with the barest of touches. His hand on the small of my back shifts a couple of inches down, grazing the top of my bottom.

At which point I go a little mad.

Up on tiptoes, I grip his shoulders and move toward his mouth. He grunts in surprise, but he's quick to adjust. His big, capable hands cup my bottom and hoist me to meet him.

There's a nano-second when my brain tries to protest but my hormones dismiss that contrary bitch.

We kiss.

Oh, how we kiss.

Only when our lips connect do I realize how much I've retained our near miss as a benchmark in my fantasies. We never made it this far, but it never stopped me thinking about it. About what it would have been like to surrender. No one ever topped the Sam Killian of my imagination, and now I know why.

He's simply the hottest man I've ever met. His mouth is fire, his body the perfect fit to mine. I'm crazy for the sweet, sexy, all-encompassing taste of him.

We're standing in the doorway to my room, or rather he's standing, and I'm curled around him like a python. With an easy strength, he moves us back a few steps and uses my back to nudge the door closed, all while kissing me like I'm his reason for breathing.

I'm suspended a couple of feet off the floor, my legs wrapped around his hips while we pour all our emotions into this kiss. My hands grip his hair, tunnel through it—it's as soft as I expected—and my comb-through yields a growl. He palms my butt cheek and squeezes, which serves to drag the fabric of my yoga pants against my pussy. I groan into his mouth.

"Cassie," he gasps, my name on his lips so desperate, before slanting his hot mouth over mine, finding new ways to drive me insane. He rocks his body into the cradle of mine, dragging his hard cock against my soft, damp core. Nothing has ever felt this good.

Maybe it's the situation, the pain we're both feeling and this need to do anything to blank it out. Not to mention what just happened with Derek.

Which is crazily inappropriate. We need to stop. The kids—

He releases my mouth, panting. His eyes still burn. "I know."

I don't think I said it, but he understands. Another surprise, this shorthand between us. He lets me down gently, but seems reluctant to break the connection entirely. My ass remains glued to his hands, feeling strangely right there.

I place a palm on his chest. "I shouldn't have done that."

"Pretty sure that was a joint effort." His eyes are still smoked over with desire and there appears to be no subsidence in the erection arena. Moving his hands away from my rear, he takes a step back and rubs his mouth, a gesture he makes when he needs time to think.

"I kind of jumped you," I say by way of apology. "When all you were doing was being kind and supportive."

"Sure. If you mean kind enough to ease that ache between your legs and supportive of your gorgeous ass in my hands. Real kind. Real supportive."

Real direct. Real dirty.

I'm doubly turned on, while he sounds annoyed.

"Are you mad at me?"

"No." He growls. "Maybe. I don't think you should minimize your actions or my response. No one jumped anyone. That was pure, white-hot instinct, our bodies doing what feels right." He moves back in, trapping me against the door, his muscled arm above my head while he looms over me. "We can blame the pain, the sorrow, the gut-wrenching hurt we're both feeling, but that's not going to change the fact I want to fuck you. I've wanted to fuck you since I met you. Every time I've sat across from you at a family cookout or a kids' birthday party in the years since, this aching need to bury myself inside you has only intensified. But you were with Derek, so I never made a move. Oh, and you hate me, so there's that."

His gaze is ferocious, pinning me to the spot. My nipples are rock-hard points, my panties drenched, my skin aflame.

He runs a thumb over my bottom lip, and I do everything I can not to suck it inside my mouth. That's not me, or at least I don't think it is. But lately, I'm a different person. With Sam, I am changed.

I haven't responded, so he continues. "It's the middle of the day and the kids are out there, waiting for us, so we won't take this all the way." He leans in and brushes his lips over mine. "For now."

That cheeky coda snaps me out of my lust fog. "For now? No, Sam, not at all. This shouldn't have happened."

His hands drop, his body retreats, but he's still looking as cocky as ever.

"It's kind of soon," he says, the first sensible thing he's uttered since the door closed behind us.

"Yes. Neither of us is in the right frame of mind. We're hurting and looking for comfort anywhere we can find it."

He holds up a hand. "I meant it's kind of soon after your breakup with Derek."

Oh. I meant that, too, though Derek was not on my mind while Sam kissed me until I forgot my own name.

"Right."

But he's caught my omission and the smirk is back. "Or maybe not so soon. Maybe you've been thinking about me for years, as well."

And we're back. "Can I leave now?"

"You can leave any time you want, Cassie. I'll be right here when you need me."

The next morning, I've just finished up one of my client Zoom meetings when I emerge to find Sam putting a jacket on Spence.

"You guys going somewhere?"

Sam points at Waffles. "Taking this guy to the vet."

"I want to see the rabbits," Spence says.

Sam looks like this is a familiar ask. "So I think we'll be visiting the petting zoo in Lincoln Park as well." He fixes me with a level gaze. "You guys okay to hang out here?"

I cast a quick glance at Maya. She seems to have recovered from her concussion, but we kept her out of school for one more day anyway. I haven't spent that much time alone with her and Sam's giving me that opportunity, which is very sweet. Or perhaps he just wants out of my orbit after our kiss yesterday.

"We'll be fine. I'll even make lunch."

Sam has the grace not to look horrified, and soon he's out the door with Spence and Waffles in tow.

I take a seat beside my niece. "How are you feeling today?"

"Okay."

"Anything you want to do? Or watch?"

She shrugs. After our conversation at the hospital about my plan to leave Chicago, she's been a little distant.

"I have an idea. Get your shoes and jacket on."

Ten minutes later, we're at the Blick Art Supplies store. "You said you ran out of pencils, so let's pick up some more. Or any other supplies you need."

Maya looks around, then heads for the drawing aisle. I let her have a few moments to herself while I take in the surroundings. Once-familiar scents tickle my nostrils: acrylic paints, just-sharpened pencils, the faint aroma of solvents and varnish. I wander around for a while, re-acclimating to what was once a space I knew so well.

Standing before the array of compressed charcoal, I pick up a pack and turn it over in my hand. This was my medium of choice, and looking at it brings back those memories in a flood. Art was my escape, the solace I sought when life was topsy-turvy. Mom and Annie knew I liked to draw, but I never told them how important it was to me. It was mine to cherish.

If I'd shared more about my hopes and dreams, would Mom have stayed? If she'd known how much I wanted to make art my life, would she have still dropped the responsibility of looking after Annie in my lap?

Probably. Selfish people don't need an excuse.

Annie marveled at my skill, but as close as we were, I never shared my heartbreak at having to give it up as a potential career. I didn't want her to feel guilty that she had to take pole position in my life. As the years went on, I drew less and less, because to continue was like a nail dragged over a festering wound. Better to slap a Band-Aid on it so I could move on.

I feel a presence at my side.

"Are you going to get those?" Maya asks. She's carrying two sketch pads, pencils, and erasers.

"I was thinking about it."

Her eyes are wide, so like Annie's. "Mom said you were an artist. You drew a picture of me as a baby."

Sam mentioned that it was still hanging somewhere in the house. I'd forgotten it existed. Preferred to, I suppose.

"I did. You wouldn't sit still so I had to use a photograph." I put an arm around her. "You were kind of squirmy. A little worm."

She looks affronted. "I was?"

"Oh, yeah. But I took a ton of photos of you so I could

have all sorts of expressions. Hungry, happy, sad, annoyed. When you have a subject that won't cooperate"—I squeeze her waist—"like a poopy baby—"

"Aunt Cass!"

I grin. "Then you, as the artist, have to come up with strategies to get to the heart of your art."

I can see her thinking it over. She likes that phrase: *the heart of your art.* I like it, too.

"You could use my sketch pad," she says, almost shyly. "If you want to draw something."

"Oh, yeah? I'd love that. And maybe some of this." I pick up the charcoal pack again. "I know you like working with pencils, but maybe we could create something together."

"Really?"

"Definitely!" I tread carefully. "Perhaps a family portrait?" Looking at photos will be hard for her, but it might also help with the healing. "Only if you want to."

She thinks on it for a moment. "I'd like that."

Twenty

Sam

This morning, when I left the house with Spence and Waffles, Cassie was acting like that kiss had never happened yesterday afternoon. Like it was some historical artifact, squirreled away under the dirt where she doesn't have to think about it.

Maybe that's how she wants to play it. Ignore it. Pretend our grief got the better of us. She can't separate that out, and I'm not going to push her.

For now.

I don't regret my honesty, though. She's a gorgeous woman, and the friction between us means that any time I see her, I imagine what it's like to fuck her. I imagine that with a lot of women of my acquaintance, but then I usually move on and forget about it.

No moving on with Cassie, though. Those dangerous thoughts have stayed with me through the years. Even knowing she has a boyfriend hasn't stopped me from thinking about her in that way. But I've also thought about what a buzzkill she is, and how annoying I find her, and the fact she doesn't like me one bit.

And then I think about fucking all those negatives right out of her.

This woman has taken up a shit-ton of space in my brain. And lately I'm never *not* thinking about her.

Holding her in my arms, comforting her, had felt so good. The feel of her mouth, the grasp of her hands, the softness against my hard-for-her dick—Christ, she's already surpassed every fantasy I've indulged in. And I needed her to know that this isn't some one-off, let's-bang-away-the-pain deal. It doesn't have to be the mistake she thinks it is.

No doubt she feels guilty because our thoughts turned to pleasure so soon after the accident. Not to mention less than sixty seconds after she gave Derek the heave-ho. (That must be some sort of record. Am I really *that* good?) But what are we to do? This condo might be 2000 square feet but right now it feels like a postage stamp.

I'm probably making this living situation worse. What the hell is going to happen anyway? It's not as if now Derek has been eighty-sixed that she'll suddenly uproot her life and come live here with us.

Though, without D-Bag weighing her down, she could move here. They have financial planner jobs in Chicago, and I've no doubt a bright, intelligent woman like Cassie could land a position easily. She could take her time looking as well because there's plenty of money assigned to the guardians. Jake and Annie made sure of it, and if they hadn't, I would.

"Is Waffles okay?" Spence asks.

We've just left the vet's office and Waffles seems to be doing fine. Apparently Irish setters often suffer with digestive issues, so we now have some medication and need to watch his diet.

"He's fine, buddy."

"Can we see the rabbits now?"

"How about we head home first and see if your aunt Cass and Maya want to come out with us?"

"Okay!" That's Spence, as easygoing a kid as you'll ever meet.

Walking into my building, I consider how to handle Cassie, especially now that I've had time to let it settle. I've already told her what I want, but I did it crudely. Like shocking her was more important than wooing her. The words just spilled out of me, colored with the frustration of years, the annoyance that she's only ever viewed me one way. A two-dimensional manwhore with little to offer beyond a good time.

And then I went and said exactly what an idiot like that would think.

I've wanted to fuck you since I met you.

Charm off the charts.

In the apartment, Maya and Cassie are on the sofa looking at the iPad. Their heads are close together, and I'm struck by how alike they are.

"Hey, guys, what's up?"

"Is Waffles okay?" Cassie asks as Waffles jumps on the sofa, proving he's very much okay.

"Yeah, we need to watch his diet and make sure he doesn't get canine bloat."

Cassie hugs Waffles and gives him a kiss. My gaze strays to the iPad screen, where my brother's smile shines back at me. The sight sends a shiver of unexpected emotion through me.

"We're thinking of creating a family portrait. Drawing something from a photo." She smiles at Maya. "Together."

"I want to see!" Spence climbs up on the sofa and touches the screen. The rabbits are forgotten. "That's me."

"You were a baby," Maya says. "Still are."

Spence forwards to the next picture, one of the family on

vacation at Disneyland about a year ago. They looked so happy, so perfect, and for a moment, I can barely breathe. I need water, so I head to the kitchen.

"Sam?"

I turn to face Cassie, realizing that I didn't even open the fridge door. That I've been gripping the edge of the sink for God knows how long while I try to hold it together.

"Yeah?" I open the fridge, fighting for composure.

"You okay?"

"Just fine." Keeping as busy as a *Law and Order* extra while being questioned by the cops seems like a good strategy right about now. I pick up a can of lemon La Croix, let myself be fascinated by it, then put it down again.

"I think this is good for Maya." Cassie's voice is closer, a soft murmur so as not to alarm the kids. Or maybe, me. "She might be able to use art to help her through the next few weeks and months. Sorry if seeing the photos blindsided you."

I'm nodding as I return to the can of water. Yeah, that's the one, the best can of water there is.

"It's a great idea," I say, meaning it, though my voice sounds like someone else's. "And there's no one better qualified to do it. I just didn't expect to see them, all smiles, the before times." I place the can down on the counter, just as Cassie moves forward and splays her hand on my back. Her touch feels like the burn and the salve all at once.

"It's okay to break down. Isn't that what you told me once?"

Turning to face her, I inhale deeply. "And I said I'd keep a lid on it. That I needed to, for everyone."

"We're in this together. No one expects you to be a robot." Which is when she puts her arms around me and gives me the best hug I've ever had.

For longer than is safe, I hold tight, inhaling her scent, molding her softness to my body, and let some of the grief swell until I feel something else swelling. I've never hated my lack of control when it comes to women more than I do now.

Moving out of her arms, I take a few steps away from her. "Sorry about yesterday."

She blinks. "The kiss?"

"No, not that." *Never that.* "The words I used after. I expect you're not used to that kind of talk."

"Did you mean what you said?" She looks embarrassed, but curious.

I could deny but I'm no longer in the mood to hide this anymore. "Every word."

Her slender throat bulges slightly. "Even when I've been rude and condescending."

"*Especially* when you've been rude and condescending."

Her cheeks flush, her tongue darts out to wet her lips. My pants are uncomfortably tight, but I don't care. Yesterday, she kissed me first, and when it turned handsy and hard, she was completely on board as I ground my body into her.

She opens her mouth, but it's Spence's yell that comes out. So much for being my wingman.

"I'd better ..." She thumbs to the living room, and I watch her back out, her color high, her footsteps unsure, and I wonder if I'm making this better or worse.

At this point, I don't think I care.

TWENTY-ONE

Sam

We're joking and joshing in the back of the truck. I'm pumped, the excitement of a first day, like starting school or meeting a woman for the first time. The eagerness to just get out there and prove yourself.

I'm holding Annie's hand, but her eyes are open, pleading with me to do something. Anything.

I wipe away the blood because that seems to be the only thing I'm qualified to do. I'm supposed to be a hotshot on Squad, but I'm too new to this. *I can't do a single thing to help.*

Sammie, please.

Annie changes into Jake. But his eyes are dead, and he won't speak to me. Like I've wounded him. Failed him.

Male vic. Not viable.

The words are an echo. Tuning them out, I manage to refocus on the one person I can save. I'm back to wiping off blood but it keeps coming back, an ever-present trickle. Annie's still looking at me, trying to communicate something, but then her eyes shutter as life seeps away in an ooze of sorrow.

"Don't go," I moan. "Please stay. They need you."

But her eyes don't open, the blood keeps coming, and someone is squeezing my shoulder.

I scent something, like a wolf to prey.

Her.

Sense-memory kicks in, hauling me out of the nightmare and dropping me into something different. Something erotic. Those tan, toned legs, the waves of sun over her shoulders, that bow-shaped mouth. Usually disapproving but not now. Now it's parted in invitation and I dive in because I'm never going to get a chance in the real world. She'll never let me in and that's for the best. This fantasy is safe.

"Sam," she murmurs, her voice so damn husky my erection pops three sizes more. "It's okay."

Fuck, baby, I know *it's okay. Because you're where you're supposed to be. In my arms, just when I need you. The way that I need you.*

My hands clutch her ass and pull her tight, and then I'm rocking into her, my cock desperate for relief. Rubbing and stroking and turning so hard I'm not gonna last.

A minute ago, I had blood on my hands and now…

I jerk awake. I'm not alone.

Cassie.

She's under me, her body soft and pliant, her thighs parted on either side of me. My comforter isn't between us—I must have kicked it off during my nightmare. But damn, I wish it *was* here, a barrier to keep her safe from me.

To keep me safe from her.

"I—" I pull back, but she holds on, her fingers curled around my biceps, her other hand on the nape of my neck. Like she's supporting the head that's about to explode.

"It's okay, Sam. It was just a dream."

Just a dream. Three fucked-up words that can't possibly begin to describe what that was.

This is the point in the proceedings where I should be rolling away, apologizing for sleep-fucking her, and sending her back to her room. I should not be flexing the hand that's palming her sweet ass, desperate to get a bigger handful, but the second I do, her body shifts incrementally. Straining toward me.

This is … fuck.

Back off. I inch away, my body, my hands, my dick. Not my mind, though. It's still engaged, sliding in deep and taking what's mine. Fucking her gorgeous body and absorbing every sweet sigh and shudder.

Lying back, I scrub a hand over my eyes. There's a faint light coming in from the hallway.

"Kids okay?" I ask, for something to say.

"Fast asleep." She's lying beside me, which I'm damn sure she didn't ask for while I manhandled her into the cradle of my body. I'm a menace, even while I sleep, which I need because I'm back on the job tomorrow.

"I woke you up?"

"Couldn't sleep. I was making myself some warm milk."

Warm milk? Even that sounds so innocent.

"And here I am, giving you night terrors to match my own."

She leans up on an elbow. "Is that what's happening? Night terrors?"

"It's just a bad dream."

"About the accident?"

We've not talked about the fact I was on the scene. She hasn't asked and I'm certainly not going to bring it up.

"I don't really rememKber the details," I lie. "The dream is different from the reality, but neither is pleasant."

She leans over, placing a hand on my pec. The pulsing muscle in my chest reacts predictably.

"I'm so sorry you had to go through that, Sam."

I cover her hand with mine, letting my thundering heartbeat speak for me.

A couple of seconds later, I mutter, "Hell of a first day on the job."

"Right. I'd forgotten that." She rubs my chest. "I-I want to ask about it, but I also don't."

I turn to her, and I'm struck by this vision mere inches away from me. She's so beautiful, so vital, so uptight, the bane of my existence. And I want her with a ferocity that scares the living hell out of me.

"Maybe one day we'll talk about it. Now, I just want to ... forget."

The energy shifts. She knows what I'm asking, what I'm begging for. But she also knows it's wrong. Here we are, the two of us, trying to find comfort in an impossible situation. Bonus: she's just exited a long-term relationship.

"Sam, I—"

"It's okay. You should go." My voice sounds rusty. "I need to be up early for work."

She inhales a breath and swings her legs to the side of the bed, sitting up.

I am crushed.

My body tenses, waiting for her to leave. Dreading it. She heads to the door ...

... And closes it.

Retuning to me, she climbs under the covers and adjusts the pillow behind her head.

"What are you doing?"

"I think you'll be less likely to scare the dog or the kids if I'm here. If you have another bad dream, just know that I'm inches away."

I barely suppress my groan. "Are you forgetting what just happened? My last nightmare placed me between your gorgeous thighs."

She hitches a quick breath. "Now, that can't have been much of a nightmare. Was I even in it?"

I smile at her attempt to lighten the mood. "Yeah, you were. Somehow the bad stuff morphed into the good stuff. The *really* good stuff."

"But it could have been anyone. Like Candy and her fabulous breasts."

Why is she insisting that she can't possibly exist in my fantasy?

"No, it was you." *It's always you.* "That scent of your shampoo is like some sort of trigger for my cock." I turn my head, eager to see if I've provoked a reaction. Needing it. "And that was all it took to have me pinning you with my body and grinding on you."

"It's probably just proximity." Her breathing sounds labored. "The two of us, here, after all that's happened ... would you prefer if I left?"

"No!" My reaction surprises us both. "But it's probably not a good idea for us to act on this. You just ended a relationship. You're bound to be feeling raw."

She remains quiet, for once the woman with no opinion. Or she knows it's best to keep it to herself.

Her hand strokes my arm. "I haven't been sleeping that well myself."

An innocuous sounding statement that I know is huge for Cassie. She doesn't like to admit to weakness, or that she needs any kind of support. All her life she's been a one-woman show from raising her sister to finishing her degree to her life with Derek.

That ends here.

"C'mere." The word is another rusty utterance. I place my arm above my head, inviting her close.

She moves in, her arm around my torso, her head against my chest. I'm doing this because I need to hold someone. I need this touch, this affection, and I think she needs it, too. My lips brush the top of her head because I'm craving an outlet for all this emotion inside me, and this seems to be the only way I'll get it.

Almost absently, her hand strokes my nipple. Her body shifts closer, her thigh brushing mine. I shouldn't have asked her to stay. And while I could have managed that, I had to go make it worse by inviting her to cuddle up to me. Then, if that wasn't bad enough, I kissed her head because I can't do anything else.

Blood rushed to my cock, oh, about five minutes ago when I woke up to the scent of Cassie and the feel of her trapped beneath my surging body. There's no letting up.

"Fuck," I mutter.

She lifts her head. "I'm making it worse, aren't I?"

"Not your fault. I should be able to sleep in the same bed as a female relative without getting a hard-on." I'm still the sex-obsessed frat boy she's always pegged me for.

"We're not related, Sam. Not in any way that ..." She peters out.

"That what?"

I hear her swallow in the dark. "Six years ago at the wedding, I was rude to you. You were so flirtatious, and I thought you were part of the problem."

"What, like the patriarchy?"

A soft chuckle. "No, the Killian problem. The charm offensive that took Annie away from me." She's still stroking my chest. "I was envious of all of you because you were able to give Annie something I couldn't. That real feeling of home."

"Cassie, that's not true. We welcomed her, of course. We loved her so much. But that didn't subtract from anything you had done for her."

"I-I know that now. But I was annoyed with you—with all of you—but especially you, for some reason. You were so carefree and oblivious, so handsome and charming, and I wanted to like you. I *did* like you. But I also wanted to take you down a peg, which is why I rejected your advances. Told you it would never happen."

I cup her jaw and draw her close, picking out the most germane parts of that admission. Our mouths are millimeters from each other.

"You wanted me back then? Really?"

She nods. "But I realized that you and I were very different. You were a party guy and I was not that kind of girl. I never have been. I couldn't be while I had to look after Annie, make sure she got the best start in life. And you were there, all charm and sun, back from your travels, like you'd walked off the French Riviera and into a fifty-thousand-dollar wedding, and that was *normal* for you. I thought about it for a second—more than a second—about what it would feel like to surrender to your sheer animal magnetism, throw away my inhibitions for a night, and be free. But I also knew I'd have to see you again at future family events and be reminded of being just another notch on your bedpost." Her faint sigh is so world weary. "I already felt like I'd lost something with Annie throwing her lot in with your family. I didn't want to lose my self-respect."

"Jesus, Cass." I don't know how to respond. "Why are you telling me now?"

When I'm burning for you.

"Because I might have misjudged you. I see how you are with the kids, how hard you're working to keep them safe. I just want you to know that I appreciate that you've changed. Or maybe that you were always this good a guy, but I couldn't see it."

My heart is beating too fast. Blood is surging to my head, my dick, everywhere. It's as if I've needed this woman's approval for the longest time, which shouldn't be right. I don't need her to validate me.

"Where does that leave us?"

"As ... friends?"

I bark out a laugh.

"Is that so strange?"

Lying back, I gaze at the ceiling, making out shapes in the tile. It shouldn't be strange. In the last couple of weeks, Cassie and I have been inching closer as we figure out the kids' needs. Co-parents, team members ... friends shouldn't be such a stretch, even if I want more.

In the silence that follows, I'm thinking about what a good guy I am, not immediately jumping her when I hear it: the gentle breathing that signifies this woman is asleep in my arms.

Despite my raging hard-on, I close my eyes on a smile, feeling some measure of contentment for the first time in weeks.

Twenty-Two

Cass

My eyes flutter open and encounter darkness. Moving my head, I realize I'm using Sam's massive chest as a pillow. It's still the middle of the night, but it feels like I've been wrapped up in this man for weeks. Years.

What did I expect? When I passed by Sam's open door and heard his distress, I knew this was a possibility. That he might invite me into his world, and I wouldn't feel so alone anymore. And when I had a chance to leave, I elected not to take it. I stayed to keep the horror away. He's been dreaming about the accident—that's why he calls out Annie's name.

He's still sleeping, and I can't help using these precious moments in the dark to map his shoulder muscles with my hand. A few hours ago, I told him things. About my insecurity where his family is concerned. About my fears of being cut out and how it's played into my attitude toward Sam. How much easier it is to see him as the incorrigible flirt, the playboy.

Because it's safer than the alternative.

That Sam might have more to offer, not just to the kids, but to me.

It takes a couple of seconds for me to realize I'm not the only one thinking in the dark.

"Hey," he murmurs against the top of my head. "You okay?"

"No," I whisper.

"I'm here," he says, soothing. "For whatever you need."

The way those words conjure a low, yearning pulse between my legs is not good. I mean, it's amazing, but it's not good for my mental health.

Now I know how he feels between my thighs, how hot that hard cock imprints on my body and psyche as it strokes my damp sex. Sure, I still had my sleep shorts on, but they weren't thick enough to hide the sensation of pure, vital male rocking his hips and pushing me to the brink.

The thought of how good it will—*would, Cass, would!*—feel without clothes is unhinging my brain. But we can't go any further. It's far too complicated between us.

He's waiting for me to respond, to play my part and tell him this is a terrible idea. It is, yet the ache between my thighs is muffling my reason.

I move my head back and brush my lips against his neck.

It's a barely-there touch but you would swear I'd jerked him off. He moans, the sound so deep and sensual, it calls to every part of me.

I try it again, this time closer to the underside of his jaw. I sense him fisting the sheet, like that's necessary to keep his hands off me. He's fighting the urge while I use my mouth to torture him.

I add my hand to the mix, coasting it across his chest and grazing his nipples.

"Fuck," he grits out. Then a heartfelt "Cassie."

My lips continue their journey, planting flags in new

territory, a conquering army seeking to subjugate. I reach his mouth, taking in the hot puffs of air he's releasing.

"Touch me," I say.

Maybe he doesn't want to. Maybe he thinks this is a bad idea.

Maybe he's right.

"You sure this isn't too soon for you? After Annie. After Derek."

"There are a million reasons why I should not be in your bed, Sam. Yet I-I can't think of a single one."

It's the thumbs up he needs. His mouth clamps over mine, claiming what I denied him all those years ago. It's not kind or gentle, which I might have expected from anyone else when faced with a grieving, recently separated woman. It's brutal and beautiful, and my lips part to take everything he wants to give me.

His groan reverberates through my body, setting off a chain reaction of shivers and shimmies.

"Cassie, your mouth. Christ." He takes it again, not giving me a chance to respond. What could I say? That he tastes like a dream, and I can't believe we're here?

Instead, I kiss him back, letting my tongue tangle with his. He covers my body, curling his hand over my ass and gripping it in a possessive squeeze, pulling me under as he positions himself between my legs.

"Tell me this is real," he whispers against my mouth. "That you're real."

Has he really been thinking of me all these years? I know it's just sex but the yearning in his voice feels like something else. Like a wish.

"It's real." About as real as I've ever experienced.

"And you want this?" He sips at my lips, softly, then moves along my jaw to deliver little nips to my ear. "Please, Cassie."

"Sam." My moan is permission. It's forgiveness. It's *yes*. "I want this. You. Please don't stop."

His hand moves from my ass to under my shirt, captures my breast, and strokes the nipple to a stiff peak. I arch into his rough and ready touch, inviting more. Needing everything he can give me.

He pushes my sleep shirt up and off over my head. "I need to see you." His tone is grated as he reaches over to the lamp and switches it on.

"That's not really nec—" The words dry in my throat as I catch his expression. His mouth is harsh with desire, his eyes scorching a blazing track down my chest. With his fingers curling into the waistband of my shorts, he pulls them halfway down my thighs. His hand follows, slipping between my legs to give me one, searching stroke.

I buck against him, the sheer, sharp sensation an electric current through me.

"That's why we need the light," he says. "I'm not missing a single second of this."

His hand is still positioned between my legs, not moving, just accepting of the growing dampness as if it's his right. I inch my thighs apart, desperate for more friction, then clamp them together again.

His smile is beautiful and evil. The swagger is back.

"That's my girl. Tell me what you need."

I shake my head, a growing fury with him for being so in tune with my desires. Reaching down I shove my shorts off and out of the bed.

"Open up for me, beautiful."

I keep my thighs shut, turn my head away, a tantrum in the making. A finger nudges inside me, then strokes up through the sensitive folds to glance against my clit.

"Ohhh!" Another arch of my back, straining for that perfect touch.

He's leaning over me, and now he takes the hand not between my legs and cups my head to face him. There's that thumb move again, the one where he brushes my lower lip, and this time I lick, then suck it into my mouth.

His breath catches. *Not expecting that, were you, Sammie?* His eyes go dark as he watches me suck his thumb. He's stroking between my thighs now, and I feel them falling open to give that big, strong hand all the access it wants.

"Oh, fuck," he says, like he can't believe what's happening. His gaze moves to his hand on my pussy, which is so hot and slick that I'm sure I can't last. It's been a long time and these days at close quarters with Sam have only amped me up for a fast ride.

He removes his thumb from my mouth and moves in for a kiss. His tongue glides over mine, just as his fingers pump between my legs, and the heel of his hand strokes hard over my clit, and I'm gone, gone, gone. Over the edge and hurtling toward oblivion.

I go still, letting the sensations buoy me through the storm. When I open my eyes, Sam is looking down, wonder etched in his handsome features.

I swallow back the emotion racking my body. "Hi."

"Hi." He smiles, and my heart flips over.

The aftereffects are starting to creep up on me. I raise both hands to my face to cool my heating cheeks.

"I obviously needed that," I mutter, noting that his hand hasn't left its post—camped out, a sexy sentry over my sex. He's still stroking softly, keeping the home fires kindling.

"Can't stop touching you." His gaze moves down my body, over my small breasts, which feel heavier than ever. Those tiny movements of his fingers between my legs are keeping me in a state of permanent arousal.

His head inclines, his mouth claims mine again, but before I can really get into it, he's moving his lips down my throat.

Feeding kisses to my neck, my collarbones, the top of my breasts, and then—oh, his tongue swipes over a nipple. It's so good. I'd forgotten how good it feels to be touched there. I've always thought my breasts were too small, not worthy of taking part in the fun times.

"You don't have to ..." I say. "I know you must be dying to get on with ... it."

He raises his head. "It?"

"I've had mine, now it's your turn."

His look is pure incredulity. "I'm kind of enjoying this, if you don't mind. Unless you don't like me loving on your pretty tits?"

"No. I mean, yes, I love it. It's ... well, they're small, so I understand if you want to move on to the main event."

"These beauties can't be the main event?"

Oh God, I didn't intend to make a thing of it. "They're not the typical fantasy fodder."

He squeezes my breast. "These babies are the perfect fit for my hand. This ass ..."—he coasts down, leaving my breast aching for more—"feels just right in my palm." He moves that same hand between my legs, clamping over my mound with thrilling possessiveness. "And here? Christ, Cassie. Nowhere feels better to me. I've got a mouth, hand, cock, so let me use them. Still want me to stop sucking on your gorgeous tits?"

He's so direct. I thought I'd hate it, but I don't. Not by a long shot.

I shake my head. "Suck away."

"Good girl." He pushes the comforter back and repositions himself, sitting back against the headboard. He's still wearing boxer briefs, but his erection is a tent-pole worthy of a three-ring circus. He pats his thighs. "Climb aboard."

"Um, do you want to strip?"

"Not yet. I have plans."

Okay. I've never slept with someone so forward with their

sexual intention. Swinging my leg over, I seat myself over his massive thighs, conscious that I'm completely naked.

With one strong hand splayed over the small of my back, he moves me forward until my sensitive, still pulsing core is flush over his fabric-clad erection.

It's divine.

His other hand runs over my chest possessively, across both of my breasts, sending every cell of my being into a frenzy.

"Lean up on your knees, beautiful. Give me those perfect tits now."

I do as he commands. He plumps one breast, swirls his hot tongue over the nipple, and feeds himself with it.

Ohgodohgodohgod, that's so fucking good.

I grip the headboard and hold on for dear life as he makes one breast feel loved, then the other. My sex is dripping, my thighs slick with desire, and that pulsing need is starting up again. So soon. I need friction, touch, anything to alleviate the ever-tightening coil of tension.

He squeezes my ass and then I feel his fingers slipping between my legs from behind and stroking through again. Just lightly, a frustrating tease. I let out a sad little whimper and earn the vibration of a laugh against my breast in return.

"Prick," I moan as I saw myself over his hand, desperate for relief.

He unhinges his mouth from my breast. "Not yet."

Now I feel him move down, kissing my stomach, the top of my pubic bone, the ...

"Hold onto the headboard. Just need a little taste."

"Oh!"

There's that tongue I've been dreaming of for days, slipping inside me, while he moans as if my taste is all he could ever want or desire. His strong fingers dig into my ass cheek and hold me in place while he sucks, spears, and licks.

"Oh-oh God." Unable to help myself, I rock against his mouth, frantic to get his tongue to where it matters. Where it can heal. *Oh please, please, just a little more ...*

He's moaning like he can't get enough of me, like I'm the best thing he's ever tasted. I'm not used to such appreciation. All this attention, and I realize that I've accepted "good enough" for far too long.

I should be adored.

I'm primed to go off, and it doesn't take long. Just a few sizzling seconds while I white-knuckle the headboard.

After a couple of shuddering moments, he speaks. "Hands off, Cassie. You'll leave dents."

And then he's scooting back up, manhandling me back into position with my soft throbbing sex centered over his still-covered erection. I'm panting, my head against his forehead, my body still spinning from another amazing orgasm.

"What are you trying to prove?" I ask.

"Prove?"

"Cass, two. Sam, zero."

He chuckles, his lips still slick with me. "Everything is a contest with you. Maybe I figured you needed it after going years with mediocre sex."

I thump his shoulder. "You know nothing about it. It was ... fine."

"Fine?" His scoff is peak Sam. "Fine is what you use to describe the weather, not sex."

"Maybe I think what happened here is 'fine'."

"No, you don't."

He's right. That was out of this world.

Now he's giving me the full Sam Killian stare, complete with a cocky eyebrow raise, and while usually I'd hate it with the heat of a thousand orgasms, tonight I'm loving it a little too much.

I squirm in his lap and yield a pained groan. Another shift, his fingers grip my ass, his lips part with desire. And then I continue, grinding now, loving how he feels against me, determined to make him crazy.

"Condoms?"

"Left drawer," he says, the words grated through his sensuous lips.

I lean over and slide open the drawer. The first thing I see is an envelope—it's the same type Annie used for her letter to me, except this one has Sam's name on it. Moving it aside to get the condoms, I notice that it's still sealed. He hasn't read whatever his brother wrote?

But that goes out of my mind on seeing a naked Sam. He's used the separation as his opportunity to strip, so when I return to his lap, his cock is springing tall and proud between our bodies.

Before I can ask, he says, "I want you on top."

There's something about this position that seems more intimate than any other. Maybe it's the subtle power shift, how Sam is in control but also making sure I won't feel caged by his bulk.

With shaking fingers, I roll the condom on but not before I run a hand over him from root to tip. Steel wrapped in velvet, he's also big, which might be another reason why he wants me in this position.

He shifts down, so he's on his back. His hands are on my hips, light at first, then firmly gripping as I move up ... to sink down.

"Oh fuuuuck!" He groans as I steal down, inch by inch.

He's halfway in and it's tight. Good, but full.

"You're ... big."

"I know. Take your time."

Another shift up and then I take him deeper. His thumb runs along my pubic bone, into my curls and circles my clit.

Just that one move makes me so damn wet that I slide easily down his cock to the base.

"Oh, yeah, that's it," he murmurs. "Right fucking there."

With his thumb still stroking, teasing, and the sensation of fullness, I'm lost in unbearable pleasure. I place my hands on his chest, needing the leverage but then I wonder if it's too much. At my softening grip, he takes my hands and says, "That's good. Like that."

I push into his pecs as I move up and down. He's guiding me, holding my hips, lifting my body, and together we're in perfect sync.

"Cassie, you feel amazing."

I don't think I can come again. This feels wonderful, but I don't think I need to. A void has been filled, a hole where my heart is, and it's enough. It can't possibly match what's happened so far, only then suddenly I'm on my back and Sam is rocking into me, somehow finding more depth.

He stops. "This okay?"

"Yeah, it's good. Perfectly fine."

"You fucking with me?" He moves out, dragging his length against my clit to the point my eyes roll back in my head, then he drills deep. "Because I need better than fine."

I wasn't joking with him, it just came out. I clutch his ass and dig my fingers in. "It's—oh, God!"

He's going slower, each stroke through me heightening the pleasure. Then his fingers slip like a thief between our bodies, pressing, milking orgasm #3 out of me and my body tightens and shudders. Needing to keep from losing it completely, I bite against his shoulder.

He buries his face in my neck as he comes with a roar. Here I am trying to be quiet while Sam wants to tell the world.

Coming down off the high, my brain re-attaches to the grid and the magnitude of it all hits me hard. Absurdly, a sob escapes me.

In a flash, he leans up on his elbows. "Shit, Cassie, did I hurt you?"

"No, no. Not at all."

He slides out of me, his face creased in horror at the idea of possibly injuring me. A quick fumble below, where I assume he's removing the condom, and then he takes me in his arms and holds me tight.

No words, just his strength and comfort while I sink into all he offers.

I cry for my sister, unleashing tears I thought spent in the wake of Annie's and Jake's deaths.

I cry for the kids, for everything they've lost and have yet to find.

I cry for my old life and the new one I don't know how to deal with.

I cry.

Twenty-Three

No one has ever cried after I gave them an orgasm. Or two. Or three.

I know sex can be a highly emotional experience for some people. Hell, this bout was highly emotional for me. I finally banged this woman I've been obsessed with forever and it was fucking glorious.

Only now I can't tell her that because she's gone into a meltdown. I'm guessing the enormity of all she's lost has come to a head, right when we connected, our bodies as one—which is either a testament to my sick skills or an example of extremely poor timing.

The sobs are quieting now, so I chance a kiss to the top of her head and a tentative query.

"You okay, Cassie?"

"It's just a lot. A lot of change." These wet words are spoken into my neck.

I shift back and tip her chin up so I can look at her

properly. She's red-eyed and sniffly, but still the most beautiful woman I've ever seen.

"I get it, but you're not alone in this. We're a team, remember?"

She nods. "But is this a good idea?"

"Making our teamwork ... sexy?"

That yields a smile. My heart sings a song.

"Worried it's going to complicate things?" Hell, I'm right there with her.

"Maybe I'm overthinking it. You don't ever let sex complicate anything, do you?"

Not the response I expected, but probably the one I deserve. Cassie's not going to suddenly take me seriously because I'm great in the sack. If anything, it only proves what she's thought all along: I'm good for one thing only.

"I try not to," I say with my Sammiest smile. "It's the perfect outlet, good for what ails you."

"Sam ..." She bites her lip. "I saw Jake's letter in the drawer, still sealed." She touches my face gently. "Is there a reason for that?"

Cowardice. Fear. Grief. "I'm not ready to say goodbye."

"Oh." Her eyes well. "If there's anything I can do to help."

"You already have." Damn. That sounds like I mean the sex, which is part of it, but not all. This closeness to her is what I need. I'm about to explain when my alarm goes off.

"You set an alarm for 3 a.m.?"

"I need to check on Maya. I'm not going to wake her, I just want to make sure she's doing okay."

Reluctantly, I pull out of her arms and grab my briefs. First, I head to the bathroom and dispose of the condom. When I come out, Cassie is re-dressed in her PJs, which is frankly, disappointing.

"I'll come with you."

She doesn't need to—in fact I like the idea of coming back

to bed and finding her there, those blond waves spread out on my pillow—but I also like that she wants to team up with me on this.

We head into the kids' room. Maya is breathing normally, snoring a little, so I'm positive she's doing fine. Spence has kicked off the cover, so I replace it, though it probably won't last. Kid's a thrasher.

Cassie stays at the door, keeping an eye on things. When we leave, she takes a step back from me in the hallway.

"I probably should head back to bed myself."

A caveman instinct to throw her over my shoulder rears up, but I smother it. Leaning against the wall, I thread my arms over my chest and aim for casual. "You might sleep better in mine."

"Not so sure about that. And you have to get up in a few hours."

She's right. I'd be unable to get through the night without pawing at her.

"Thanks for earlier," I say. "Seeing me through the bad dreams."

"No problem. And thanks for the orgasms."

"Cassie, three. Sam, one." I run a finger down her cheek. "Plenty more where they came from."

"The Orgasm Fairy?"

"Making all your sex wishes come true."

That makes her laugh. That's me, purveyor of sex and chuckles.

"Night, Sam."

"Night, Cassie."

I watch her walk to her door, like I'm seeing her home from a date.

Wishing that was even possible.

I wake up early, before 5:30 a.m., my body a mix of numb and aching. Sex with Cassie was amazing, and while it's complicated things, I know once won't be enough.

Anyone who's observed my relationship with this woman up until now would assume we're finding comfort in each other during this difficult time. Maybe even that the roommate situation is contributing to a cauldron of sexual tension and that banging it out kills multiple birds.

I don't think that.

I was honest with Cassie when I said I've had it bad for her for years. But that never translated into wanting more than a chance to rumple that prim and proper exterior. I've done that. I should be satisfied.

Yet.

I'm not. There are all sorts of reasons why this can't continue—the guardianship arrangement, the kids' well-being, how we're oil and water, that she just got out of a long-term relationship. How she doesn't even live in this city.

Yet.

The kids will do better if they have two strong and loving presences in their lives. It would be easier if Cassie lived in Chicago. Not just in Chicago, but here. With us. As a family.

I sit up quickly, in an agitated state that I do not need especially as I'm back at work today. Sure, I want Cassie. I want her body and her pretty little tits and that sweet ass. I want those hard-won smiles and the way she challenges me. But do I want it ... forever?

Or am I justifying this to make things easier for me in any custody fight? If it all goes south, that's what she might say. That I tried to use sex to keep her sweet.

I need to psych myself up to have this conversation with her. Coffee will help. I'm about to head out to the kitchen, when I hear a noise coming from my sneakers' closet. I'm guessing Waffles is in there sniffing around and looking for places to lay gifts.

I nudge open the door and find Spence. He's sitting on the floor with one Nike Air Max shoe on his left foot, the other nowhere to be seen. He's playing a game on the iPad, his little face scrunched up in concentration.

"Hey, buddy." He looks up, and I'm pretty sure that's disappointment. He's expecting his dad and starting to wonder why he's never here. Jake has a sneakers' closet just like mine—he copied me, actually—and Spence loved hanging out there.

I take a seat beside him. "What are we playing?"

"Game."

It looks colorful, something with dragons and a maze.

"Up kind of early, huh?"

He turns to me, his blue eyes big and troubled. "I want Daddy."

I hold out my arms, and he climbs into my lap. I no longer have the resources to keep duct-taping my heart daily.

"So, you know how we said that Mommy and Daddy are on vacation?"

"Disney. With Mickey and Goofy."

"Yep. So something happened." I strive to push through, say it quickly. But when I speak, it sounds like it's coming out of my mouth in slow motion. "They had an accident. A very bad accident and they can't come back because they ... died."

"Like the dragons?"

"Dragons?"

He points at the iPad.

"Kind of. But the dragons can usually come back in the game." I'm guessing that's how it works. "That's not going to happen here. Mommy and Daddy have gone away for good."

"To Disneyland?"

My chest caves in. "No, not Disneyland. Another place, where they can't come back from."

"I want to go."

I haul in some air, but my lungs refuse to fill. "You can't, buddy."

He looks completely lost, his little mind trying to figure it out. Where is this place and why isn't he allowed there? The resources I consulted said you shouldn't use euphemisms or tell your preschooler that the people they love are in a special or better place. Use plain language, even if they don't understand the full nuance.

Because I'm committed to this clusterfuck, I try again.

"They're dead, Spence." My voice cracks. "All gone."

"Sam," I hear in a low voice. I look up to find Cassie in front of me, still in her sleep shorts and tee, but that's where the resemblance ends. This is not the woman I left at her door last night. This version is staring at me with eyeballs of burning coal. "What are you doing?"

"It's time, Cassie."

She picks Spence out of my lap. The sneaker falls off and hits the floor with a louder-than-expected thud. "You want some cereal, Spence?"

He nods. "Mommy and Daddy are gone. They're dead."

She glares at me over her shoulder and takes Spence into the kitchen. Sighing, I follow, feeling guilty, though I'm not sure why. While she feeds him, I start the coffee, then I pull her aside.

"He's been asking about them. There's only so much longer we can put this off."

"We should have told him together."

I touch her hip, marveling that she lets me even though she's upset. That must mean something.

"The opportunity presented itself and I thought it was as good a time as any."

"But, without discussing it ..." She shakes her head and folds her arms. "We're supposed to be a team."

"We are. And sometimes decisions are made in the moment because they make sense. It's not a competition."

She makes an exasperated noise. "This isn't the first time you've made unilateral decisions. Moving the kids here, sending Maya back to school. What part of 'co' in co-guardian do you not understand?"

Jesus, I can't get anything right. Anger flares, but I do my best to rein it in. "So, maybe I jumped the gun here, but it was never gonna get any easier. I already broke it to Maya and let me tell you that was a hell I wouldn't wish on anyone." I lower my voice. "To be honest, I'm not sure how much he truly understands. We'll probably be telling him this more than once, so you'll get your chance to break the news. Again."

She looks appalled. Good. "Sam—"

"I need to shower and get going for my shift. Can you manage here?"

"Yes. I can."

Sure sounds like it. What I've probably done is drive her back into Derek's arms. The minute I get home from my shift, she'll be on a plane back to figure out how to make a life there with my brother's kids.

TWENTY-FOUR

Cass

"When are you coming home?" Gina squints at me on FaceTime. "I want to hug the hell out of you."

"Probably a couple of days? Sam's back at work today and we still need to figure out childcare."

"God, I know what that's like." Gina has two kids, a useless ex-husband, and a parakeet. "But it does sound like you guys are working things out?"

"Things are kind of in flux right now."

She smiles sympathetically. "Of course they are. It's been an awful couple of weeks."

"I broke up with Derek."

Her eyes go wide, and she makes all the appropriate noises while I take her through the story. I leave out what happened with Sam. I'm not proud of my behavior—any of it.

I broke up with my boyfriend, immediately jumped into bed with the enemy, then got mad at him for doing the hardest thing anyone should have to do.

"So does this mean you're going to move to Chicago?"

"No, not at all. My job's in New York—I hope. I need to talk to Joanna." Joanna's my boss at Beacon and she's given me a lot of leeway so far. "But more than that, my life is there, even if it's not with Derek anymore."

Gina's nodding but looks like she has *opinions*.

"Okay, spill it."

"Whatever you do, I will support you one hundred percent. But being a single mom is tough. I know this to my core. Which is romance-speak for the vagina that's not getting any. You'll never date again."

I don't care about that. Or at least I don't care about it at this moment.

"I'm fine with being on my own." I always have been, which might speak to how I've felt these last couple of years with Derek. Or maybe I'm the problem—I'm not meant to be in a committed relationship.

She eyes me critically. "But you have this family in Chicago. I can't imagine they're on board with this. Or that it's the best move, to be honest."

Another person who thinks I'm screwing up. "So I should up sticks and move here?"

"I'd hate to see you leave me. Honestly. But maybe?" She cocks her head, curious. "How are things with the hot firefighter?"

"He's charging ahead, thinking he knows everything."

"Okay."

I blow out a breath. "We might have had sex."

Her jaw drops. "*Might have?*"

"Okay, we did." I rush on. "After Derek and I broke up."

"How soon after?"

"That's not the point. There's been a lot of tension and it just happened. But it won't happen again." No more visits to soothe his pain in the middle of the night. He'll have to make his own way through.

"But it was good, right?"

So. Good. "It was fine. Perfect way to blow off some steam."

Her face softens because she assumes that seeking comfort during this terrible time was a major part of it. Better to stick with that story rather than this bone-deep desire that feels so dangerous.

Feeling a touch guilty that I might have implied it was *merely* sex, I move to amend. "Sam's been ... great, to be honest. Much more invested in the kids' care than I expected. But he also has a habit of making unilateral decisions without running them by me."

"Like?"

"He told Spence about his parents this morning. About them being gone."

"Oh, honey. That's got to be hard."

It is, and it must have been so difficult for Sam to do it. "I thought we would do it together."

"Right. How did Spence take it?"

I put my face in my hands. The volume is low enough that he shouldn't react on hearing his name. "I'm not sure he understood. But the books all say not to sugarcoat it. Try to use plain language. Sam said he saw a natural opening and it felt right to tell him." I look up to find my friend eyeing me gravely. "I just think he should have run it by me. He's a shoot first, think later kind of person, which is not how we should be doing things."

"Okay, so you have different parenting approaches. But maybe there can be some middle ground. It doesn't have to be so ..." She trails off.

"So what?"

"Competitive?"

"We're not competing. He's always going to be closer to them." Is that why I'm upset? Because I want to be the one who's supporting the kids emotionally and I'm jealous of Sam's relationship with them? "He mentioned that he had to tell Maya about her parents, and it was awful."

She shakes her head. "It must have been. And he did it again with Spence."

"I didn't ask him to."

"Maybe he thought he was making it easier for you by taking this on. You're not really used to asking for help. I remember when you started at Beacon, you thought I was patronizing you when I offered to be your mentor."

So I have a stubborn, independent streak. I've had to figure stuff out and I'm not used to involving other people in the fundamentals of my life.

"I've never been good at that. But I don't need Sam to take on the burdens of co-parenting just to make things easier for me."

Gina considers this. "Why not? So yes, he should have discussed this with you. That kind of communication takes time, but the takeaway here is that Sam did this terribly difficult thing in telling Spence and that should be acknowledged. Like him coming to New York to tell you about Annie and Jake in person. That was a nice thing to do as well."

It was, and I never thanked him for it. Sam's been doing all the hard things while I'm behaving like a jerk.

"I feel so prickly around him." Mostly because everything he does either (a) annoys me or (b) turns me on. There's also the (c) where I feel safe with him. Cared for. Maybe that's what I'm afraid of, relying on someone, and I'm dressing it up as some mansplaining slight.

"It sounds like he's willing to step up and not shirk his responsibility," Gina says. "That's solid gold right there. Look, I'm not going to tell you that you should be moving to another city, but this kid stuff takes a village."

"You hate that phrase."

She grins. "I know. But it's never been more apt right now. There's this ready-made support system in Chicago that would make the transition smoother. And this is about the kids, too, right?"

"But Sam and I—that can't happen again."

"Because?"

"Because it just muddles everything." It's also possible Sam has an agenda and is trying to keep me hormone-happy while he gets what he wants. "I want to keep a clear head and not think with my vagina."

Gina grins. "Okay. But maybe think a *little* with it while the going is good."

After my call with Gina, I'm left thinking about the events of the last twenty-four hours. I think I messed up here. Spence has been asking about his mom and dad so much and we've been fobbing him off with little white lies.

But there's only so long we can do that.

I'm also realizing that we need to get him into preschool or kindergarten (I'm not sure of the difference). I can spend some time with him, playing puzzles and reading his favorite books, but I can't do it all the time. I'm already neglecting work calls and emails, and even a morning without Sam makes me realize how hard this is for one person. For the next fifteen minutes, I keep one eye on Spence as he fits colorful blocks together and I research nanny agencies, which turns out to be a rather involved process. Once on an agency's books, there are resumes to review, interviews to conduct, and background checks to run. I'm not sure how this can happen on a timeline that allows me to return to my previous work schedule.

Around noon, I bring Spence his PB&J and glass of juice.

The little stinker turned on the TV when I wasn't looking. "Hey, Spence, what's on?"

"*Frozen*." He looks up at me. "Olaf is melted."

Sure enough, the funny little snowman is milking his death scene. But if I recall correctly, Ana brings him back to life with magic.

"Remember Sam told you about where your mom and dad went?"

"Are they melted?"

As that sounds horrifying, I won't be going there. I'm realizing now that Sam did me a huge favor by taking on this responsibility, and that he's probably ten times better at it anyway. Spence might not completely understand, but the concept has been introduced and the next time it comes up might be easier.

My insensitive handling of the situation is weighing on me when Waffles wanders to the front door and gives a couple of light woofs.

"What's up, boy?"

I hear a scratching sound. When I open the door, there's a giant basket, the whiff of jasmine, and a woman tiptoeing away.

"Oh, hi!"

Charlie from the penthouse turns and waves. "I didn't want to disturb you. I just thought you might like a few treats."

The basket is shrink-wrapped, tied up in a bow, and bigger than Spence, who's come out to see what the fuss is all about.

"Present!" He pulls on one of the ribbons.

"Wow, this is so generous."

Charlie waves it away. "Not at all. If I had any homemaking skills, I'd have made you a casserole. That's what people do, isn't it?"

"Some people. I think I like your approach better. Did you want to come in?"

"Only if it's not a bother."

"It's not. I could do with the company." I pick up the basket, but I don't get far because Charlie has stopped by the photos in the hallway.

"Annie's wedding," she murmurs.

"Six years ago."

"Gosh, Maya was so cute. Of course, she still is. And Sam, wow!"

Sam, wow? I'm not sure how to respond, so I offer a feeble "there he is."

She pulls a face. "You're not seeing this?"

"What?" I take a closer look.

"He's got his eye on you in this photo."

I re-focus on the framed image. Sam's smiling, his head turned slightly as he takes in Maya, who's in my arms. "Eye on his niece, more like. She was the center of attention that day, even more so than the bride."

"Hmm, maybe. He was what age? Twenty?"

"Twenty-one. Mental age of ten."

She chuckles. "Oh, they're all like that. So handsome, though, and even better now. He's really grown into those muscles."

I'm not enjoying this objectification of my co-guardian. Everyone seems to view Sam a certain way.

She scans the wall, her gaze alighting on the other photo of me with Annie, the one I had never seen before moving in here.

"This is lovely. Did Sam take it?"

"I don't know." But I think I do. He probably did or at minimum, he liked it enough to feature in this prominent spot in his home. Whatever the answer, it's a precious acknowledgment of my close relationship with Annie. "Would you like coffee or juice?"

"Coffee would be great." She follows me into the kitchen where I place the basket on the table. Spence stands on a chair to check it out.

"Spence, baby, let's get you down from there." I scoop him up and put him on the floor. The basket is filled with treats like macarons, shortbread, crackers, dips, wine—quite the collection. "This is really nice of you." I can feel my eyes getting wet.

Charlie smiles. "How about you take a seat and let me make the coffee? This Keurig works, I assume."

I didn't sleep well after sex with Sam. It should have been the perfect release, relaxing all my muscles, but something felt wrong about returning to my room instead of staying in his arms. Our fight this morning has me on edge, and Gina's obvious disapproval over my plan to return to New York and split up this family is making me even more upset.

Charlie's expression softens and she urges me to a chair with a "Hey, hey, take a load off," then sets about making coffee. She's obviously trying to give me some space while I swipe away stray tears.

"Where's Uncle Sammie?" Spence asks.

"He went to work."

He lets out a weary sigh, which makes him sound like a little old man. "I want to go to work."

"Maybe later." I rip open the macarons and hand a blue one to him. "Want to try this? It's French."

Charlie chuckles as she loads up the Keurig. "Start those high-class dessert tastes when they're young."

I run a hand through Spence's hair, dark like his dad's. Like Sam's.

"So, I'm not stopping you from doing something

important, am I?" I'm conscious that it's the middle of the day and she probably should be at work.

"Oh, no. I nipped home for a little alone time with the hubs. And I'd had the basket delivered a couple of days ago and thought it would be a good time to bring it down."

A couple of minutes later she takes a seat at the kitchen table. Coffees in hand, we watch as Spence moves his fire truck over the floor.

"How's living with Sam?"

I sip my coffee. "Infuriating. But he's great with the kids."

"What's infuriating?"

"All that cockiness."

She chuckles. "Hmm, he can kind of back it up, though, can't he? Reminds me of Max. God, you wouldn't believe the swagger when I met him."

"All gone?"

"God no!" She laughs, a little ruefully. "But now the swagger is mostly for me."

"I can't imagine Sam limiting himself in any way." Not that he should. Seeing Sam with other women, like the attractive ER doc or that dog owner in the park, or witnessing his sexting practices, has inched under my skin in an unfortunate way.

This seems to amuse her. While I sip my coffee, we chat, and before long I'm telling her about my job with Beacon.

"So they're a boutique outfit, right? No branches here?" Charlie asks. "But I'm guessing you could find a job like that in Chicago."

I'd be lying if I said the thought hadn't occurred to me. While I've told Gina that my life is in New York—even without Derek—I can't get away from the notion that Chicago is the place to be, especially if I want a real relationship with the kids.

"I like working with a smaller client list. It's more personal, even if it's not exactly the dream job."

"What would you prefer to be doing?"

I'm not even sure why I said that. It's been so long since I thought about those distant dreams. "Once upon a time, I wanted to study art. It wasn't very practical, so I gave it up."

Charlie looks pleased, as if it's the answer to a puzzle. "Well, we have some great art schools here. Columbia, the Art Institute. Maybe you should look into that, even just part-time. Assuming you're sticking around."

I take a breath. *Assuming you're sticking around.* Even with the communication issues between Sam and me, I'm starting to realize that everything is conspiring to keep me in Chicago for the foreseeable future.

And I'm not sure how I feel about that.

Twenty-Five

Sam

At Engine 6, everyone is thrilled and slightly horrified to welcome me back. The crew do their best to act like it's perfectly normal for a bereaved man who witnessed his closest family members die to be back on the job.

Abby pulls me aside and hugs me hard. "Hey, I have something for you from Kathleen."

"Is it fruit cake?" Abby's aunt Kathleen spends every waking hour making corned beef and cabbage or doorstopper-dense fruit cakes.

"You know it." She smiles. "We miss you at Sunday dinners."

For the last year, any off Sundays were usually spent at Kathleen's with Jude and Abs. That schedule has suffered now that Abby and Jude are coupled up, but I usually try to get out to Bridgeport once a month.

"I miss you guys, too. Not sure I miss fruit cake, but the kids might like it."

Abby's eyes light up at the mention of my niblings. "How

are they? I'm happy to babysit to give you guys a break. Any time."

"Thanks, Sullivan. I might take you up on that. We really need to find a more permanent solution for childcare."

"How are things with Cassie? Is she heading back to New York?"

I slept with her and she's mad at me. These two things might be related.

"She's still here. For now."

Abby's lips kick up. "Interesting."

"It's not. Today's the first day alone with the kids and she also has to do online consults with clients as well. It's going to be tough on her."

Abby nods. "Sounds like she could do with some help."

I'm still thinking on what happened this morning. Maybe I handled it all wrong, but I truly believe Spence needed to hear the awful news at last. Bonus if I can spare Cassie any more pain.

Not that she saw it that way.

I'm in the lounge cooking up a pot of stew when Jude comes in. He was out this morning at a doctor's appointment.

He puts an arm around me and kisses my temple. "Nice to see you, Sammie."

I launch right into it. "I might have screwed up, Garland."

His gaze dips to the stew. "Definitely. Needs more carrots."

"I slept with Cassie."

Flipping to a casual lean against the counter, he delivers a slow nod. "And now you're in love with her?"

"What? No!" People in love are always so ready to assume the worst for everyone else. "It's just made things complicated when I need it all to be simpler. She's still determined to go for sole custody—"

"She said that?"

"She hasn't *not* said it. And she's not going to change her mind because I've bedazzled her with my dick. Even if she wanted to, she'd hold her ground just to prove my sex skills played no part in her decision-making."

Jude squints at me. "That's kind of overthinking it, isn't it?"

"I'm trying to stay several moves ahead of her. That's how she'll think. That I'm trying to control the situation when all I wanted to do is make it better."

"Now I have no idea what you're talking about."

I fill him in on what happened this morning with breaking the news to Spence. "And now I'm the bad guy because I saw an opening. No one wants to tell their three-year-old nephew that his parents are dead. I took that one for the team and she thinks I'm cutting her out."

"That's not what she thinks. Listen, both of you are trying to navigate this terrible situation with as much grace as possible. You're not going to get everything right—"

"So you think I got it wrong."

He shakes his head. "No. There's no right way to do any of this. You're experiencing it all for the first time—death of someone you love, having to be strong for your family and these little ones, this battle you think you're in with Cass. And then there's the fucked-up fact that you were on the ground when it happened." He squeezes my arm. "Maybe you should talk to one of the CFD counselors?"

"I don't need that. It's better if I work. And it gets me some space from her."

He doesn't say anything, just gives me a moment to breathe.

"Hey, Sam." I turn to see the firehouse's admin, Kathy. "The captain would like to see you."

"Take over here?"

Jude assents while I head in to see the cap. Wyatt Fox raises his gaze to mine.

"Have a seat, Killian." When I do, he asks, "How are you?"

"Kind of numb, but I'm ready to return."

"Sure about that?"

I shoot a sharp look at him. "You think I shouldn't be here?"

Captain Fox gives me his famous Wild West squint. "Not saying that. But I know what it's like to lose a brother. It's not easy to spring back."

Wyatt lost his brother Logan as well as his foster father, Sean Dempsey, in a high-rise fire over ten years ago. It was devastating for the entire Dempsey family of foster kids, but it spurred them all to join the service. To follow in their steps in honor of the fallen.

"Is there something about how I acted at the scene that makes you think I'm not ready?"

"No. You acted the way anyone would. But it was the worst first day on the job anyone could have."

I flex my hands. "I need to replace the memories with better ones."

It's already getting easier because Cassie's here, making it so and giving me plenty to think about. I'm not sure how to feel about that.

"Okay. But if you need anything—a break, a timeout, someone to talk to—tell me."

"Will do."

It's a busy shift for Squad, with a call-out in the morning for a hazmat situation, then another one in the early afternoon for a car that went for a swim in the lake. No casualties for either, so a good day. Staying active is having the desired effect.

Somehow, I'm managing to compartmentalize my life, living in the moment for my job, and keeping everything else on the backburner of my brain.

Tomorrow morning after my shift is done, I'll go home and apologize to Cassie for jumping the gun with Spence. She's right. We should have discussed how we were going to tell him, instead of me acting on my gut.

Just after a late lunch (the Irish stew went down a treat, though I added some paprika, so it was more of a goulash), I'm in the locker room, drying off after taking a shower—eau de Chicago lake water is a tad odorific—when I hear a slight cough.

I look up and there she is: Cassie.

Panic climbs my throat. "Where's Spence? Is Maya okay?"

She steps inside quickly, hands raised. "They're both fine. Spence is with Jude right now. He's showing him the fire truck."

"I just thought—"

And then all thoughts leave my brain because she's in my space, her hand on my chest. I'm wrapped in a towel, but I may as well be naked.

"I did text to say we were stopping by. Jude said to find you in here. I didn't realize ..."

Her words peter out, perhaps the knowledge of how close she is seeping into her bones.

"I usually leave my phone in my locker, and I haven't had a chance to check. Why are you here?"

"Two reasons. Spence was asking for you. I think after this morning's conversation he feels a bit clingy."

"Well, I'm awesome."

She smiles, though it crumbles a little around the edges. She's nervous. "And the other reason is ... I wanted to apologize for how I reacted. You know the kids better than me, so of course you're going to sense the right time to tell them. I wanted to share that burden with you, I suppose. Not try to micromanage it, but so we could work out a plan."

I blow out a breath, mostly of relief. It's so good to see her here, back on my team.

Our team.

"I'm not really a planner. I tend to go on my gut, always have. But I get where you're coming from. I took the shot because damn, his little face, you know. He looked so fucking sad when I walked in, like he was expecting his dad. Spence used to spend a lot of time in Jake's sneakers' closet. He loves the big shoes and I guess that space reminded him of his dad." It reminds *me* of him. "And when he asked, I thought, I can't do this anymore."

Her eyes well and she starts sniffling. I rush to catch her tears.

"Cassie, I'm sorry."

"No, you did the right thing. I don't know why I felt it could have gone any better with my input. It's not like I know them any better than you, or at all."

My laugh sounds like a bark. "It would have been a hundred times better if you had been with me. As soon as I started talking, I knew you should have been by my side, giving me the strength I need to explain to a little boy that his parents are gone."

It's true. With Cassie, I feel vital. Alive. Like there's a chance I can make it through this terrible time. Together, we are solid.

Only now, I'm a mess. I put a heel to my eyes and shake my head.

God, look at us.

"You did good," she says. "You took that off my shoulders, just like when you showed up in New York so I wouldn't be alone. I never thanked you properly for that kindness. You're a good man, Sam Killian. And so amazing with the kids. I've underestimated you and I'm so grateful we're in this together."

Jesus, how can that be a turn-on? Do I need her approval so much? Apparently, I do. My cock *loves* getting that endorsement.

My hand is still curled around her neck, my thumb on her still-wet cheek, and my lungs and heart will fly apart if I don't kiss her.

Can't have that. I need those internal organs in tip-top condition. So I do the only thing that makes sense: take her mouth with mine.

She responds with crazy, soul-stirring hunger. I grasp her ass and pull her flush against me. Just the feel of her body against mine, and I'm lost. She clutches at my shoulders as we kiss and kiss and fucking kiss like this is not the worst idea and there's no tomorrow.

She came to see me—and in doing that I feel she actually sees me.

Knowing that sends me higher, my body screaming for release, but I'm also aware that we're in the locker room of my workplace and anyone could walk in.

I pull back, panting. "Jesus, you wreck me, Cassie, you know that?" She's looking a little wrecked herself. "Something about you apologizing has me hard as a rock."

"My apology turned you on?"

"Yeah. Anytime you admit you're wrong, I want to fuck you."

She raises a saucy eyebrow. "And when I don't admit it?"

"I want to fuck you harder."

She wants to be annoyed but my crude charm wins the day.

"There's something else I need to tell you." She runs a hand along my chest, like she's checking I'm real. She takes a breath, maybe psyching herself up. "I think the kids should stay in Chicago. It makes the most sense."

I struggle to react. Does that mean—? "You won't fight to take them to New York?"

"No, this is their home. I'm still not sure how I fit in, but I know that taking them away from everyone they know and love is not the best thing for them."

The huge weight crushing my chest lifts, though something else she said niggles. About how she fits in, and her doubts on that.

"And you're staying?"

She looks unsure, vulnerable. "For now."

Though it sounds like a compromise, I decide it's best not to push my luck.

She gives a small smile that I think she'd like to be a bigger one. Maybe her guardianship decision is a weight off for her, too.

I kiss her forehead. "Let's go see our nephew."

TWENTY-SIX

Cass

Out in the truck bay, Jude and a couple of the other firefighters are hanging with Spence. Jude is carrying him, letting him run his little fingers along the ladder hitched to the truck's side.

"I want to drive it!"

"Hey, what's going on here?" Sam asks.

"Uncle Sammie!" Spence reaches for his uncle who scoops him up and lands a big kiss on his cheek.

"No kissing!"

"Since when? You *love* kissing."

Everyone laughs, then a couple of people seem to notice me. Or maybe they already did but were being discreet because of the halo of cartoon birds circling my head. Sam Killian has that effect.

I told him that the kids should stay here, that there won't be a custody fight, that I'll be on hand at least for a while. I don't know what this future looks like. I hope I've made the right call.

Spence is insisting that he get to drive the truck. Sam hops up into the driver's seat so Spence can sit in his lap with his hands on the steering wheel.

"Cassie, you want in on this action?" Sam calls out.

"No, I think I'll stay down here."

"Good call," Jude says. "Hey, Cass, have you met the crew?"

Introductions are made, or re-introductions, because I recognize most of them from the funeral service. Luke Almeida is Sam's lieutenant, an imposing figure with shocking blue eyes and a hard-ass demeanor, which softens as he shakes my hand. Alexandra Dempsey, who I later learn is Luke's sister, is a tall, striking woman with dark hair, streaked with auburn waves.

"How's Maya doing?" she asks.

"Okay." Though I hope more than know it's true. "She's back at school. We're trying to give her the support she needs."

"It's good that she's back. Good that Sam's here as well. Except it leaves you on the hook with the childcare."

"Sure, but I don't mind."

"Are you working right now?"

"Yes, and I can do some of it remotely." But that can't last. Now that the kids are staying, I'll have to start thinking about what that means for me in the long-term.

"Childcare can be tricky with both parents working," Luke says sympathetically.

Jude speaks up. "I checked in with the Rebels and got some nanny contacts for you."

"Oh, thanks." Those must be the feelers Sam said he'd put out.

"And if you need childcare in the meantime, you could always drop them off at my place," Alexandra says. "We don't live that far from you."

"You'd look after Spence?"

Luke snorts. "She might have given birth to two kids, but that's where the maternal feeling ends."

"Luke!" Alexandra thumps him in the arm, which Luke rubs theatrically. "I am perfectly maternal, but I sure as shit cannot spend 24/7 with my angels. Women want fulfilling careers, asshole." She turns back to me. "I have two kids of my own, three and a half and six months. We have in-house childcare, so she's already vetted. You'd have to pay her, of course. I think she'd be open to it. Someone else does the cooking, though, so no need to worry about her attention being diverted."

Luke cups his mouth as if telling me a secret. "My sister isn't really housewife material. Not sure why she bothered to get married at all."

"Right, because your better half Kinsey is the ultimate housewife, whatever that means these days." She rolls her eyes affectionately before continuing. "Spence is close enough in age to my Logan that he'd have some socialization." She smiles at me. "Sorry, I'm getting carried away, organizing your life for you."

"No, that's so kind of you." It is. And it would give us some breathing room while we figure out a more permanent solution. "Let me talk to Sam about it. Maybe you could run it by your nanny?"

"Katya. She's Swedish. And as hot, blonde, and efficient as that sounds."

Someone honks the horn of the fire truck, which is followed by Spence's giggle. Two minutes later Sam hops down with Spence in his arms.

"What'd I miss?"

"Just your crew figuring out a solution for our childcare issues."

Sam's eyebrows dip in a V. "Ah, is Spence gonna come to work with me every day?" He nuzzles his nephew's nose. "You want to be a fireman, little guy?"

Spence yells his approval while I continue. "Before we put the kid to work, we might be able to piggyback onto Alexandra's arrangements."

"Oh, yeah? Thanks, Alex."

Alex smiles. "I need to convince my nanny that three kids are no more work than two. Stay tuned. But I think the both of you could do with some breathing room."

Sam shares a quick glance with me, and something about it makes my body thrum. No surprise there. I avert my gaze far too late but catch Jude's lips rolling in on a suppressed smile.

A siren goes off, followed by a robotic announcement. "Engine 6, Squad 3, Ambulance 16," along with a location and some code I don't understand.

Everyone jumps into action, while Sam passes off Spence and gently pushes me back to a safer spot near the wall. "Spence can see the trucks leaving the house from here."

And so can I, which suddenly worries me. "You'll be careful, won't you?"

Sam's brow crinkles, then relaxes. He smooths Spence's hair, looks like he's going to touch me, then changes his mind.

I wish he would kiss me. Instead, he says, "Don't worry. I'll see you tomorrow morning."

"Or just text to let me know you're okay." What is wrong with me? He could have spent the entire day here without me knowing a thing. But something about seeing him in his natural habitat makes me nervous. He runs into burning buildings, for God's sake.

"I'll text. Drive home safely, beautiful."

He called me that when we had sex the first time, and now it feels just as intimate. Maybe more so because it's outside the bedroom.

I head outside with Spence in my arms, and we watch as the various vehicles leave the bay. Jude's driving and he honks the horn which thrills Spence. Sam lifts a hand in a wave, and then they're gone, leaving behind an eerie quiet and a woman who's not sure what she's getting herself into.

———

When we return home, I set Spence up with a puzzle game while I make a snack for him in the kitchen. A text comes in from Sam.

SAM

Back at Six, safe and sound. I saved a duck.

He sends me a picture of him holding a duck that looks like it's having a day. Its feathers are singed and wet.

ME

I need this story.

SAM

Well, a duck, a goose, and a rooster walk into a bar …

ME

Sounds like it would be better in person.

SAM

Yep. I definitely am.

So cocky. Why am I suddenly enjoying this aspect of his personality? My phone rings with a call from the man himself.

I hit accept. "Are you worried your charm doesn't translate by text?"

"Fuck, no. I'm a charm machine in every communication medium."

I chuckle. "To what do I owe the pleasure then?"

"Just wanted to hear your voice."

Oh. That's unexpected—and unexpectedly sweet. "Was it a bad call-out?" That must be why he's calling. A need to ground himself with the familiar.

"No, fairly routine. I wanted to thank you for your visit today."

"Well, Spence loves seeing you."

"And I love seeing him. But I also loved that you were able to think things through and agree that you might have made a mistake. It's good that we're able to communicate like that, don't you think?"

I do. And I love that we're in sync about the kids' needs. Maybe even about our own needs.

I suddenly feel very toasty. "It is."

"I've been thinking about the childcare issue—what do you think about going in with Alex's nanny until we come up with something more permanent? I know your job must be suffering."

"It would help, I think. My boss is trying to be supportive, but I don't think she likes how long it's taking to figure stuff out. I just want the kids to be safe."

"I know you do. I think this is a good idea, at least for the meantime. Even when I'm home, I'm gonna need to sleep for a few hours when I first come back. That leaves a lot on your shoulders. Running Maya to school, which is a pain in the ass because the school's so far away. And we need to start thinking about preschool for Spence. He's at that age."

I take a breath. "Okay, but I'd like to meet this nanny and make sure she's (a) okay and (b) not being railroaded into this."

"I'm sure that can be arranged."

As plenty of people have told me—even Derek—Sam has a better support network. I need to start acknowledging this.

"You've gone quiet, Cassie. Talk to me."

Now that the decision to keep the kids here has been made, it's starting to settle on me. What exactly that means.

This isn't my world, and I'm trying to shoehorn myself in where I don't belong. Maybe that's why I got mad at Sam this morning—he has a special relationship with Spence and telling him about his parents came naturally. What do I have to offer?

"Just thinking about work."

"About that? I know you need some space and time to catch up, so I'm sending someone over to help."

"Wait—what?"

"You met my friend, Abby, after the funeral service. Today's her day off and she offered to pick up Maya and watch the two of them so you can get some work done."

I'm floored and not sure if I should be annoyed or not. It's nice not to have to ask, though.

"Doesn't she need to sleep after her shift?"

"Yeah, but she said once she's put in some nap time, she can help out."

"That would be great," I say, meaning it. "I can call Maya's school and let them know Abby's on the way. What's her last name?"

"It's Sullivan. I'll send you her phone number so you have it. You just look after our boy and take a breath, okay?" There are indistinct murmurs in the background, then the sound of the siren going off. "Gotta go. I'll check in later, Cassie."

And then he's gone, and I'm left wondering if I'm truly needed here.

Twenty-Seven

Cass

"All the financials are looking good," I say over Zoom to Tegan Glazer, one of my clients. "At this rate, we could be looking at retirement in eight years, which is amazing for someone so young. You'll be out of the game before you hit forty." Tegan works for an investment bank on Wall Street and has been planning her exit strategy for a few years now. She's the same age as me, thirty-two.

She makes a face. Oh dear.

"Have I said the wrong thing?"

"No, not at all. It's just—" She hesitates. "I'm not sure I've ever told you what I'd like to do when I retire."

"You've said you want to travel, see new places."

She nods. "Yes, there's that. But more specifically, I'd like to teach yoga on a Mexican beach and live in a shack."

This is news. "You've never shared that."

"True. Most of my friends think it's crazy and I suppose I worried you might agree. Everyone says I'll miss this life, but I kind of want to start ... now."

I'm not supposed to be judgmental—is that how I come off?—but I have to be realistic. "What kind of income would you need to live in a shack on a Mexican beach?"

"I think I could do it for less than twenty-five grand a year. And I know the funds I have would support me for the first few years. If the yoga thing takes off, I'd have that income, small as it might be. But the idea of another eight years at this job ..." She shakes her head. "Do you love your job?"

"Sure—well, it's a job. Very few people get to do their dream job."

Financial planning wouldn't have been my first choice. I had to do something stable and goal-oriented. What if Annie's marriage failed and she had to move back home? It's all well and good to fantasize about a different life, but you have to come down to earth eventually.

"Exactly!" Tegan says. "But now I have a chance to pivot. I'm lucky to be able to save a lot of money so I can cut and run earlier. Could you run the numbers again with this new information?"

"Happy to." We sign off, with a promise to reconnect in a couple of days. I sit for a few minutes, thinking on dreams dashed and career goals and how a life can change in a crash of burning metal. Most of the clients I work with have the means to make these big changes, pick up where a dream was delayed, work towards that kind of fulfillment. Is that something I should be thinking about or am I grasping at the threads of a life that was never mine to begin with?

Feeling unsettled, I head out to the living room with a nebulous plan to make dinner, only to smell the delicious scent of cooking. Abby's in the kitchen, heating what looks like meatballs in a pot.

"You cooked?"

"Well, no. While you were on your call, my fiancé Roman brought over his special meatballs."

I grin. "Sounds like the start of an SNL sketch."

"Yep. Working in a male-oriented environment, I can run with balls jokes all day."

"Balls!" Spence's contribution.

Abby mouths "sorry" and I wave it off. She showed up a couple of hours ago, having picked up Maya from school, and brought with her an air of calm efficiency and girl-can-do.

"You hungry?"

"Starving."

"Wine?" She already has a bottle of Pinot Noir open. "Don't let me drink alone. Roman's picking me up in an hour so I can splurge a little."

"Sure. Happy to help."

Maya and Spence are all over the spaghetti and meatballs, so I know what I need to be cooking up for a once-a-week Italian treat. Over dinner, Abby asks about my job and my life in New York, and when the kids head to do homework (Maya) and play a puzzle (Spence), I share about Derek.

"So you're unencumbered?"

"I wouldn't have called a long-term relationship an encumbrance."

Abby holds up a hand in apology. "Sorry, I didn't mean to make it sound like a life sentence without the possibility of parole. Just that, you have less tying you to New York." Her blue eyes sparkle with the possibilities.

"I'm not sure I'm ready for that much change. I need to work. Pay the bills."

She cocks her head. "I'm sure there's plenty of money to help support any major decisions you make. You can take your time, not rush into it."

"Yes, but it's the Killians' money."

"Which your sister would want you to have so you can take care of the kids." She shrugs. "My best guess."

She's right, though I wonder how she knows these details. She and Sam must be close.

"You met Sam at the firehouse?"

"At the Fire Academy during training. He was so cocky—well, you've seen it. He hit on me, probably because he can't *not* hit on anyone." She chuckles in memory, though all it does is remind me that Sam is a player to the core. "Anyway, I wasn't there to get laid. I had too much to prove."

"What you do is amazing."

"Thanks. My mom was one of the first female Chicago firefighters back in the day, so I've wanted this since I was a kid. But my dad wasn't a fan of the idea because Mom died on the job when I was a little younger than Maya."

"I'm so sorry. That must have been awful."

"It was, but of course you understand. You're going through it and doing your best to support your little ones. I'm so glad you and Sam are working together—he makes a good team player. I'm not sure I could have made it through the Academy without him and Jude having my back."

Sam certainly seems to be a different person when it comes to his job and his friends. Or different from how I saw him all those years ago.

Then I remember that he brought a very casual date to his nephew's birthday party, was still sexting with her up until a few days ago, and I'm confused all over again.

"He's still the guy with all the swagger, especially when it comes to women."

"That's our Sammie. But a guy that good-looking is going to get attention." She takes a sip of her wine and eyes me over the glass. "Doesn't mean he can't be a good dad to these kids. Or good at other things. Though to be honest, I don't know how he's able to come back to work so soon. That had to be the toughest run."

"You mean the accident?"

She nods. "Sorry, I shouldn't bring it up."

"Sam doesn't talk about it." I'm afraid to ask him. Maybe Abby can tell me more, a perspective that's once removed. "Were you there?"

"No. Not my shift, but Jude was. He said Sam was there for Annie, right at the end. Jake was already gone."

"For Annie," I repeat, uncomprehending. *Right at the end* ... "I thought—oh, I didn't know that." Why didn't I know that? I thought it was over in an instant. "You mean Sam was with Annie when she ..." I can't say it.

Abby grabs my hand and squeezes. "I'm so sorry. I thought you already knew this. Me and my big mouth."

"No. That's fine. Sam and I have been so focused on the kids"—*and making sex-eyes and more at each other*—"that we've been avoiding talking about what happened. He told me it was quick. But people like to say things like that, so we don't think our loved ones suffered."

It must have been so painful for Annie, holding on by a thread.

And now torture for Sam.

Because the word he called out hoarsely in the night was "stay."

TWENTY-EIGHT

Sam

I open the door to my apartment at just after 9 a.m. and start at the quiet. Cassie already texted to let me know Alex's nanny can take Spence for a few hours and that she'd dropped Maya off.

"Cassie?"

Nothing.

I shouldn't feel disappointment. The woman is probably running a circuit around Lincoln Park, reveling in her freedom. She could've brought Waffles with her, though. The sad-eyed pup gives me the look then rubs his nose in my hand.

"Did no one feed you?"

I check and his bowl is half-full. Just needing some attention. I know the feeling.

I head into the living room, surprised to see a giant hamper filled with treats on the coffee table. Something else, too: a sketch pad. At first, I assume it's Maya's—she and Cassie have been working on a family portrait—but a closer look indicates otherwise. The style is different, but one I recognize. It's Cassie's work.

I pick it up and flip back a couple of pages. The initial sketches are of Waffles in pencil, though the lines are tentative, unsure. The latest one brims with confidence, reminding me of that framed portrait of Maya as a two-year-old hanging in Jake and Annie's house. I love that picture.

Behind me, the door to the apartment opens and in walks Cassie in sweats, her hair in a high ponytail.

"You're home," she says, sounding pleased to see me. I love that she called it *home*. She holds up a bag. "I bought bagels." Her eyes dip to the pad in my hand, and for a moment, she looks exposed.

"This is amazing, Cassie."

Two spots of color appear high on her cheeks. "Just doodling."

Hardly. "You were always so talented." I can tell she doesn't want to talk about it. I gesture to the basket. "What's this about?"

"Oh, Charlie brought it over. Your neighbor."

Alarm pings me. "You met Charlie? From upstairs?"

"Yeah, we had coffee. I ran into her in the elevator one day. She's lovely."

I shouldn't worry. Max would never discuss my situation with his wife—client confidentiality and all that—so I probably shouldn't dwell on it. Now that Cassie has said she won't fight me for custody, my conversation with Max shouldn't be an issue. Yet I'd rather keep it to myself.

"How are you enjoying your first morning of freedom?"

She smiles. "It's kind of strange but I miss Spence. Leaving him off at Alex's was so weird, but I had a chat with Katya and she's about as perfect as Alex promised."

I take a seat on the sofa. "It'll be good for him to see other faces. Not that your face isn't worth seeing—"

"Thanks."

I grin. "But he could do with some variety, and let's face it, we need a break."

I take a seat on the sofa, and she sits beside me, a few feet apart. The urge to touch her is almost overwhelming.

"How was the rest of your shift?"

"Good. A couple of call-outs, nothing too dramatic." I move closer and run a finger in the hollow below her throat. Her breath hitches at my touch, yet she also seems distracted. "You okay?"

"Sam, why didn't you tell me you were with Annie when she died?"

Her question is like a punch to my heart. Abby texted me earlier to tell me she might have put her foot in it with Cassie, but I haven't had a chance to get the details.

"Did Abby say something?"

She nods. "I know we haven't always gotten along, but why would you keep that from me?"

"Are you telling me you'd like *more* detail about how your sister died?"

She looks shocked at my tone. "Not because I need to know. But because it's been weighing on you. Your dreams ... they're about this, aren't they? About Annie?"

The generosity of that floors me. I don't want to burden her. My goal throughout this entire process is to keep the hard stuff from her, to protect her and the kids. And in a way, protect myself. She needs to think I can do this. Hold it together and not risk a meltdown.

If I let her in ... if I tell her how bad the terrors get, then it's another black mark in the column. I'm not saying she'd use it, but I can't know for sure. She could change her mind about going for sole custody.

"Not now." I get up and head to the bathroom, peeling off

my Henley as I go. I drop it on the bathroom floor and fumble for my zipper.

"Would you rather talk about it *after* I come across you calling out Annie's name in the night?"

She's behind me, watching my reflection in the mirror.

"I'd rather not talk about it at all." I drop my pants and kick them off, along with my socks. Standing in my boxer briefs, I turn to her. "Talking about it won't turn back the clock. It won't make you feel better."

"But it might make *you* feel better."

"Not interested in conversation, beautiful." I run a hand over the front of my underwear, a taunt to return us to before, the slight touch sending my cock to life. "If you don't mind, I've got an appointment with the shower and my dick."

Just as I intended, it pisses her off and sends her packing. She needn't think I'm as evolved as Derek, ready to spill my guts about my problems. No. The only thing I need right now is a shower jerk-off and a few hours between cool sheets.

Divested of my boxers, I step under the hot shower and fist the tile.

I should be glad she left, yet I'm absurdly disappointed. *Nicely done.*

She wants to help, but the trust between us is tentative, a gossamer thread that could snap at any moment.

Running a hand over my hardening dick, I close my eyes and try to empty it of anything erection-blocking. I should have known sex with this woman would complicate my situation—everyone told me—yet I jumped at the chance to be with her because I may never get another one. Remembering the feel of her in my arms, the clasp of her around my dick, the sounds she made as I plunged into her again and again, is enough to get me close.

Only the dream of Cassie can't quite displace the nightmare of Annie.

She's gone. My beautiful sister-in-law, in truth, more a sister to me, is no longer here.

Jakey's gone, too. The brother I love so much has vanished from my life. I know I couldn't do anything. I know this shit happens all the time.

But I sure as fuck am not appreciating it happening to *me*. To my parents. To Cassie. To Maya and Spence. We should have my brother and his wife in our lives, so we don't feel like shit all the time.

The bright spot is her. Cassie. Yet the hard truth is that she wouldn't give me the time of day if we weren't currently trying to piece together our lives after this tragedy. I would still be the man-child that she turns her nose up at, while she'd be the prim and proper schoolmarm who pisses me off to distraction. It's not right that out of this emotional rubble, I'm getting what I want: a shot with the woman of my dreams.

The door to the shower opens and I turn.

There she is, naked as a babe, those shamrock-melted eyes burning the truth into me. Tragedy might have brought her here, but I'm not going to look that treasured gift horse in the mouth. She stands before me, warm and beautiful and so fucking alive.

Like a fool, I ask, "What do you want?"

Her answer is to move into the arms made to hold her and kiss below my pec, right over my heart.

Ah, fuck.

I freeze for a second, conscious that my heart is thumping, in a mad scramble to exit my chest. I'm not sure I can cope with such tenderness, so I'm grateful that she moves to my nipple and sucks on it. Jesus.

I need her mouth. I need every part of her to be connected to every part of me. Gripping her ass, I hoist her upright and back against the tile. Then I kiss her, my tongue thrusting, my lips alternating between sucking and sipping.

Because this is Cassie, who never lets me get away with anything, she moves back, her eyes sparkling.

"How's that appointment going?"

"What?"

"With your dick."

I drag one of the parties to this meeting along the heated seam of her, loving how her soft folds feel against my cock.

"Pretty well." I shake my head, feeling a smile touching my lips. Feeling like the Sam of old. "I was a jerk before. Sorry."

"Maybe I like this jerk side of you. God knows I see enough of it, yet I'm still here."

"For the kids."

She tilts her head. "Not just for the kids, Sam."

That's enough to send me into a crazy attack on her mouth. My cock gets in on the action, rubbing and stroking. Then, gently I place her feet down and drop to my knees in worship.

"Stand wide."

She does, but it's not enough for me. I lift her foot onto my shoulder and explore the angle I've created. Pretty, pink, wet, and mine for the licking. Slowly I move my fingers over her lips, parting that slick, hot flesh with penetrating efficiency and getting the lay of the land. Her hand reaches into my hair and there's the slightest nudge.

"You in a hurry, Cassandra?" Looking up, I see the shower spray hitting her breasts, bringing her rosy nipples to hardened peaks. I can't wait to suck on those beauties again but for now, I have another feast before me.

"I'm not used to this kind of … patience."

"Get used to it. I like to take my time before I take what's mine." I move my lips in a soft brush over her pussy, absorb that shudder, then go in deep with my tongue. The sweet taste of her goes straight to my dick.

She moans, and now my licks become broader, taking in as

much of her supple flesh as I can. The nub of her clit feels huge against my tongue, and I hold her still while I focus my efforts. Sucking, licking, drinking in the tangy juice of her as it coats my mouth.

She tastes perfect. She *is* perfect.

She shudders again, but this time it's the precursor to her coming, so I stay with her, drinking in those lovely little shivers and moans.

I raise my gaze to her and for a moment, I'm frozen by the sheer beauty of what I see. This perfect wave of woman who I can't get enough of and for whom I might never be enough.

I stand up and kiss her. Better that than tell her how I feel. Undeserving.

She's here because we both lost something precious. This isn't real. It comes from pain and cannot last.

She pulls back, her hand coasting down my chest. At some point she soaped it up and now she runs taut, erotic circles over my chest and my abs. I place my hand against the tile behind her and let her take care of me.

When she gets to my dick, she says, "Turn around."

I do, and she lathers up again over my back and ass, and just the tenderness of it does me in. I feel tears coming, so I rub my face to stop their descent.

"So good," I murmur, anxious to move it back to sexy times.

She gets the memo, using her hand to grip my cock and give me a frothy stroke. Leaning my head against the tile, I let her jerk me, let her take me out of this dark space I seem to have found myself in.

These people I love are gone.

Yet somehow, I won the prize.

Twenty-Nine

Cass

Sam might be direct about his needs in the bedroom, but that's where it ends. I know he's in pain, and that I can help him. But he's chosen to withdraw rather than let me be the one to assuage his grief, like he's done for me.

He needs to know he can tell me about Annie. He can talk about Jake. If anyone understands, it's me.

But right now, talking is not on the menu. If he won't speak the words, then we'll have to communicate another way.

"Sam, turn around."

He doesn't. My hand is still cupping his girth—barely—and moving in a soapy, slippery trail from root to tip.

"Sam, please."

He pivots, wiping a hand over his face. Not because of the shower spray, this is something else.

Oh, my love.

"It's okay. I'm here."

He pushes my hand away and lifts me, changing our positions so I'm against the tile. And then he's inside, easier than the last time, like my body is made for him. I groan into his neck, then recall that there's no one to hear us and I can let loose. On his next thrust, I moan louder than before.

"Yes. God, yes."

His strength in keeping me off the ground at the perfect height to be plundered is such a turn-on. I never thought I'd be a fan of the big guy-petite woman dynamic, yet here we are.

His eyes are open, a raging sadness in them. "Sam," I whisper. "I've got you."

He looks a little surprised by that. Another thrust, this time deeper, like he has to prove how much he can pleasure me. That this is his purpose.

I don't need proof. I already know this man is an expert at pleasing a woman.

But there's more to him. A good man, an amazing son, uncle, co-worker, and friend. Any woman would be lucky to have him in her life.

I'm lucky.

Not that he's in my life in a way that could ever be more meaningful than our current arrangement. Eventually we'll tire of this, or our hearts will heal. I'm not sure which will come first.

Because this pleasure can't last, not when we're using it to mask the pain. Eventually real life will intrude, and I can only hope regret won't show up as shotgun.

"What time do we have to pick up Spence?"

Sam is lying on his bed, looking very relaxed after that shower. He also looks like a bronzed god I want to lick. This lust fog he puts me in every time I see him is so distracting.

"*You* don't have to pick up anyone. You'll be sleeping."

"What time, Cassie?"

I relent. "I'll pick him up at 2 p.m. I have an online consult with a client at noon and I need to tidy the kids' room before then."

He pats the bed. "C'mere."

"Oh, no. We've already had our fun."

"Come on, beautiful. Just lay with me for a while, until I fall asleep."

I can't deny that request, not when it comes with that look of vulnerability. I'm used to closed off men, which has always suited me because I like to keep things tight to my chest. As long as no one is asking the hard questions, we can all stay in our emotional bubbles.

Sam pulls back the covers and I slip inside, my head on the pillow to face him. It's strangely intimate. I like it a little too much.

"Do you like your job?" he asks.

"Where's this coming from?"

"We haven't talked about it. I love my job, but you're quiet about yours."

"I like it, though I don't know that I feel it's a vocation like you do with yours. I love working with people, and I love connecting people's money with their goals. A lot of people don't really understand how money works, even when they have tons of it." I shrug. "It might come from growing up with very little of it. I've always craved stability, and working in a job like this means I have control over my financial goals and well-being."

He runs a finger over my shoulder, along my collarbone. "And if you weren't doing this job, what would you be doing? Something with art?"

"I spent six years doing a degree part-time so I could get a job like this. Art isn't really a job."

"Even though you wanted to go to art school."

"How did you know that?" No one knows that.

"You told me the night of the wedding. We actually talked, y'know."

I'd obviously put that out of my head. Let lust and disapproval be the prevailing memory.

I never even told Derek, so sure I was of his disapproval. But art wasn't my only ambition. I'd also dreamed of motherhood. Being part of something greater than myself, a big family, a life busy not only with a career but with personal fulfillment.

"What's that?"

"I didn't say anything."

He touches my nose. "You twitched. That's your tell."

"I do not have a tell!"

"Ya do. That little nose twitch tells me that you're hiding something. I spotted it the first night I met you when my aunt Jenny tried to set you up with my cousin, Nathan."

Something else I'd forgotten. I wonder if I've reshaped that night in a way that reflects better on me than Sam. Our memories are tricky beasts.

"So I didn't want to date your cousin."

"Yeah, and you still do the twitch. When you don't approve of something, or something bothers you, or you're hiding, which means your nose is like *Bewitched* on steroids. So many secrets, Cassie. I saw it there. You had something else in mind other than your job."

"It—it doesn't matter."

He leans in and cradles my jaw, so gently that I melt into him. "It all matters. Tell me."

"It's going to sound weird."

He squeezes my shoulder and I'm encouraged to go on.

"When Mom left us and I became sister-mom to Annie, it was hard. Harder than I've ever admitted. My life changed dramatically. No dates. No hobbies. My schooling delayed because I had to work. A shift in my priorities because I wanted security. Constantly having to watch her every move to make sure she didn't suffer."

"You resented the sacrifice?"

"I thought I would. Sure, I missed some things, but there was something very satisfying about taking on that role. I loved Annie so much. And I realized that this suited me. I was born to the mom role." I feel my cheeks heating in embarrassment, but Sam nods his approval. "Things were delayed for me, but Annie had lost her mom. I had to make that right for her, be everything Aileen refused to be. And when she got into college at Cornell with a full ride, I was so proud. Like it was just as much my achievement as hers."

"It was. You did that."

My breath hitches at hearing it acknowledged so readily. To think I've come to crave this man's support and validation of my choices.

"And within six months she got pregnant. Everything I-we'd worked for gone in a positive pregnancy test. Not only that but she was moving to Chicago, to the city where I'd thought I'd be." I sneak a look at him, feeling small and foolish. "I had a place at the School of the Art Institute that I had to give up when Aileen left us."

He looks surprised. "You'd already got in? When you talked about it the day of the wedding, it was more like a 'in another life' thing."

"Well, it was in a way. While Annie was still in school, I worked in a bank so I could support us both. I always thought I was just putting off art school, that I'd eventually get back to it. But one year passed, then two. Soon, that dream turned into a long-lost mirage, distant, barely remembered. I convinced myself that it was never meant to be. That everything happens for a reason. I decided to do a business degree instead, to aim for security."

Assuring myself this was the right call was the only way to move through the sadness of my dreams dashed and life tilted.

"You could have gone back to it," he says. "Once you knew Annie was settled with us."

"It would have been like starting over. I didn't have the luxury of doing that. The expense, the investment of time, the fear of failure." Mostly the last one. "I'd already started down another road, the one more taken. I drew that picture of Maya, first as a cheap wedding present, but also as a farewell to that part of me."

He rubs along my arm, making me shiver with pleasure. "Now you're saying hello to it again."

"I thought it would be a good way to connect with Maya."

He sees right through that. "And maybe yourself. It's great that you have this common language. You're better with her, with them both, than you realize. My focus is on making sure they're fed and bathed and rested. Yours is making sure their brains don't rot."

I chuckle. "You're underestimating how important you are. All you do to keep them safe."

To keep me safe.

I suspect Sam has underestimated himself for years. I've not helped.

"We're both winning here," he says with a wry smile.

I love that we recognize each other's contribution. "We are. We both need to be in their lives. And when you find some big-breasted floozy to be their stepmom, I'll still need to play a part."

"You think I'm gonna replace you? No chance. I need someone with the important mom-skills. Like yours."

"Glad to hear I have some use."

"Cassie, I could hire an army of nannies, bring in a gaggle of busty girlfriends, and make Jude and Hudson babysit every night, but it still wouldn't match what you mean to the kids.

Annie and Jake are gone, but you're here. I'm here. We can make this work whether you're in Chicago or in New York, but it would be better if you're here."

Of course, the continuity of care would be more stable with both guardians in the same city. But the idea of it—the bigness of it all—terrifies me.

"Everything I know is in New York."

"But everything you love is here."

My heart catches, though I'm not sure he realizes what he's said. The depth of it. Because he's right. Everything I love is in this place. The kids, my dog, this burgeoning reconnection to the girl I used to be.

Sam.

No, that's not—that can't be. This is just intense sexual attraction, which is confirmed when he rolls over and pins me.

"There's the twitch again."

"No. Maybe. Change is hard."

He brushes a thumb over my cheekbone. "I know. But it's easier with the right support."

"That goes both ways, Sam. We've talked a lot about my relationship with Annie. Anytime you want to talk about Jake, I'm here."

I think on the letter in the nightstand drawer. Perhaps he's already read it. Perhaps he's starting to heal.

"What did Jake's letter say?"

He goes still. "I haven't opened it."

"Any reason why?"

"It's so … final." He meets my gaze directly. "Did it help? Reading Annie's letter?"

"I'm not sure. I'm still pissed that she's gone."

"Amen to that."

And then his mouth is on mine and we're kissing like this might mean something. It terrifies me how fast we've moved after so many years of antagonism. Perhaps this connection has always been there, lurking beneath the surface, an itch waiting to be scratched.

I don't know what it means, but I find myself hopeful for the first time in a while.

The pain is still there but Sam makes it hurt less.

Thirty

Cass

"Avast, matey, you're a no-good scurvy cur!"

That sends Spence into a flurry of little boy giggles.

Sam adjusts his tri-corner hat and pokes gently at Waffles with his plastic sword. "Time to walk the plank, ya landlubber."

Poor Waffles peers up from beneath his own eye patch (we're all wearing them). Instead of heading to the plank, which is really a table runner spread out on the hardwood floor of the living room, separating the boat (sofa) from the ocean (the hearth rug), he settles down, clearly tired of the pirate shenanigans.

"No? You dare to resist me? Captain Sam Stinksalot?"

Maya chuckles and murmurs approvingly, "Stinksalot." She leans into me on the sofa, where we're trying to stay under the radar and not be pulled into a pirate skirmish.

Waffles remains unmoved, so Sam points at Spence. "Argh, you'll have to take the cur's place. What's your name?"

"Spencer!"

"That's not a pirate name. From now on, you're known as Poopdeck Pete!"

Spence is absolutely thrilled to be so christened. He jumps off the sofa and picks up the tiny, and very safe, plastic sword that Sam bought this morning at Party City.

"Hey, Spence, hold on." I pull him toward me. "Let's fix your eye patch."

"It's Poopie Pete!" But even pirates need assistance from their aunts, so he lets me help him out while Maya tells him, "Your name is Poopdeck."

"Enough from you," Sam says, pointing his sword at Maya. "I won't have my first mate makin' trouble. Up you get to teach this scallywag how to fight."

"No more plank walk?" I ask.

Sam shrugs his huge shoulders. "We're a flexible lot aboard the Jolly Killian. I need a crew who works hard and will get me all the booty I require. First mate?" He gestures to Maya. "Shark Fin Suzie, let's show the landlubbers how it's done."

Maya smiles, obviously pleased with her uncle's name for her. She jumps up and adjusts her hat and eye patch.

"So, does everyone lose an eye in this business?" she asks Captain Stinksalot.

"Only if you're doing it right," Sam says, picking up Spence and planting him on the table runner. "Let's see if you can handle yourself on the plank, Poopdeck Pete."

"Poopie!" Spence is enjoying himself so much, and my heart lifts at his laughter.

Next Sam turns to me, a wicked gleam in his eye. "Everyone on the Jolly Killian has to work for their supper. What have you got to offer ...?"

"Salty Sadie." Not sure where that came from, but I'm feeling it.

"Salty Sadie, huh? I've heard of you. You have a reputation

for associating with bilge-suckers of the worst degree." His accent is impeccable along with his pirate vocabulary. "We'd be happy to have you come aboard."

"The honor is mine, Captain Sam."

"That's Captain Stinksalot to you. Show some respect." He curls a hand around my waist and lifts me onto the table runner. "Show us yer best plank walk, Salty Sadie, while I check out yer booty."

I shoot him a heated glare, which he counters with a heated look of his own. God, he makes a handsome pirate.

Someone pokes a sword in my stomach. Spence—I mean, Poopdeck Pete—is scowling at me. Or as much as the little guy can scowl.

"Walk the plank!"

I raise my hands in surrender. "Okay, okay." Spence pokes me in the butt, moving me along, so I follow the table runner to the hearth rug and hover on the border.

"What if I tell you where the booty is?" I sneak a glance over my shoulder. Poopdeck Pete checks in with the captain.

"Think I might have already found it," the scurrilous villain says, his scorching gaze on my ass. I mean, really. "But even if I didn't, I'd figure out a way to make you pay for all your crimes, Salty Sadie." To Maya he says, "Let's tie 'er up."

I spend the next ten minutes lashed to a chair with a Rebels scarf—it's very soft and my situation eminently escapable—and then the captain and Poopdeck Pete have a sword fight while Shark Fin Suzie circles me, prodding every minute or so to keep my attention.

"I have an idea!"

The pirate fight stops, and all eyes are on me.

"I could ... bake a cake."

"Pirates don't eat cake!" the captain yells, but a quick glance at his cake-loving crew has him on the back foot.

"Unless it's made by a scurvy landlubber like this one! Send her to the galley to rustle up some vittles."

With my release, I inform Sam, "Cake will always win, Captain."

He pulls me into his body and says softly, "Argh."

We're in a good place. It's been almost a month since Annie and Jake left us, and while the hurt hasn't gone away—I'm not sure it ever can—it's starting to morph into something else. Something real.

And that has everything to do with this man here.

Sam pulls me close and kisses my temple. It's affectionate but not overdoing it in front of the kids. "It's okay. I won't make you walk the plank."

I smile, so grateful for his strength. "I should check to see if we have ingredients for baking." I head into the kitchen, but a few moments later, Sam appears, a small shopping bag in his hand.

He places it on the counter. "I got you something."

"I don't need to be bribed to make cake."

"Oh, I know. It's not much, but I was passing by the store the other day and thought you might like it."

I peek inside, my heart hammering at the idea Sam thinks of me outside this house and not just as co-parent for the kids. Inside is a packet of colored charcoal.

"I'm not sure it's the right kind," Sam rushes on, sounding a touch nervous, "but that old picture of Maya was in charcoal so I figured you can never have too much. Are they the right ones?"

I can't speak. They can't have cost more than ten bucks, but it's one of the most thoughtful gifts I've ever received.

"Cassie? Did I get it wrong?"

"No." I peer up to find him looking concerned. "They're perfect."

"In your hands they are. I don't think you realize how

good you are at taking raw materials and transforming them into something ... amazing."

Is he talking about my art? Or Annie or the kids?

"I've missed this." I take a closer look at the charcoal, my mind bubbling with ideas. Returning to my art has opened new neural pathways in my brain.

Just like spending time with Sam and the kids. It's strange to feel this buzz of life so soon after Annie's death, and I wonder what to do with it.

"Thanks, Sam."

It's for more than art supplies, but they're as good a proxy as any.

Thirty-One

Sam

"These seats are amazing!" Cassie looks around, her mouth agape at all the sights and sounds. I love seeing this side of her. I get the impression she missed out on a lot while she raised Annie.

"Oh, look, it's Theo Kershaw!"

Maya shares an amused glance with me. "Aunt Cass really likes hockey."

"Yeah, I do." She puts an arm around Maya, who is decked out in Rebels gear, gifted by her uncle Jude. (He got it all for free, but still, it's cool to have connections.) I love seeing my girls getting close. "And you look amazing in your Rebels jersey, Maya. I kind of wish someone got one for me."

I smile over my niece's head. "If I knew this was all it took to get you to like me, I would have got you some Rebels merch years ago."

"Years ago you didn't know Hudson Grey—oh, there he is!" She waves as if Hudson can see her. The seats are good, but not that good. "And I don't care about your hockey connections. It doesn't change my opinion of you."

Her smile is a little superior, which I take to be a clue into her state of mind vis-à-vis yours truly.

Cassandra Ferguson might like me.

And I like her. In a big way.

On my other side, Jude leans in. "This is interesting."

"Is it?" I mumble while I check in with Spence, who might get bored soon. My parents offered to watch him, but he's been clingy with me lately and I'd rather he was here where I can see him.

"Oh, very." He inclines his head. "She's kind of into you."

"No, she's not. And even if she was, it's just a lust thing." I need to minimize, likely because I'm feeling nervous about it.

His look is all sympathy, but by now the puck has dropped and talking is only of the smack variety. We get some top-notch action right from the start. Cassie certainly thinks so. She's up on her feet the second Reid Durand connects with the puck and line-drives it all the way to the goal, only to be foiled by the Detroit tender.

"Oh my gosh! That was close. And wow, Reid D is so handsome!" She takes a seat but is up again within seconds when Kershaw gets the team out of trouble with some incredible defense. Seeing her let it all out is very sexy, though this yo-yo business goes on for much of the first period and by the time the break is in, I'm tired just looking at her.

"What?" she asks when she catches my eye.

"Pretty hot."

"What's pretty hot?" Maya asks, while Cassie gives me the stare down of "not in front of the children."

"Me. I'm pretty hot."

Maya looks at me with suspicion. "You're weird, Uncle Sam."

"I know." I tweak her braid, the one I learned how to do

on YouTube a couple of days ago. I did an excellent job, I think. "We're all kind of weird, though."

"I'm not weird," Spence says, looking up from the game he's playing on my phone.

"What? You're the weirdest of all!" I kiss the top of my nephew's head, which draws the inevitable, "no kissing!"

During the break, there's the usual hustle and bustle as people head out for bathroom and beverage breaks. Spence needs to go, so I'm scooping him up onto my hip because it'll make for a faster and safer journey up the steps when I lock eyes with a woman descending in our section.

Madison Maitland.

She sent me a nice handwritten note of condolence after the accident, and for a moment I thought of using my grief to get back into her bed. That's the kind of jerk I am, apparently. Then forced proximity with Cassie evicted all notions of anyone else.

Madison is with another woman I recognize, Kinsey Taylor, who happens to be married to my LT, Luke Almeida. Kinsey and Madison run a PR firm together, and if memory serves, Kinsey is also friendly with Jordan Hunt, a sports reporter married to one of the Rebels players.

"Sam," Madison says warmly, leaning in to kiss my cheek. Kinsey busses my jaw as well, says something about my loss, then heads down to a few rows in front of us, leaving me with Madison.

She looks good, but then she always does. At least ten years older than me, she's twice divorced and too independent to need a stud like me. That's what she used to call me: her hot young stud.

"How are you, Mads?"

"Not bad." Her gaze dips to Spence and brightens a touch. "Your nephew?"

"Yeah, this is Spence. Hey, buddy, say hi to Madison."

He's suddenly shy, but he reaches a hand toward her knife-straight hair, styled in a black bob. I had such a crush on her last year. I won't say she hurt me when she said we'd run our course, more that she bruised my ego. She made it clear I'd never make the grade as a potential partner.

"Kinsey told me you're busy with your family."

"I am. Spence here, and that's my niece Maya and my sister-in-law, Cassandra." I gesture over my shoulder. "We're figuring out the co-guardian thing."

Madison dips her curious gaze to Cassie and Maya, then turns back to me. "Sounds like you are. It's good to see you, Sam. Take care."

When I return from the bathroom and retake our seats, Cassie is smiling at me.

"What?"

"Jude told me you used to date that stunning woman."

Fucking Jude. He's disappeared at the minute, which is typical. Drops the turd and exits.

"A while back. She thought I was too much of a frat boy."

"Got what she wanted and kicked you out on your fine ass?"

That's pretty much the gist of it. "Can't get no respect," I mumble, trying to make a joke of it. Madison never saw me as serious partner material, and even with all this newfound responsibility, I doubt Cassie does either.

I'm mulling this over just as a woman with pink-streaked blond hair turns around and smiles at me. She looks familiar and my first instinct is to wonder when I banged her. Christ, I'm the worst. No wonder Cassie can't see me as anything other than a sex-obsessed playboy.

"Sam, right?"

"That's me."

"You probably don't remember. We met at a cookout you

co-hosted with Jude and Hudson last summer. It was on the roof of your building. I'm Kennedy, Reid's wife."

As in Reid Durand, one of the players in tonight's game. *Phew.* Leaving the condo inevitably runs the risk of crossing paths with old flames, so I'm relieved this is not one of them. I'm also relieved that's not my life anymore.

Now to convince Cassie.

"Yeah, I remember. You had that super cute dog." Bucky, I think. "How's your brother-in-law doing?"

Reid's brother Bastian was signed to the Rebels over the summer and made his Rebels debut last week. Only it ended in disaster when he sustained a re-injury to his wrist during a clash with the Rebels mascot. I mean, what are the odds?

She makes a face. "Having a hard time of it, I'm afraid. But he'll get there." She arcs a gaze over the kids. "Yours?"

"My nephew and niece. This is Spence, and Maya is an uber-fan. Though maybe not quite as much as Cassie." I mouth at her, "busted."

Cassie is blushing up a storm. "I'm a big fan of the team," she mumbles, obviously embarrassed about her comments on this woman's husband's hotness.

Kennedy giggles. "It's okay. I'm used to everyone having it bad for my husband."

"Oh, I don't have it bad ..." She trails off.

"Just kidding. Besides, it looks like you've got your hands full anyway. You guys are so cute together. Well, you all are."

Cassie seems to be at a loss for words. Maybe she can't see what I see—that she and I are good together and not just because of how we're here for the kids.

Kennedy is still talking. "Are you guys going to visit the locker room after the game?"

"If the invitation is open, sure." Then I wink at the woman everyone thinks belongs to me.

After the game, we visit the locker room, and on our way in, I nudge Cassie.

"Don't embarrass me in there, okay?"

"Oh, shut up," she says, laughing. "We're doing this for Maya."

"Sure. For Maya."

Cassie rolls her eyes affectionately and turns to Jude. "Hudson was a beast out there." Hud scored a late goal in the third period that broke the 2-2 stalemate.

"He was. He'll be impossible to live with for a couple of hours." He grins. "Shall we?"

In we go and spend the next few minutes chatting with Hudson and Jude before Theo Kershaw stops by.

"You're Maya's favorite player," Cassie says with a smile.

I've met Kershaw before, not that I'd expect him to remember, but somehow he does because he's a class act. He's super friendly, an all-around good guy, and he takes the time to sign Maya's jersey and chat with her about hockey.

"Cass is a big fan, too," Hudson says. "Though I hear Reid's your number one. I'm not offended."

Cassie blushes, which makes me laugh.

"She already got into a fight with Kennedy in the stands."

"I did not! So I might have been thirsting after her husband without realizing she was right in front of me, but she was very nice about it."

Theo looks over his shoulder. "Hey, Durand, get your fine ass over here. Women want to tussle for you."

Cassie moves behind me, her hand on my hip. "Uh, no. Leave him be."

Reid must not have heard because he stays put—or he just doesn't answer to Theo Kershaw.

I place an arm around her waist. "Cassie, I'll protect you.

But if you really need the hall pass, I'm happy to let you go for it—"

"I do not!" She giggles, and God I want to kiss her so badly.

"Why would you need a hall pass?" Maya asks.

"That's where I give permission to your aunt to talk to other guys."

Maya frowns. "That's silly."

"Sure, Killian. Like I need your permission." To Maya she says, "your uncle's just joking around."

Seeming to realize how handsy we are with each other, she pulls away. "It might be time to get these two home to bed."

We say our goodbyes and head out to the Rebels Arena lobby area.

"That was fun," I say to Cassie. "Your face, though, when Kershaw called over Reid Durand ... priceless."

"So I'm a fan. But I'd rather be a fan in my own way, not be forced to fangirl in the man's presence." She nudges me. "Thanks for being my protector all the same."

I smile at her, while the wings on my heart flap away with joy.

"Any time, beautiful."

THIRTY-TWO

"I want to be a pirate," Spence says, his voice sleepy. "Then I could go to Disneyland and see Mom and Dad."

My heart cinches at his innocent words. Sam has just finished reading *How to be a Pirate*, one of Spence's favorites. He was tired after the Rebels game but not so much that he didn't want a story—and it had to be Sam who told it.

"Well, buddy, that's a great idea except your mom and dad aren't there anymore. Remember I said they died?"

"Like Goldie?"

"Yeah, like Goldie."

"But we put Goldie down the toilet."

Sam rubs a hand through Spence's hair. "That's what you do with goldfish, but with people they go somewhere else. They have to stay there forever but it's not a bad place. It's a good place and Mom and Dad are together, looking after each other. They just can't come back."

"Are you and Aunt Cass going there?"

Sam throws a quick look of desperation at me. I move in

and sit behind him on the bed, my cheek to his back. "Your uncle Sammie is going nowhere. Neither am I. We're going to take care of you and your sister and Waffles."

He sniffs and his little eyes grow large with unshed tears. "But I want Mom. I want to see her. It's not fair."

Sam picks him up, gathering him close. "I know. I know it's not fair."

He cries a little, and the two of us wait with him, joined together in grief, until Spence falls asleep. Sam lays him down gently and pulls the covers up to his chin before thumbing away the tears still staining his cheeks.

Maya is standing at the bedroom door.

"Hey, honey, you okay?"

She places her arms around my waist. "Do you mean it?"

"What?"

"Are you staying?"

I raise my eyes to Sam, who's watching me avidly. "That's the plan."

Her body softens, all the tension seeping away from her bones, and I hug her tight. I don't think I realized how adrift she's felt, not knowing if I'd relocate to Chicago.

A couple of minutes later, Sam and I are in the living room. I have my back to him because I can't look at him. If I do, I'll break.

I feel his strong hand on my hip, moving toward my stomach, pulling me against him. The possession in his grip both soothes and ignites.

His lips brush against my neck, my body molds to his, chest to back, and we're locked together. I can think of nowhere I'd rather be, no one I'd rather be with. His strength gives me hope that I can be as good at this as him.

I turn in his arms and place my hands on his chest. "You're so great with him. With them both."

"So are you," he says, placing a hand over one of mine and

moving to kiss my wrist. "And now you've promised to stay, you can't take it back."

"I don't want her to worry about anything"—not that it's a lie, but I'm not sure I can commit to it completely—"and I've already said I won't stand in your way."

"But what does that mean exactly?"

I nod. "The kids are better off here in Chicago. The rest are mere details."

"The details matter, Cassie."

"We can live our lives and still care for the kids. Be civil to each other. Friendly, even."

His grip tightens on my hand. "Civil? Friendly? We've already established that you need to be here in Chicago with the kids. What I need to know is what it means for us."

There he is, Mr. Direct again. I don't know how this would work, but I do know that if Sam and I took this further and it all went south, that would be awful for everyone involved, especially Maya and Spence. And if Sam and I aren't together, could I handle seeing him moving on?

An image of that beautiful woman at the hockey game swims into my mind. She was older, sophisticated, beautiful. I'm not sure I could compete with that or any of the other stunners Sam can attract with the click of his fingers.

But I am committed to the kids.

"I could get a place here. Look for a job."

He smiles. "Or you could just live here while we look for a bigger house. I'd suggest we all move into Annie and Jake's place in Winnetka—nearer to Maya's school and my parents—but city employees, including firefighters, have to live in Chicago. So either we live here, which is probably big enough but you'd have to move into my room officially so the kids can have their own spaces, or we look for a house in the city." His hand moves to fondle my cheek, and not the one on my face. "I think we could make a go of this, Cassie."

"You want me to move in, permanently?"

"I want us to try."

Trying could be disastrous. "And if it doesn't work, that would be confusing for the kids, wouldn't it?"

He looks stricken. "You're already giving up?"

"I don't know what this is yet, Sam. I've just lost my sister, exited a long-term relationship, and jumped into this with you. It's a lot to reckon with."

"Only if you overcomplicate it."

"But it is complicated. Up until a month ago we hated each other. Of course, I can see that you've changed—"

"Changed?" His expression grows hard. "Maybe that's what you want to see. Yeah, this has been a learning experience, for us both, but I haven't always been the irresponsible lightweight you think I am. As for hating each other up until a month ago, I guess that's just the opinion of one of us."

What does that mean? I don't get a chance to ask because he's already moving away.

He holds up a hand. "I don't want to fight, not after this fun night out. Let's sleep on it and talk tomorrow."

I nod, feeling like I've offended him deeply. How can he not see that the kids are paramount here and that any decisions we make about us can't be taken lightly?

He's already left the room before I can marshal a defense.

I can't sleep, so I'm sketching in the pad I bought a couple of days ago. In the old days, my medium of choice was charcoal, but I chickened out of buying any at the art store when I visited with Maya. It would've looked like I was taking it too seriously, or I was trying to recreate a time in my life when potential was ripe and anything was possible.

Pencil is safer. Pencil can be erased.

I'm sticking to drawings of the kids and Waffles, though my fingers itch to capture Sam when I'm not sure he can be caught.

We took selfies at the game, and now I'm using them to sketch Maya and Spence. My niece looks so serious, even at a hockey game. Spence, on the other hand, has a mischievous gleam in his eyes. It's tough to nail down, but I think I'm almost there.

Sam bought me some charcoal a couple of days ago, though. He has faith in my ability to find that part of myself again. More faith than me.

That's where we differ. Sam is an optimist, a believer in all that's possible. He sounded so wounded when I didn't take his offer to move in seriously. But how can I commit when everything is rushing by like a fast-moving stream? It would be so easy to be pulled under by his enthusiasm, but if it fails, I'd be left on the opposite riverbank again like when Annie left for Chicago, or worse, dashed to pieces against the rocks.

I push the sketch pad aside and reach for the lamp on the nightstand. That's when I hear it.

Sam.

For the last few nights, he hasn't had the nightmares, or at least none that woke me up. But now, when we're apart, he's back there at the accident.

I don't hesitate to go to him.

"Sam, it's okay." I lie beside him, over the covers, but he won't come out of it.

"Stay," he says again. He's talking to Annie. He was with her at the end, and I might be resentful of that. He got to have that final moment with her, and I never got a chance to say goodbye.

I sneak under the covers and throw an arm around his torso, snuggling in tight to absorb the pain.

"Cassie?" He sounds confused.

"It's okay. I'm here."

That's usually enough to soothe him, but it seems to have the opposite effect. He inches away from me.

"Sorry I woke you—did I wake you?"

"I wasn't asleep."

He gusts out a breath. "I'm okay now. You can go back to your room."

So, keeping the distance between us, the one I instigated when I told him I couldn't just jump in feet first, not without knowing where I'll land.

"Can you tell me about it? The accident?"

His answer is quick. Practiced. "You know all there is. My first call-out, nothing to be done, too late."

"You were there with Annie, though. At the end."

"She didn't say anything. She couldn't say anything."

I tighten my hold on his body and lay my head under his chin. "But you said something, didn't you? You asked her to stay."

He's quiet for a moment, his lips touching my hair, and I wait in the secrets-laden dark for him to tell me something. Anything.

"I held her hand. She squeezed it, so I knew she was still here. Still fighting."

A sob erupts from my throat. He squeezes me tight and waits a moment for me to get it together. Somehow, he knows when I'm ready to hear more.

"We'd pulled her out of the car, placed her on the gurney, and were about to head to the hospital. I knew as soon as we arrived, she'd be rushed into triage to see if they could stabilize her before taking her to the OR. I might not see her for a while, or at all. So I talked to her, not sure if she could really hear me."

"She could hear you," I say.

"Yeah, as soon as I started talking, I could tell. Her eyes got a little brighter—you know how she had that mischievous look when you said something naughty. Like Spence. Not that I said anything or she was feeling mischievous. I-I don't know what I'm trying to say."

I rub his chest. "That she knew who you were. She was listening."

"She was."

"What did you say to her?"

"I told her—" He breaks off, then takes a second to find the words. "I told her we loved her. All of us. That she had to hold on because Jake needed her. The kids needed her. Her sister needed her."

My breath catches. Maybe he's just saying that to make me feel better. Even if it's an untruth, I'm grateful.

"I think she knew Jake was already gone. I think she'd seen that before we pulled her out of the van, but I said it anyway. I had to ... lie."

I raise my head, catching his shining eyes in the dark. "That wasn't a lie. Jake did need her, even if he was no longer alive. He needed her to fight for the kids. For all of us who couldn't imagine a world without her."

He touches my face, like he can't believe I'm here. I want to tell him I'll always be here, but I'm not sure I can. Not in this way. I've been insisting that making a go of this with Sam could be potentially disastrous because of its impact on the kids. But that's not the real reason.

I would be gutted if we fail.

"She didn't make it to the hospital," he continues. "She knew she was slipping away, getting weaker. No words, but she held my gaze and told me with her eyes what I needed to do."

"The kids."

"Yeah. Take care of her babies. She went into cardiac

arrest, and I begged her to stay. Don't leave. I was kind of an asshole about it, to be honest."

Oh, Sam.

"But she couldn't hear me anymore. She'd already delivered the message she needed. Held on long enough for that."

I lift my head and face him directly. "What's happening in the dream, Sam?"

"I'm trying to wipe the blood out of her eyes—that happened. And then she changes into Jake. He's mad at me about something. I don't know what. Probably because I didn't save his ass when I've always been such a cocky motherfucker about it. Then it's Annie again, only this time she's begging me to save her, but the blood keeps coming and —fuck!" He looks up at the ceiling and wipes a hand over his mouth. A tear falls from the corner of his eye.

"Sam, it's okay. There was nothing you could have done."

"That's what everyone says. I was so fucking excited to be on a call, pumped up to be playing the hero. I've always known my enthusiasm for my job is happening at the expense of someone else's worst day, but it's been abstract. A separate thing. And then the two worlds intersected in the worst possible way."

I touch my lips to his chin and hold them there. "It's okay to be excited about your job. You want to help people. You're great at it."

He doesn't answer that. "Tonight's dream was different."

"In what way?"

"Usually, I'm asking Annie to stay but tonight it was ... you."

My pulse picks up. "Was I hurt?"

"No, but you were out of reach. Unattainable. Like always."

My mouth parts while my brain searches for the right words. "Like always?"

"Tonight, you said something about how we used to hate each other. How up until a month ago, that was the sum total of our relationship."

"I was too harsh. Hate was too strong. I'm sorry."

He's staring at me, peeling back the layers of my skin and bone and heart. Seeing right into me.

Time to be brave. "You said that was just the opinion of one of us."

"Oh, heard that, did ya?"

"I wanted to ask what you meant, but I was too much of a chicken."

His lips curve. "You? Chicken? I don't believe it."

"What did you mean?"

He shifts his position so he's leaning over me. "I think you know. I think you've always known."

My heart is thunder in my chest.

"I've wanted you since the moment I met you. I was crazy about you, which I neatly covered by making cracks about your mom credentials and generally pissing you off. It seemed the only way I could get close to you was by telling you I wanted to fuck you. And when you told me it would never happen, it crushed me for a while."

His honesty topples me. "It wasn't about you, or not only about you."

"Okay." He sounds skeptical.

"Once she was married, Annie belonged to all of you. Officially. I felt like I was on the outside, the urchin at the window, looking in on this perfect family. I didn't want to feel like that. I didn't want to like you, to fall for your glimmer, so I decided not to. That's why I rejected you."

I've always been sense to Annie's sensibility. I've always had to be the responsible one.

"I get it. I wasn't a good bet." There's a melancholy to his words. "I was a stupid, horny kid, looking for the next thrill, the easy entertainment. You were always going to be suspicious of someone with such selfish motives."

He's not just thinking about a missed connection at a wedding. This goes to the heart of who Sam is and the man he's become. I've accused him of being self-involved, and he might have been once, but that's no longer the case.

"It's not selfish to love your job, Sam, or to want to enjoy that feeling of saving people. Of being good at it. Just as it's not selfish to want a night off or for your life to resemble what it used to. It's not selfish to wish for the easy way out, especially when you're doing everything not to go that route. All of that is perfectly normal. You're a wonderful man, Sam —an amazing uncle, son, friend, and now father. You're the best partner to me in this. What happened before between us, all those years ago, it doesn't have to dictate how we handle things going forward."

I'm not making any promises about a future with Sam, but I'm finding it harder and harder to deny what's happening here. How much I want him. How much I want *this*.

Tonight, he told me about Annie. I'm so glad he was there at the end. I can't think of a better person to have held her hand as she took her last breath.

When he places that healing hand between my legs and gives a hard, dirty rub, I lean into the reprieve he's gifting me. Neither of us wants to push, to upset the tentative peace and perfect moment.

I arch into him, unable to help myself. "Sam," I moan. "I can't think straight around you."

"Then don't think." He kisses me, capturing my mouth with a hunger I can more than match. Not thinking sounds wonderful right now.

THIRTY-THREE

Sam

We're in a strange place, Cassie and I.

We've reached an understanding. She's staying in Chicago, she's even looking for jobs, while I try to figure out if one of the Chicago Rebels nanny options could help us out. Yet neither of us wants to discuss the next steps: where we should live more permanently and what that looks like. Knowing how skittish she is, I'm playing her game while thinking about what needs to happen to bring her crash-landing into my orbit.

Mostly, I'm choosing to believe in the possibilities of us. Unfortunately, my face hasn't got the memo.

"You okay?" Jude takes a seat beside me on the bench in the locker room at Engine 6. "Sorry, stupid question."

"No, it's fine. Of course it's still tough and it's only getting more complicated."

"Is Cass back to talking about taking the kids to New York?"

"No. She's agreed that Chicago is the best place for them.

But whenever I try to talk about what that looks like—one house, two houses, city, burbs—she gets squirrely."

Jude studies me. "And what do you want to happen?"

"I want her to move in with me, sleep in my bed, and we co-parent and fuck each other's brains out."

A small smile. "Sounds like a good plan to me. But Cass is an overthinker, isn't she? She's like my Hudson in that respect. You need to lay it out there. Tell her what you think. How you feel." He squeezes my shoulder. "I know you're still in so much pain at the loss of Jake, but something kind of wonderful has come out of it. You've been in love with this girl for years."

My heart jumps sky-high. "Now, wait a sec—"

"Sammie. All that blister-in-law and bitchin' about the witch talk never disguised the fact you've had a heart-on for Cassie since you met her."

I scoff. "I think you mean a hard-on. I don't deny that."

Jude laughs. "But you'll deny when your feelings are involved? That's so difficult for you? Keep it simple, stupid. You're in love with her and you want her to live with you. It's got nothing to do with gamesmanship or the kids. This is just you and her and what you'd like to see happen."

I told her I've been crazy about her since the first moment I met her, but I never used the L-word.

That's—shit, that's fucking huge. I've never been in love before. I love Maya and Spence, I love my parents, I love Jude and Abby. I loved Jake and Annie. I still do. I have a lot of love to give, but I never doubted I'd get it back from any of these people.

That's the rub here. The fear that Cassie might not feel the same way. Given the tension of the last couple of days, telling her that all-important thing terrifies me.

Because Jude is right. I do love her. So fucking much.

Admitting that is scary and liberating at once. I want to

hold onto this feeling for a while; once it escapes into the real world, it'll take on a life of its own.

"You think I should just ... say it?" I have no experience here. Is that how it's done? Or do I need to take her out to dinner first, buy her flowers, prime the pump?

"So you're admitting it," Jude says. "'Bout time. Now you need to say it out loud."

"I love you, Jude. To the ends of the earth and back."

He grins. "Not what I meant, but I appreciate the sentiment. Right back at ya, Sammie. Now, how about you try some of that honesty on your girl?"

Honesty? Fuck, when has that ever worked for anyone?

I'm in love with Cassandra Ferguson, and it's going to be brutal.

By the time my shift is over, I've given it some thought. Okay, I've thought of nothing else in between an elevator shaft rescue—my specialty—and a three-story fire in the Pilsen neighborhood. Once I get home, Cassie should be back from dropping off Maya at school and Spence at Alex's place. We can sit down and talk about the future.

I'll tell her how I feel.

I'll lay it out, just as Jude suggested. Give her the specificity she needs to make a decision, because that's Cassie. She's a planner. A details person. If necessary, we'll create separate households to ease her into life in a new city. I'd hate that, but I'll give her whatever she needs.

I'm just about to turn onto Belden from Lincoln Park West, heading for the building's parking entrance, when I spot Cassie coming out of the Gloucester's front door.

She's not alone.

I recognize her companion, and it's the last person I need to see right now.

Fucking Derek.

What the hell is he doing here? Cassie has barely mentioned him over the last couple of weeks, mostly because I'm too busy extracting orgasms from her tight little body for her to spare a thought for that loser. Now here he is, coming out of *my* building with *my* woman.

I roll the Ducati a few more feet and pull alongside them.

"Cassie."

"Oh, hi." A flush tags her cheeks, which I would usually find ultra sexy, but right now can only interpret as guilt. "Derek just flew in," she adds unnecessarily.

"So I see."

"Sam." Derek comes forward, his hand outstretched, and I have no choice but to accept it because any other reaction would be churlish. He pumps once, twice, and adds a manly chin jerk.

I want to punch his throat, then run him over with my Ducati.

"Just got in from Tokyo, actually," he says, though I didn't ask. "I was about to head back to New York, and I had this crazy impetus to change my ticket to Chicago, which is why I'm so early. Luckily, I was able to get plenty of rest in business class."

I turn to Cassie. "The kids okay?"

"Yeah, I just got back from dropping them off and Derek was in the lobby chatting with Benji."

Derek smirks. "I wouldn't say chatting. That's a nice building you live in, Sam."

"Thanks. So why are you here?"

"Sam," Cassie says, her tone one of warning.

I ignore it. "Are you here to win her back?"

Derek raises a cool eyebrow, like he can't believe I'd go there. *Well, Derek, I did and I've no problem going there again.*

"Sam, Derek and I are going to the Belden for coffee." She sounds annoyed, but I'm beyond caring. I came home, ready to declare myself, and I'm not letting this fucker slip into the space I've created.

"Sure. I'd like an answer from Derek, though. Because last I heard, he wasn't interested in giving you what you need." I make sure everyone knows that I will have no problem catering to Cassie's every need.

Cassie flaps a hand in frustration just as Derek speaks up.

"Cass isn't some trophy, Sam. She and I have some unfinished business and I'd like to talk about it in person. So much gets lost in translation through text or even a phone call."

"Seems you made your position clear before."

He divides a look between Cassie and me. "You and Cass discussed our relationship?"

"We're living together, Derek. We've become quite close."

Good old D-Bag needs to know that I'm not going down without a fight.

Cassie turns to Derek. "Would you mind walking to the coffee shop on the next corner and getting the drinks in? I'll catch up with you in a second."

Derek puffs up. "I'm fine with waiting."

"I'll just be a second," Cassie says with a smile that Derek does not deserve. Those fucking smiles belong to me.

He splits another look from Cassie to me, then back to her. "Really, Cass? You and the himbo?"

"Derek!" Cassie's color is high. "I will see you in a moment."

Evidently satisfied with the damage he's done, he eases back. "Good to see you, Sam. Hopefully we'll get a chance to chat again."

Not if I can help it. I say nothing as he walks away, but I didn't miss that pointed jibe about me. *The himbo.* Which means Cassie thought that at one time.

A month ago, I'd have laughed about it. People have been underestimating me my whole life. I have looks and money, so smarts come a distant third in the eyes of most. What did I care what others thought of me when my life delivered big in every way that mattered?

But now … now I care about this woman's opinion. And if it's that I have little to offer beyond my bedroom technique, then how am I going to overcome that?

Once Derek is out of earshot, Cassie turns back to me, hands on hips.

"Really, Sam?"

"What, I'm supposed to just stand by and watch him slobber all over you?"

"That's not what's happening. Things ended between us without a lot of discussion, and it would be good to close the loop."

Sounds like business speak, the kind of blah-blah Derek would say during his merger negotiations. I'm still sitting on my bike. Leaning in, I grasp her hip and nudge her forward. "I just don't like this timing. I don't like him."

Her chuckle calms me somewhat. "That much is obvious." She turns serious again. "But you can't go around asking whether he's here to win me or implying you're taking care of all my needs." She points at me. "Yes, I got exactly what you meant by that and so did Derek. It's such a caveman move."

"Which you like."

"I do not." But her nose is twitching so I know she does, and knowing this puts me more at ease.

What I really should do is tell her all the stuff I discussed with Jude. That I want her to stay, to live with me as my partner, to complete our fragile little family.

That I love her.

But it would look like gamesmanship, a desperate power grab. She would assume I'm only saying it because Derek is back in the mix and I'm jealous. Which I am, but I need to be more subtle. She won't believe I love her—and I need her to believe.

"Don't forget all the reasons you broke up with him." I'd like to outline them, but again, I need to play it cool. Less caveman, more urbane.

"We're just going to chat over coffee."

Fair enough, but I have to make some sort of statement. Curling a hand around her waist, I pull her flush to my body and claim her mouth. I wish Derek was still hovering, so he could see how good I—

No, I don't.

He doesn't need to see this. I've nothing to prove to him.

If I keep telling myself that, maybe it'll be true.

With great reluctance, I release her. I hope she keeps that lust-blown gaze for her coffee date with Derek. Let him know he can't satisfy her like I can.

"Later, Cassie."

Thirty-Four

Cass

There's comfort in the familiar, especially when your life is filled with the strange. Seeing Derek again has unfurled a safety net beneath me, a link to the stability I knew before.

"I can't believe you're here."

We've taken seats at the window in the Belden, though I wonder if maybe we should sit in the back in case Sam decides to do a drive-by.

He sounded jealous, though knowing Sam, it's just annoyance at any competition for my affections. He's used to getting what he wants.

Derek smiles, all boyish charm, though obviously a little strained after his long-haul flight. "What I can't believe is that we've gone two weeks without talking."

"We've gone days without communicating before."

"Sure, when I'm in the middle of a deal." He takes my hand and rubs the palm. "Cass, I've missed you."

"You haven't texted or called so you can't have missed me that much."

"Work has helped to mute the hollowness I've been feeling. This void you left."

The void *I* left? I inhale a breath, removing my hand in the same moment. "What's changed, Derek? Other than missing me?"

"Isn't that enough?"

"But nothing's changed about my situation."

He frowns. "About that. I might have been too quick to dismiss the possibilities. Of course, I can't expect you to abandon your sister's children. They're your flesh and blood." He stops for a second. "I ran into Joanna. She said you put in your notice. That you're moving to Chicago."

"It seemed like the best move for the kids."

He shakes his head. "You don't need to do that. Let's engage the lawyer, make a plan to get the kids to New York."

"Derek—"

"Cass, I need you. And I think you need me. You'll always be on the outside, looking in with the Killians. They're the kind that suffocate with affection, and they'll squeeze you out. Like they did with Annie. With sole custody, you can be more to the kids than just a passing presence in their lives. Bring them home. Let's raise them together."

What I wouldn't have given to hear this support right after Annie died. But he's wrong about the Killians. Once Annie moved here, I chose to hold myself back because I was resentful of the all-encompassing love they gave her. I chose to see it as Annie taking sides when really, she was just focused on her growing family.

Derek can only see the custodial arrangements in business terms, as winners or losers. I might have been of that mindset once, but no more. I'm not taking the kids away from their family in Chicago. I'll move here to be closer to them, but I can't think beyond that.

"Derek, Chicago is best for the kids. And for me."

But he's not listening. He has an agenda for how this negotiation will go and he's about to reveal what he thinks is his ace.

He falls to one knee. I catch the barista's eye, who is all agog.

"Don't do this."

He ignores me, which is par for the course. "Cassandra Ferguson, will you marry me?"

Oh God. Again, information I could have done with a month ago.

"You don't mean this. You don't want this."

"I want us to be together."

Which doesn't really address my concern. "Derek, please get up."

In a rather ungainly scramble, he stands and retakes his seat.

"I can't marry you," I affirm, in case my objections weren't clear.

His expression turns stark. "It's him, isn't it? I could tell something happened." His mind is in Merger & Acquisitions mode, thinking on how to salvage the deal. "It's okay. We were on a break."

Oh, fuck off. "Derek, I'm not going to insult you by pretending there's nothing between me and Sam. We've become close."

"Sex. That's all it is. The man's a walking hormone receptacle, all brawn and smiles. But that's not important. That kind of attraction can't last. Things are muddled because of your grief and the kids and how long we've been apart. You're bound to be lonely. I've been doing a bad job of tending to you."

Like I'm a weed-ridden garden.

"You and I have grown apart." Even I can't help the analogy! "We've been on separate paths for years. I'm not coming back to New York, but that doesn't mean I'm jumping into another relationship immediately."

"I should hope not!" Said rather indignantly. I'm not convinced he cares all that much for my rejection of his marriage proposal—I did do that, didn't I?—but is more concerned that I might be with Sam in some capacity.

Neither of these men like to lose.

"Because?"

His expression is incredulous. "The hot idiot? You've never had a kind word to say about him, Cass. He's just a brainless bruiser born into money, which is lucky for him because looks fade, don't they?"

I've said things like that, both to Sam's face and behind his back, but that was my own insecurity talking. There's so much more to this man than I ever gave him credit for.

"No need to be cruel, Derek, or to remind me that I've been kind of a jerk to Sam. I didn't know him well back then. But now I do, and he's been nothing but amazing with the kids."

And to me.

Derek blows out an annoyed breath. "It sounds like you've made up your mind."

"I have. I'm grateful you came here, and I'm glad we got to talk again after how things ended sort of abruptly. But this is where I need to be."

I'm unloading the dishwasher when Sam comes into the kitchen, freshly showered and smelling like a dream. I don't imagine the look of relief on his face.

"Aw, did I miss Derek's exit?"

"He was sorry he couldn't say goodbye in person."

"Sure he was." He leans against the counter, looking cockier than ever. He's loving this. "So how did *that* go?"

"He asked me to marry him."

That wipes the grin off his face. A muscle tic starts up in his cheek. "Did he now. And what did you say?"

"Well, I wasn't sure what to say. We've been together so long and it's a dream I've had forever—"

He looks wretched, so I rush in to correct his assumption. "I'm kidding. I said no."

He's staring, and I wonder if perhaps he hasn't heard me.

"Sam, I said—"

"No," he finishes.

Next thing, his hand is curled around my neck and his head is inclined to mine, his kiss all-consuming. He clasps my ass and hoists me up around his hips. I gasp at this display of strength, though I should be used to it by now.

"Sam, what are—"

"She said no," he murmurs against my lips, like it's the most wonderful thing. And then he's kissing me again, while carrying me back to his bedroom, kicking the door behind us so Waffles doesn't get to watch. My clothes don't last, and neither do his.

The kiss, however, is forever.

He yanks open the drawer and suits up quickly. I'm already arching up to meet him, my core flushing to accept him, my lips parted on a groan as he enters me. He interlocks his fingers with mine and fucks me deep and true.

"She said no," he repeats, the words filled with wonder. Like this is the best thing to ever happen to him. I didn't choose Derek.

I chose Sam.

That's what I did in rejecting Derek's proposal. Maybe in

breaking up with him in the first place. I was already in deep—with the kids, with this life I've craved, with my grief.

With Sam. Always with Sam.

He rocks into me, his chest rubbing against my breasts, the friction wild and frenzied. Everything feels so good, so right. Pleasure is radiating through me, starting with where our bodies are connected. He squeezes my hand, and I squeeze his cock, and he pumps again and again.

"Sam," I gasp.

The way he looks at me is so real, so clear, I can't believe we've made it to this point. A moment of doubt flutters across my consciousness, trying to ruin this good, true thing. He has so much power over me. This is his city, his apartment, his family, his world.

He'll break your heart, just like Annie did.

But then it floats away on the rush of an oncoming orgasm. That's the thing with sex. Good sex wipes your brain. Great sex destroys it.

Sex with Sam Killian tears me asunder.

He follows me over, sounding torn apart himself. His groan is primal, a wild animal unleashed, ending with a whispered, "Cassie."

When he leaves to clean up in the bathroom, I try to piece my brain back together. He emerges with a smile, covers me with the comforter, and pulls me into his arms. I'm mush again.

"She said no," he murmurs against my temple.

"I think I did."

He turns his head, his brow furrowed. "What?"

"Basically, I told him to get up off the floor and recognize that he and I are not to be."

"Sure sounds like a refusal." He's staring at me intensely.

"Sam." I meet his gaze, my heart thumping wildly. "I'd

already decided I'm moving to Chicago. There is no me and Derek."

Another kiss, which like all things Sam is intense, focused, perfect.

"We need to start looking for a house in the city," he says, adding more kisses. "But in the meantime, we should bring all the kids' stuff over here because house-hunting takes time. Spence can have the guest room and you can move in with me. We'll sit the kids down and explain it—"

"Sam, slow down."

"There's no time. There's a lot to do and I want to get started ASAP."

I place my hands on his chest. "I've said I'm done with Derek and New York, but that doesn't mean that I should jump right into something new."

His eyes narrow. "But you're here. You will be, officially. There's no obstacle to ... us."

I withdraw from his arms. "We need to be careful about doing anything rash."

"Like what? Finding comfort in each other?"

"Exactly that. What if that's all this is? Just a temporary relief from the pain."

He looks hurt. "Is that what you think? Sammie the himbo gives good lovin' but isn't for keeps?"

Damn Derek and his thoughtless words. But mostly damn me. I'm just as guilty. "I'm sorry. He shouldn't have said that."

A storm cloud has settled over his features. "Your opinion of me isn't exactly a secret."

"No, that's not—so I've been critical of you in the past."

"Sure. The past."

"Neither of us had good things to say about the other. What am I? The blister-in-law? St. Cassandra?" Annie told me about the nicknames because she thought they were funny and my antipathy toward Sam would soften the blow. It didn't. It just made me feel like more of an outsider. "I'm sorry I hurt you, and I want to be sure I don't do that again. I've always chosen carefully. I've had to."

"And when you think hard about a life with me, the numbers don't compute. Is that what you're saying?"

A united life, apart from what we need to do for Maya and Spence? "It's a big risk. And the kids—"

"Don't use the kids as an excuse. The kids are resilient. Whatever happens between you and me, they'll understand. But I won't force you into something you can't commit to 100%."

He's talking about commitment, the man with a different woman for every occasion. So he hasn't strayed outside the lines since Annie and Jake died, but that seems more likely a function of grief and busyness than a complete personality change.

That I even think that means I'm not ready to trust him.

"Sam, we're in this bubble right now. It's intense and lovely and filled with a carefully curated life for Maya and Spence." He opens his mouth and I hold up a hand. "But eventually we have to burst it and stray outside. We have to return to some semblance of normality."

"Which you can't envision with me?"

I want to. I want to take the chance, but I'm already risking so much by giving up my job and moving to Chicago. Some people might say it's not much of a risk when the funds are there to support that move. Still, it's a wrench from everything I've known. Ensuring the kids get through the next few months as painlessly as possible is the ultimate goal.

Thinking about something personal, for me, is dangerous. It could be ripped away in an instant.

"I want to take it slow. I know that's not your MO, but it's always been mine. I can't change my personality overnight, not when there's so much at stake."

"So what do you want to do?"

He sounds so wounded. I want to hug him, but I have to be strong.

"When you have your next 48 off, I'll go to New York and pack up. When I come back, I'll move into Annie and Jake's place in Winnetka. I can be here for the kids, but we might want to talk to them about going back to the house. It's closer to school for Maya and closer to your parents."

Even though he can't live there while he's a city employee. The bottom line is that he and I can't live together in the same house. It's too confusing.

"Sounds like you've given it some thought." His tone is cool now, shields back in place.

"The kids come first."

His mouth twitches, like he can't believe I'm still running with that tired excuse. Perhaps he's right. But it's the cover I need for now.

"Sure," he says, his voice weary as he pulls back the comforter and swings his legs out of the bed. "The kids."

THIRTY-FIVE

Sam

Can you break up with someone even if you were never truly together? I feel like I've been dumped but Cassie would probably explain it differently, in a way that sounds like we had some mutually convenient uncoupling like you read about on TMZ. I wouldn't care for whatever words she comes up with because the bottom line is the same: she's not ready to make a life with me.

Maya was reluctant to move back to the house in Winnetka, but when we explained that this made things easier for the school run and visiting her grandparents, she relented. This is good. The kids will have their own rooms again and it'll bring Cassie closer to them. That's important to her, and I'm totally on board with it.

We've settled into a new routine, splitting the childcare duties, drop-offs, meals, appointments, visits to my parents'. While she's looking for a job and we're interviewing nannies, she can be with them all the time, and I see them on my days off when I sleep in the guest room at Jake and Annie's place.

On those days, Spence usually crawls into my bed. I wake up and there he is, usually wearing oversized sneakers from his dad's closet (sometimes smeared with chocolate, which gets all over the sheets) and cuddled up between me and Waffles, who should not be on the fucking furniture. That dog is an outrageous opportunist.

The nightmares about the accident have receded, only to be replaced by something else. I wake up, agitated, knowing something is missing. It's not hard to work out what. I miss her, even though she's usually not more than a couple of walls away.

I've won, but it doesn't feel like it. The kids are staying in Chicago, but not having her in my bed is torture.

A few days into our new world order, I arrive home after my shift to the house in Winnetka to find her sleeping on the sofa. It's Sunday and the kids aren't up yet—I checked, surprised to see them so tuckered out.

I take a seat in the armchair and watch like a creeper. She looks peaceful, like she's sleeping just fine without me. But then her nose twitches and I get a little boost to my heartbeat at the notion that she might be lying to herself in her dreams.

On the table are sketches, mostly of the kids, some of Annie and Jake, even a couple of me. They were done while I was sleeping, which makes me feel like I'm some object, good enough for drawing but not for real life.

Her eyes flutter open. "Hi," she says shyly. Her gaze flickers to the sketch in my hand, which I place down. "What time is it?"

"Just after nine."

She sits up, giving me a prime view of her perky nipples pushing against the thin fabric of her sleep shirt. Seeming to realize she's exposed, she pulls the comforter up to cover.

"How come you're sleeping out here?"

"We were up late watching a movie and then I stayed up to work."

To work. I like that she calls it that. It makes her art as important as it should be.

I stand. "I'll start breakfast."

"You don't have to do that."

Ignoring her, I head into the kitchen, wash up, and start the morning routine. Usually it calms me, but I'm feeling nothing but agitation when she's around.

When she's not around.

All the fucking time.

A couple of minutes later, she appears with a yawning Spence, who's wearing one of his many Spider-Man PJs. On spotting me, he yells, "Uncle Sammie!" and runs into my arms.

As I scoop him up, he says, "No—"

"I know, I know. No kissing."

"No cereal. I want jelly on toast!"

I eye him. "What about kissing?"

He nods and plants one on my cheek. This kid is going to be the death of me and my sore heart. I hug him hard, thankful for the joy he gives me, and kiss him back. I catch Cassie's shiny eyes and we share a smile.

"Did you know about this?"

She shakes her head. "No, you're the first to be so blessed."

I turn away, trying to rein in the emotion that's running rampant through my veins. It's only a little boy's kiss but it feels like more. Like a new phase in all our lives.

"What kind of jelly, buddy?"

"Saw-belly!"

"Saw-belly? That sounds delicious."

Maybe this will be okay. I'll get over her, and we'll focus on being there for the kids because right now, they matter the most. Or so everyone keeps telling me.

Maya appears, rubbing her eyes. "Hi, Uncle Sam."

"Hey, bug. Slept in, huh?"

"We watched a movie."

My nephew chimes in. "Spider-Man!" Did I tell you that Spence loves Spider-Man?

"Into the Spider-verse." Cassie smiles at me again, tentatively, like we don't know each other's bodies intimately. "I know they should have been in bed earlier but—"

"It's okay. No need to justify all the decisions."

Her smile fades, taking that as criticism. I don't want us to be sweating the small stuff. It's exhausting.

We spend the next thirty minutes in a haze of breakfast, detailed explanations of the Spider-verse ("they have a spider pig!"), and catch-ups on Maya's classes. Earlier, we explained to the kids that I'm working a lot so I won't be here as much, and they seem to be okay with it, but Maya can tell that something is different. Every now and then I catch her looking at the two of us, like she's trying to figure out what's changed. I wish I had an answer for her that makes sense.

While I snag a few zzzzs, Cassie will finish up some job stuff before flying to New York later this afternoon, a wrap-up trip to get her life out there packed and stored before she moves to Chicago more permanently. I assume Derek will make one last ditch effort to win her back—he'd be a fool not to.

I wonder if she'll tell me. Probably not.

We're the definition of perfect co-parents, civil and agreeable. The kids are here, safe and healing. I got my way. So why am I so pissed about it?

In the guest bedroom, I'm peeling off my shirt just as there's a knock.

"Yep?"

Cassie pushes the door ajar. "Oh, sorry."

"It's okay. What's up?"

"Your mom asked what I was bringing to Thanksgiving

dinner on Thursday, which was interesting because it was the first time I realized I was going to your parents' for the holiday."

I scoff. "What were you planning on doing? Sitting all alone with a Whole Foods pumpkin pie?"

She smiles. "That's actually not *un*appealing." Her gaze takes in my body, then switches to my face.

"I know it's hard, Cassie, but you gotta try. I can't cover up for you all the time."

"You're such an ass."

I move in closer. "You mean, you *love* my ass."

"Okay, that, too."

There it is: the spark, the chemistry, the I-want-you-all-the-time, that I don't think will change any time soon. Joking about it should be a relief; the dull ache in my chest says otherwise.

"So you'd rather not spend Thanksgiving with us?"

"Actually ..." Suddenly she looks vulnerable. "I'm really looking forward to it. The last couple of years, I missed celebrating because Derek was out of town for business."

"But you could have come to Chicago and joined us. You would have been welcome."

"Really? The blister-in-law, a boil on your Turkey Day plans."

A joke, but there's truth in there. "I would've loved to see you, Cassie. I'd have been a little bitch about it, but underneath I'd have been thrilled. Just like I'm thrilled you'll be there this holiday with us. And Christmas, too. No Charlie Brown rinky-dink shit, either. You, me, the kids, my parents, turkey, presents, the whole nine yards. Where you belong."

She snatches in a shallow breath, which is when I realize how alone she's felt all these years since Annie moved to Chicago. On the outside, wishing she had a bigger role. In losing the people she loved in such tragic circumstances, she's gained something precious, but what a terrible way to emerge with a win. It's not unlike the self-reproach I've felt that this awful situation brought Cassie and me together.

We have this in common, what they call survivor's guilt. Our people gone, this beautiful thing between us struggling to bloom. We could talk about it, but I've missed my window. I've never felt I deserved her, and when I got my chance, I didn't fight hard enough to keep her.

I had it all planned out, after that chat with Jude.

I love you.

But Derek showed up and fear took over; I was too worried about it not being enough, that she'd see it as some sort of pathetic land grab in the face of her ex's reappearance. That she wouldn't trust the words or the sentiment behind them. She's afraid of feeling isolated again. Removing me from the equation as a viable partner—in all things—is her way of protecting herself.

So even if I can't say everything I feel, I can say some of it. Let her know she's wanted.

"You're family, Cassie. You always have been."

I close the gap, gratified when she stands her ground, and that dizzy lust sizzles through my blood. I get it: I'm not serious enough for her. I'm just the guy who knows how to bang her brains out and not much else.

"I'm not ashamed to admit I want you, that I want those perfect thighs wrapped around my hips. I might not be endgame for you but damn, we worked over there." I thumb over my shoulder at the bed, even though it's a different bed.

"We did," she concedes.

I incline my head, so my lips brush her ear. "If ever you need some relief, you can call on me."

Her palm lands on my chest. "You have more to offer than that, Sam."

"Not sure I do."

"What I said before—you're none of those things. I didn't know you. I'm sorry."

"It's okay. I said some things, too. About how you're an officious rule-follower, absurd perfectionist, a total buzzkill, and a pain in my ass."

"Hey!" Her green eyes light up like mini-lamps.

"You're also kind and generous and a great mom to our littles."

"Oh, wow." She blows out a breath. "Don't lie to me."

"You *are* a pain in my ass. No lie."

Her eyes sparkle with tears. "Thank you," she whispers.

I nod stiffly and stand back to let her go. I need her out of my orbit before I fall to my knees and beg her to stay. I tried that on one sister with no luck; I sure as hell won't be trying it on the other one.

Thankfully she takes the hint, yanking my heart out of my chest as she leaves.

THIRTY-SIX

Cass

After a week of packing up my possessions in New York, it's with little joy that I take on the task of packing up my sister's. I figure I'll get a head start on it before I mention it to Sam. I know he'll want to help and deal with his brother's belongings, but for now I'm content to spend this time alone and try to find peace in the pieces of their life.

It was certainly a good one. I see it in every framed photo, every scribbled fridge-door reminder, every squeaky dog toy underfoot. I spend several hours clearing out Annie's closet—she had a quirky style that matched her independent personality. It makes me question if I got it all wrong with her. Did I push her too hard toward college? Try to make her conform to my wishes? She certainly found the ideal way to rebel against the structure I tried to create for her. Always led by her passion, she made a life separate from me. Distinct, and all her own.

I wish I had her bravery.

I've never been impulsive. I'm the responsible one, though

some people would call it boring. Sam's attraction to me can't possibly last, not when the artifice of our mission to take care of the kids is stripped away. All that's left will be me, the stick-in-the-mud. Sam might want me now, the woman he placed on a pedestal all those years ago, but I'm not nearly exciting enough for him.

I'm a couple of days into it. Annie and Jake have a lot of art, some of it original and expensive, but I'm looking for something unoriginal and cheap.

The charcoal sketch I did of Maya when she turned two.

I had just graduated NYU with a major in business when Jake and Annie married. Laden down with student loans, poor as a church mouse, I couldn't afford anything off their registry, so that was my gift to them. After that, I didn't draw anymore.

That's when I met Derek. Not to say meeting Derek crushed my love of art, but once I'd assured myself that Annie was secure, that I didn't have to take care of her, I closed the door on that part of my life. Old Cass, the artist, the dreamer.

But I'd like to have that last drawing I did, from a time when I hadn't completely capitulated to the pressures of the future. Sam said it was in Jake and Annie's bedroom, and when I come across it, my heart hitches.

It's awfully good.

There's something in the lines that speaks to the emotions raging through me at the time, all this repressed love I had for Annie and her little girl. At the time it felt like goodbye, but seeing it again feels like hello.

Maybe ...

On my phone, I check out the website for the School of the Art Institute of Chicago. The idea of returning to school for another degree is crazy but ... *yes*. They have summer school programs. Classes with names like Narratives in Acrylics, Introduction to Drawing, Plein Air Painting.

I sit on the bed, thinking about crafting a new life. Not

one circumscribed by my love for Annie or her children, by sacrifice and responsibility. Something that gives me pure joy. Something for me.

My phone rings with a FaceTime call from Gina. We managed to get together for a drink in New York and she's fully supportive of my decision to move to Chicago. I'm worried that it's going to be a lonely one, possibly even more so than the last few years because Sam will eventually move on.

Gina smiles. "Hey, what's up, friend?"

"Packing up my sister's clothes for Goodwill."

"Oh, that's got to be so tough. Do you want to get back to it?"

"No. Happy to take a break. How's work?"

She launches into a breakdown of the usual office politics, who put a tuna casserole in the microwave (*why is it always fish?*), and how a used condom was discovered in the copy room. *Ugh.*

"How's the job hunt going?"

"It's not." A decision I came to just this instant.

"Ah."

"To be honest, I'd like to be a stay-at-home mom for a while." I don't mention the art classes. I need to think on it some more. "You probably think I'm betraying the code or something."

Gina shakes her head. "Not at all. Believe me, motherhood is a full-time job, my friend. With your firefighter's shiftwork, you want to be there for them. I get it."

"Sam's doing his best. I can't think of a better parent for them, actually. But the nanny search is going slowly. I'm lucky that I have the means to be able to make the choice. It's a luxury I'm very conscious of possessing."

"Okay, enough with the privilege awareness. We get it." Gina grins. "And what about Sam?"

"We've reached an understanding. I want him to be able to get back to his life."

The smile fades. "Like dating?"

The words are ash in my mouth. "If that's what he wants. He led a very active sex life up until he had to take this on. He got some stress relief with me, but I don't expect him to be a monk."

I'm imagining Sam Killian in a dark brown robe, taking a vow of chastity. Hilarious. After a few seconds of my chuckling, Gina frowns.

"What?"

"That sound out of your mouth. It's, uh, kind of creepy."

"I'm laughing at the idea of Sam staying celibate. Can you imagine?"

More squinting, followed by silence.

"Oh, come on, G! The man is a sex machine. Believe me, I know. Can go all night without quitting, so you know he must be thrilled to be back on the market. Of course, he still doesn't have much time but when he's ready to spread the Killian love, I'll be there to watch the kids."

I can hear my voice getting higher, possibly even squeakier, but that's because everyone talks loudly on FaceTime, don't they?

"Cass," she says pityingly, "you don't want to see Sam with anyone else."

"Correction: I don't want him bringing anyone else to meet the kids, at least not until he's serious about them. Which won't happen because this is Sam we're talking about." I swipe away a pesky tear. "I don't know what's wrong with me."

"Yeah, ya do."

I'm shaking my head, struggling to form words. "I think I miss the camaraderie most. These quick looks we shared when one of the kids did or said something that made us laugh, or the way he texted to check in. It was nice having that link."

"You were lonely with Derek."

I was. We led very separate lives, and now it looks like I'll be doing the same with Sam. Or *not* with Sam.

"But it's more than just camaraderie, right?" Gina sounds hopeful enough for both of us. "You two had something. Maybe still have it."

"Chemistry, Gina. Sexual. That kind of connection can only last so long."

She considers this. "While others last for six years."

"There's no comparison."

She smiles, all knowing. "Exactly."

At the front door to the Killians' house, Sylvia throws her arms open wide. "My babies! You're here!"

Maya rolls her eyes, which makes me giggle. She's so like her mom.

"Be nice," I say while we're still a few feet out from her grandmother. "Your grandma is crazy about you."

"Or just crazy," she mutters. On the way over, she asked why I didn't like Uncle Sam anymore. *First you didn't like him, then you did, and now you don't. I don't get it.* I told her we're still friends, and it was for the best. I'm not sure she believed me.

I'm not sure I believe myself.

Sylvia's already unbundling Spence from the back seat while I take the apple pie I made from Maya (it took me four hours but I think it turned out well, if a little lopsided). She held it on her lap all the way over.

"Grandma, you can kiss me now," Spence announces.

"Oh my. I'm honored." Sylvia smiles warmly at me, then

gives Spence a kiss on the cheek. To me, she says, "where's Sam?"

We walk toward the front door together. "He wanted to spend some time at the house, make a start on boxing Jake's things up." The kids have gone ahead, screaming for Granddad, so they can't hear. "I'm sorry. I know that's hard for you."

"It has to be done," she says stoically. "I'm just glad he's not leaving it all to you."

"He finished a shift this morning, so he needs to sleep. He'll stop by late—" My words falter as my gaze collides with my surroundings. It's already Christmas at the Killians' and it is magical.

"But Thanksgiving isn't over yet." The rule-follower in me isn't sure what to do with this.

"I know, but Sam said you missed out on big Christmases when you were younger. He thought we should start it early for you and the kids. Came over the day before yesterday to set it up."

For me? And the kids, of course. That's so thoughtful, but then that's Sam.

I walk by the large Christmas tree in the foyer and follow Sylvia through into the kitchen. Gingerbread scents assault me, and I think I might cry.

"We'll probably do mac n' cheese tonight," she says. "The kids love that—and I'm including Sam in there. He and Jake used to try to outdo each other with the hot sauce on every meal. Sam even put it in Jake's toothpaste once." She shakes her head at the memory, tears welling. "You should have heard him screaming. They were such a pair."

I place my arm around her. "You know we're going to get through this. Together. The kids will be here, and you can stuff them with mac n' cheese and cookies to your heart's content."

She takes a deep breath and meets my gaze. "You're definitely staying? For good?"

"Absolutely. This was Annie's home and it's where the kids will thrive. I think I'll be happy here, too."

She clutches her chest. "Oh, Sam is so lucky to have you, Cass. I can't imagine how they'd get fed or bathed or off to school if you weren't around. He'd be a mess!"

I've suffered Sylvia's digs about Sam for too long. I can't be the only person who sees how amazing this man is.

"Actually, no one is better at all that than Sam. He makes the drop-offs, does all the cooking. Reads stories, plays puzzles. Last week he created this pillow fort that the kids adored—"

"Well, he's a big kid like they are," she says cheerfully.

"Sylvia." I hold her gaze because I need her to hear me. "Sam is the glue holding this little family together. I know he was kind of wild when he was younger, but he's not that irresponsible kid anymore. These days, he's a rock, at his job and in his personal life. He's there for his friends, his family, for me. You think he can't do this without me? It's the other way around. I can't imagine doing this with anyone else."

She looks a little shocked by my effusive praise. "He's always been so different from Jake, and I guess I can't help comparing them."

"Which isn't fair." I worry I might have overstepped but I can't let this go on.

"You're right. I haven't been fair to him."

"It's okay. I just want him to get his due. He needs to know how much we appreciate him. How much we love him." I can phrase it like this, a generic, familial-type love.

Though my love for Sam is as real as the pine-scented Christmas tree in the entryway. Gosh, it hurts more than I thought possible. Breaking up with Derek didn't feel like this.

"You're right." She looks around and grabs her phone from beneath a turkey-themed dish towel. For a good minute, she works on a text, stopping and correcting and muttering about how bad she is at it. Finally, she says, "There."

"Did you just text your son to tell him you love him?"

"No, I was reminding him to pick up whipping cream." She winks. "And that I love him."

That makes me laugh.

Her lips twitch. "I must say, Cass, this is kind of a surprise coming from you. Now you're his number one fan?"

"When you go through something like we have, it changes your perspective."

Sylvia gives a slow-dawning smile. "I guess it does."

THIRTY-SEVEN

Sam

Dempsey's Pub in Wicker Park is a traditional hangout for firefighters based on the North Side, not least because it's owned by my captain, my squad leader, and the rest of the Dempsey clan. I wave at Gage Simpson, who's behind the bar, then head to a corner table where Abby and Jude are already installed.

Good friends that they are, they've grabbed a pint of Sam Adams Winter ale for me. Perfect. I'd rather not make small—or big—talk with anyone at the bar.

Abby stands to give me a hug, then Jude. To be honest I didn't want to come out tonight, but tomorrow is Thanksgiving, and it's a rare evening where we're all off and the kids are staying the night with my parents. For once, I'm a free agent.

It's been six weeks since Jake and Annie died.

Ten days since Cassie moved out.

Six years and two months since I first laid eyes on her.

I've never been good at math but those numbers shouldn't be living rent-free in my head.

"So how's the wedding planning going? Uh, both of you?"

Jude and Abby share a look, then Abby speaks. "Let's talk about Cassie."

I groan. "Do we have to?"

"Yes!" said in annoying unison.

"What's the latest?" Abby asks.

"The latest? We're doing what we said we would do. Co-parenting, being perfectly polite to each other, keeping the kids' needs front and center."

Jude nods. "And how are the kids doing?"

"Spence has stopped asking about his parents, which I'm not sure how to feel about. I don't want him to forget them, yet reminders are just as painful." I turn to Abby, who was a little younger than Maya when she lost her mom. "What should I be doing here?"

"When my mom died, my dad was so devastated he never talked about her. It created an atmosphere, like memories of her were forbidden."

"I don't want to do that. I want them to feel they can talk as much or as little about them as they want." Even though it hurts because I miss them, too.

"Then you're handling it right," Jude says. "My dad and I got along well after my mom died, but we lost that when I came out. You just want to be there for them no matter how they handle it. Don't be prescriptive about their coping strategies."

I nod, accepting the wisdom, grateful to have these two on my side.

Abby rolls back her shoulders, cracks her knuckles, and coughs.

"Jesus, Sullivan, you are a total ho for the goss."

"Can I help it? I'm practically an old married woman and

this one"—she thumbs at Jude—"is a drama-free zone these days. Spill it, Killian."

I blow out a breath. "I love her. That's all."

Abby's big blue eyes get impossibly bigger and bluer. She can't believe I said it out loud, in front of God and everything. "That's ... all?"

I shrug and take a sip of my beer.

"Sammie ..."

"Don't get me wrong—it sucks. Big time. I want her all the time, I miss her like crazy. I think I might have been in love with her since the first time I laid eyes on her, and I coped by employing a classic strategy of immature quippery and fucking anything that moves."

Abby looks stunned. Jude, not so much. He's borne witness to more of the Sam-Cassie dynamic over the last few weeks, and he's already called me out.

"But this is great!" Abby flaps her hands. "Have you told her?"

"God, no."

"But ..." She looks to Jude for assistance. My man of business merely shrugs which earns Abby's plaintive whine of "Jude!"

He puts his pint down. "It's not as easy as just laying it out there, Abs."

I acknowledge with a hand gesture toward the honorable gentleman to my right.

"But why not? You're being all forthright and honest with yourself. With us. Why can't you do that with her?" She sounds so wounded, like I gave her the recipe to the male psyche secret sauce then told her she couldn't slather it on her man-burger.

"To paraphrase Obi Wan, I'm not the man-ho she's looking for. I can admit my feelings to you guys. To myself. But she's got a certain idea of who I am. Sure, I've given her flashes of the Sammie potential over the last few weeks. I'm good enough to co-parent the kids but not good enough for her. She doesn't trust me to love her like that. Unconditionally."

Something pings in my brain. I'm not sure what, but I let it settle to analyze later.

Abby's frowning. "You can still tell her all these things."

Jude scoffs. "And risk rejection?"

I stare at my friend. "You think she'd reject me if I laid it all out?"

"I've no idea. But this way, you never have to worry about it."

"Not helping."

He grins. "Oh, you wanted help."

Abby's expression is stormy. She clearly doesn't like the tenor of the conversation. "We need to be serious here. How is Sammie going to get the girl?"

"I'm not, Abs. Sometimes it doesn't work out. Sometimes cowardice and fear and grief win the day. Otherwise, there would be no wars or crime, and everyone would be walking around with sappy smiles on their faces. I can't make her come around to my way of thinking, and I sure as hell don't want to force her to go against her nature. She's a rule-follower and she's already indulged in some coloring outside the lines. Now it's back to her safe space because I sure as shit am not it."

"But why?" This is Jude.

"Why, what?"

"Why aren't you her safe space?"

I laugh, though I feel about five thousand miles from the state of cheerful. "Because, my dear deluded friend, I might leave."

Abby's face brightens like she's found a loophole. "But you won't."

No, I won't. I'm in so deep that nothing can stop me from

loving her. "People have left her. Her mom. Her sister—well, Annie moved here, but Cassie saw it as abandonment." She chose a guy like Derek who gave her just enough of a routine to maintain the stability she craves but no more love than she felt she deserved.

I shift uncomfortably in my chair and take another draft of beer. All these facts are known to me, yet I've never strung them together with such startling coherency. It feels remarkably like I'm doing "the work."

I hate doing the work. Navel-gazing and deep reflection have always felt a touch precious, but right this minute, my heart is racing with insight. Is this how Einstein felt when he discovered the theory of relativity?

"But you won't leave her," Abby repeats. "That's what she needs to hear. That you're in it for the long haul. You're not a flight risk."

Maybe she'll see that while we continue to cooperate in this family unit we've formed. It means biding my time, letting her know I'm here for when she needs me.

But what's to stop her from meeting someone else? Another Derek who meets her criteria for safety, security, and boredom? Chicago Dereks litter the streets in the thousands.

Jake would know what to do here. He'd understand if I have a shot.

Actually, I have no idea if he'd know, just as I have no idea why he asked me to take on this responsibility. Why he trusted me with such an important task—and with Cassie, of all people, as my co-captain.

"I'm going to head out."

"Want us to come with you?" Jude asks.

"No, you stay here. Happy Thanksgiving, friends."

Abby smiles, her eyes a little misty. "You can do this, Sammie."

"Sullivan, no pep talks."

"Too late!" She jumps up to hug me, Jude does the same, and we hold each other a little too long. I'm so lucky to have friends like this.

If only friends were enough.

I don't want to go home to the Gloucester. My condo has felt empty since the kids moved back to the house in Winnetka. I could head over to my parents' and spend time with them all, but I'd like to talk to someone else first.

The air is bracing as I motor the Ducati down Western, then onto Ridge, before I join up with Sheridan, each curve dipping toward the lake and back again. When I finally reach my destination in Wilmette, I'm chilled to the bone and acutely aware that I've screwed up.

Cemeteries are only open at night in teen-driven horror stories. Of course, I can't visit my brother's grave at 9 p.m. in the evening, the night before Thanksgiving.

Faced with a locked gate, encroaching night, and the November chill, I contemplate my next move.

I remove the letter from my inside pocket, thumb under the flap, and break the seal. It's one page, which is about right for a man's final words.

Hey Sammie,

I'm praying to fuck you never have to read this. But no one knows what the future holds. And the future—especially that of my kids—is too important to treat casually.

Cass, being the total responsibility nerd she is, "encouraged" Annie to make a will, which meant we had to think hard about stuff no one wants to dwell on. Like cemetery plots. And do-not-resuscitate orders. And the kids growing up without us.

It sucked. But it also made me realize how good my life is and that includes all the people in it, not just Annie, Maya, and Spence. (I'm talking about you here.) Mom and Dad don't give you enough credit, but I know how hard you've worked to get where you are. So you're a cocky asshole about it, but it doesn't change the striving or the intent. You didn't have to do it. You could have coasted on Granddad's money for the rest of your life.

You're a hero, Sammie. My hero.

I'm hoping that I'll be drunk one night and tell you some of this stuff to your face. But if I don't, there's this letter to lay it out there (again, thanks, Cass). This letter, to tell you that we're good, you and I. I trust you with my life—and my family is my life. I can hear you arguing with me that you're not qualified, not responsible, not good enough. No one is until they're thrown into the deep end. That's how it felt when Annie told me she was pregnant. I might have claimed to be cool with it, but I was terrified. Like I'm guessing you are now.

That's okay. You'll make mistakes, but you'll also make my kids happy because you have the biggest heart of anyone I know. Trust your instincts, Sammie. You have great ones.

I hate the idea of not being around to see Maya try ballet until she becomes tired of that and goes for hockey. I'm crushed that I'll miss Spence's Little League games and when he loses his baby teeth. It kills me that I won't get to see you fall flat on your face when the woman you want cuts you off at the knees and rips your heart out. I would've loved to see that, you and Cass figuring it out.

You think I didn't know? I'm your big brother. I know everything!

I won't say you can do this, but you know it's what I'm thinking.

I love you (yep, only in writing as I ponder my mortality),

Jake

Fuck me. Are those some *Minority Report* precog skills or what?

I refold the letter, put it in its envelope, and return it to my pocket. I look through the gates, though I can't see their graves from here. They're behind a tree on the northwest side, a shady spot that's perfect for them. Picnicking in the afterlife.

I miss them, but I don't have to do this alone.

I don't plan to.

Thirty-Eight

Cass

The doorbell chimes.

If someone buzzed my apartment intercom in New York late at night, I'd grab a knife from the butcher's block before I even checked who's calling. In the Chicago suburbs, I should feel safer, but I still make a move toward the kitchen all the same.

Then, I get a text.

SAM

Hey, I'm outside.

I open the door and there he is, in jeans and leather, his dark head silhouetted against the fat, full moon. The Ducati is parked at a jaunty angle a few feet away.

Seeing him like this takes me back to when I met him the first time, that moment when we were introduced at the rehearsal dinner, the day before the wedding. I had never seen someone so handsome in the flesh, and for a moment I was bowled over by it. Then, suspicious. It was our story for a long time.

Now I'm feeling bruised again by his beauty. I also know what it's like to be the center of this man's world for a while. I miss it—and him.

"Is everything okay?"

"The kids are fine," he says, holding up his hands. It seems we need to preface every conversation with a statement like this. "Mom texted to say they're all watching *another* Spider-Man movie, which you know she won't understand."

"Kid gets bit by a radioactive spider. What's to understand?"

He snorts. "She's in a weird mood. Actually texted that she loved me earlier in between demands to run errands."

"That's sweet."

"If you say so." He smiles. "Could I come in?"

"Of course." It's just after nine but feels later because of the cold and inky-blue night sky. I stand by to let him in, but not far enough back I can't get a whiff of that citrus-cedar Sam scent I live for.

The door closes. We're both standing in the foyer, unsure of next steps. Do I take his jacket? Ask him if he wants a drink? Kiss him?

I really want to do that last one.

"Come in. We have a fire, though I'm not sure I know what I'm doing. It was a bit smoky while I figured out the flue damper thing."

Walking in, he looks around, and I wonder what he sees. He made a start on Jake's closet earlier but apart from that, I've divided things into piles for keeps, for discarding, and for Goodwill. I'm hoping that he and maybe, Maya, could go through it to make sure they don't want to retain something important.

He hasn't said anything, so I pick up the conversational slack. "What's up?"

"I wanted to make sure you were okay."

Oh. That's—I'm not sure. Lovely. Unexpected. The essence of Sam.

"Thank you. I'm ..." I shrug. "Not sure how I am, to be honest." I take a breath. "I miss you."

I wait for a cocky grin or smug comment. *Of course you do. I'm awesome.*

Instead, I get a somber, "I miss you, too."

Then I ruin it with an explanation. "Because it's easier when it's the two of us. I know it's still the two of us, switching off, caring in tandem, but it's easier when we're in the same house at the same time, all the time."

"True."

Then silence.

I struggle for a neutral conversation topic, but Sam speaks first.

"Why do you think they didn't tell us?" At my querying look, he clarifies. "That we were *both* on the hook as guardians."

I knew, though I had no idea about Sam, and it's clear he was in the dark as well.

"Because they expected we'd bitch about having to work together. To them, which they probably would've hated. We spent a lot of time criticizing and thinking about each other, didn't we? I wonder if they knew something we didn't." At his frown, I rush on. "Not that something would happen to them. But that something would happen to us."

He moves in closer, his expression a little wild-eyed. "Something did happen, didn't it? These last six weeks weren't my imagination. I've been living in a fog of pain, but the most lucid moments were the ones with you. The best ones were with you." He rubs a hand across his mouth. "If they did know or thought this would be a good way to bring us together ... hell, I'm not sure I can accept that. If the only way this could happen—*we* could happen—is because they couldn't be here, how can that be right?"

The guilt still remains for us both. "Who's to say we wouldn't have come together some other way? But I can't help thinking that this tragedy produced a fresh bloom from the salted earth. It brought me into the heart of your wonderful family."

It brought me to you.

I swallow my fear and plow on, blindly. "I've felt so terrible. I wanted to be closer to all of you—Annie, Jake, the kids, your lovely family. And now I am, but they're not here to share it. That's not right, Sam."

"No, it's not. It's the fucking worst. But here's the thing. I wanted you and only got a chance to be with you when this horrible thing happened because we needed something drastic to make us see each other in a different light. Like you said, this fresh bloom from a pile of shit."

My chuckle is pained. "Not sure I put it exactly like that."

He moves in closer, overwhelming every sense as he always does. "Tell me what you're afraid of."

Alarm pings me. "Afraid of?"

He nods. "Just spell it out."

"The kids getting hurt. Screwing this up. Failing my sister and Jake."

"What else?"

"Isn't that enough?"

He takes my hand and leads me to the sofa. Shrugging off his jacket he turns to me.

"Those are normal things for parents to feel. That's what you are to Spence and Maya—their mom in all but name. Maybe one day, in name. Now tell me what you're afraid of when it comes to loving me."

I try to catch my breath. So direct, so Sam.

"Losing myself in this. In you. I spent so much of my formative adult years making sure Annie got the best start. I'm not as worried about that with the kids, but when I'm with you it feels like I could fall down a rabbit hole where everything I want is set aside."

"And what do you want?"

The words come to me more easily than expected. "Room to explore who I am. Who I wanted to be before life's events took over and sent me down a different path. Made me so cautious."

Saying it aloud sounds a little pretentious but oddly right.

He takes my hand and squeezes it. "Take it. Take the time to explore. But I also think you can do that with me at your side. At your back. Over and under you." He gives me a wicked smile with that addendum. "I'm going to support any decision you make but I'd love to be with you on this journey."

It's so supportive, everything I've ever wanted in a partner. And then I realize that I never asked for that from anyone before. From my mom or Annie or Derek. I've only asked for it from Sam because he encouraged me to do so.

There's something else. Something else gnawing at me.

"I worry that I won't be enough for you." I look toward the flames of the open fire, searching for the answer in the flickering firelight, then back to him. "You're such a catch, Sam. Brave, handsome, kind. You could have anyone."

"Not anyone." His gaze holds mine unerringly.

"Yes, anyone. But *this* anyone is worried about giving her heart, about going all in. I always kept myself at a certain distance from Derek. It was a little staid, a little dull. No highs or lows. With you"—I place a hand over my heart because it's suddenly thrashing about in my chest—"it's mostly highs. Every beautiful moment. Even the bickering, the disagreements, it's all jet fuel that burns through me every second I spend with you. But the low with you—the not being with you—has hurt so much. I can survive that, if it's just this once. No more highs, but I won't have to experience another dip that might kill me."

His expression is as intensely heated as the fire behind me.

"I'm not going anywhere."

I swallow. "Well, I know you're here for the kids."

He shakes his head. "Not talking about the kids. I'm not leaving. I'll be around forever, annoying the fuck out of you when I drop the kids off from ballet practice and Little League games. I'll be drilling them for information on who you're seeing and then using that information to ruin any dates with Chicago Dereks—"

"Chicago Dereks? What the hell are Chicago Dereks?"

"Oh, you know what they are. Dull guys you feel safe with, who can't give you highs or lows or decent orgasms." He looks furious. "You're worried about being left alone, Cassie? That I might leave you? That should be the least of your concerns. I'm going nowhere." He cups my jaw, a possessive grip on my neck that makes my entire body thrum in anticipation. His hand is as cold as his gaze is hot. "Because this is where I'm meant to be. We came together, fell apart, and you're still here. The kids are yours. My family is yours. My heart, yours. If you want it."

Oh God, I do.

"Sam," I whisper.

Still staring at me with those super-nova suns, he says, in a slow and measured tone, "Tell me again what you're afraid of so I can tell you how it gets fixed. How *I* will fix it. Because I'll do whatever it takes to make you feel safe and wanted and loved. To give you the room to grow. To make you feel like you belong."

And just that one word—*belong*—is enough to break me. A sob escapes, barely, because it's smothered by Sam's kiss.

I love you, that kiss says.

I'll take care of you.

I'll never leave.

And for the first time in my life, I believe it. Sam Killian has made me a believer.

We separate for a moment, needing some air, and I take this respite as a chance to tell him what he means to me. Not just as a co-parent and team player and pain in my ass. But as the man who means more to me than anyone.

"I love you," I whisper, then louder. "I love you so much."

My heart is full, blood pumping, my entire body seized with awareness and love for this man. Again we kiss, and it doesn't take long for the love to manifest physically as want. As need. As blinding lust.

But there's more. With this man there always is. There's affection, which I've missed, and laughter as we come together in waves. We're clumsy and desperate in removing our clothes, and then we're rocking and rolling into each other, seeking with tongues and lips. When he pierces my body, I cry out at the rightness of it.

No competition, no trying to prove anything. We are one, and I finally understand what it means to have someone at your back.

It's Thanksgiving morning, and we step outside the front door to Annie and Jake's house. It feels like a new day, in all the ways that matter. We're heading over to his parents' place to spend the holiday with our family.

He leads me to the Ducati.

"Um, really?"

"Do you trust me?"

"Yes," I whisper. I'm taking bigger chances these days.

He smiles. "I thought we could visit the cemetery first, if you're up for it."

"Yes, let's."

He hands me a helmet and straps me in, his fingers brushing the underside of my chin. "Hold on, Cassie."

I do, for dear life. I sneak my hands under his leather jacket and snuggle in close. The streets are deserted, the cool air a balm to my hot thoughts. It's still scary—I'm not immediately cured of my terror of dangerous machines—but holding tight, I make it through, a test of the faith I have in Sam and this love we've found.

At the cemetery, I scramble off, glad to be once again on solid ground, and hand the helmet back to him. Briskly, we walk to the graves and stand before them with hands held tight.

"Would it be weird if we talked to them?"

I turn to him, wondering if he's serious. Knowing that he is but wanting to look at his beautiful face anyway.

"No, not at all."

"Well, dummies, here's another fine mess you've gotten us into."

"Sam! You can't call the recently deceased 'dummies'."

"How long do I have to wait?"

"Six months. At least."

He sighs. "We miss you guys. So much." He turns to me, and I nod. "Still a fine mess, but we're doing our best."

"Better than that," I say. "After the earthquake, we found each other in the rubble. I'm not sure what I do for Sam, but I know what he does for me."

"I keep it interesting. No more 'fine' orgasms."

A woman standing at a grave a few feet down from us sends a sharp look.

"Sorry, lady, I'm taken," Sam calls out, while I shake my head. In a lower voice, he says to the gravestones, "She gives me love worth fighting for. That's what she does for me."

I squeeze his hand and lay my head against his bicep.

"I love her, Jakey. This flat-on-my-face, cut-off-at-the-knees kind of love you wished for me. It'd be nice if you'd wished an easier road for me, but the hard one has been so worth it. Thanks for having faith in us. For trusting us with your precious littles. For bringing us together."

He releases my hand and shifts to gathering me into his side. We stay like this for a while, until the chill starts to penetrate our clothes and into the marrow.

Kissing the top of my head, he murmurs, "You ready?"

I nod.

"Let's go home, Cassie."

EPILOGUE

EIGHT MONTHS LATER
JULY

Sam

"I still think we could have doubled up, Garland. Or even tripled up if Sullivan wasn't so selfish."

Abby sips her champagne and eyes me with a cool expression. "Sure, you explain to my hot Italian husband that you'd like to share his nuptials because you think 'threesomes are cool'."

"RoRo would have been fine. I think you're the one who wants to play diva." I pull on the poorly knotted bow tie. "Why can't I do this?"

"Sammie, let me." Jude steps up and takes over from my shaking hands. We're in a room at the Hendersons' lakeside mansion—that's Max the lawyer's parents—which they're letting us use for the wedding. My parents' house is awesome but Casa Henderson fronts the lake, so it wins. (My mom didn't talk to me for a full twenty-four hours when she heard.)

"How do you even know how to do this?" Jude's bow tie skills are astonishingly good for someone who has only worn a tuxedo once that I recall, at his wedding to Hudson last month.

"Just good at everything." He pulls it tighter and tweaks it. "You nervous?"

"Fuck, no. This'll be a cakewalk."

Abby snorts. "Even now, Samuel." She knows different. I'm a bundle of nervous energy, a bag of nuts-and-bolts, planning to vibrate my way down that aisle.

"Anyone seen the bride?" I ask casually.

"I have!" A new voice enters the mix. Charlie Love-Henderson, our wedding planner, has just walked in with another guest.

Spence has never looked cuter, though he's grown two inches in the last eight months. Walking in, wearing a tiny tux, he releases Charlie's hand and runs toward me. I scoop him up and breathe in his coconut shampoo.

"You made it, buddy! Thought you were off rescuing people in the Spider-verse."

"No," he says with a grin. "We're twins."

"We are. Only I like cake and I heard you don't."

Spence looks alarmed. "I like cake."

"You do? Are you sure? I thought that was a different Spencer."

He nods his head enthusiastically. "No, it's me. This Spencer!"

"Phew. Thank goodness. I won't have to give it to another big boy in a bow tie." I turn to Charlie, who runs a hand over her swollen belly. She has a couple of months to go. "So when you saw Cassie, was she by any chance running in the opposite direction or maybe tearing her hair out wondering if she'd made the worst decision of her life?"

Spence is unraveling my bow tie, which is what you get when you give a curious kid access to a complicated puzzle.

"No, she's still here and looking fine." Charlie gives a low whistle and gestures with her fingers to her lips. "Chef's kiss." Another quick smile, then a slight frown at my undone tie. "We're ready for you to go out there."

"Got it." I plant a kiss on Spence's cheek and put him down. "You're going to be good for Grandma, right?"

He shakes his head, the little rascal.

"Okay, I tried. Everyone heard it."

Charlie grins and leaves, holding Spence's hand, ready to deliver him to my mom in the front row.

I turn to Jude and point at my tie. "Garland, help me out here."

Five minutes later, we're waiting at the top of the aisle in front of the floral bower. Jude and Abby, my best people, are by my side. I look out over the assembly at the various pockets of my life—firefighters, EMTs, my family, a famous hockey player. Cassie has her people here, too, mostly from New York. No Derek, though I encouraged her to invite him. It's childish, but I won, and here we are.

I spot Maya approaching in her flower girl outfit, but she's not moving slowly like she would if she was starting the ceremony. She's barreling toward me in a way that disturbs me because what if Cassie has come to her senses and changed her mind?

When she reaches me, I bark out, "Is everything okay?"

"Yeah." She throws her arms around me and gives me the tightest hug imaginable.

There are a few "aws" from the crowd because she looks fucking adorable, and everyone knows our story and how much these kids mean to me.

She peeks up with those green eyes so like her mom's and aunt's. "I just wanted to wish you luck."

"You think I'll need it?"

She considers my question in that grave way of hers. "Maybe. We all need a little luck."

"Not me. I've got you and Spence and Cassie. I'm already the luckiest guy in the world." I kiss the top of her fair head. "But I appreciate you coming out here to calm my nerves. Say hi to your aunt for me."

She smiles. "See you in a bit, Uncle Sam."

Off she trips back down the aisle. About thirty seconds later, the music starts, and there she is, my Cassie, standing with my dad, who's giving her away and looks proud enough to burst.

She's been amazing this past year, the perfect mom to the kids, the best partner I could have. We just closed on a house in Chicago. I knew it was the right place when I saw Cassie's eyes light up at the sun-filled studio, a place for her and her art. In there, I hope she can explore the person she kept under wraps when she took over as Annie's mom, the dreamer she wants to be. Still cautious, she's refused to jump right into a Fine Arts degree, instead taking evening classes at the School of the Art Institute. She says she wants to build a portfolio she's proud of first. Whatever she decides is fine by me.

Come fall, Maya will be starting a new school in the city and Spence is already in preschool. I'm still rocking it at Engine 6, though I never stay past my shift end. Why would I when I have this gorgeous woman and my littles to get home to? It's a busy, heart-full life, and I wouldn't change a thing, except to still have Jake and Annie with us. It can't happen but my gratitude that something beautiful was borne from the pain knows no bounds.

I pat the letter from Jake in my pocket. He saw something in me I couldn't see in myself and trusted me with his entire world. I wish he was here, if only to see Maya and Spence thriving like the little weeds they are.

I'm not a man of religious faith, but I would be a fool not to look around and realize I'm blessed. And as Cassie begins her procession down the aisle, her eyes shining with love, I know she sees it, too.

Inhaling deeply, I send a prayer up to Jake and Annie. I know they're watching, the guests of honor at this celebration for the family they made. This gift I'll treasure forever.

Thanks, guys. They're safe with me.

Thanks to my amazing editor, Kristi Yanta; my proofreader, Julia Griffis; cover designer, Lori Jackson; and Wander Aguiar for the wonderful cover images.

To my agent, Nicole Resciniti, and my husband, Jimmie Meader, thanks for always having my back.

Finally, thanks to everyone who encouraged me to head back to Engine 6 and write more firefighter romances. It's been a blast creating additional steamy stories, set in the most romantic firehouse in Chicago!

About the Author

Originally from Ireland, *USA Today* bestselling author Kate Meader cut her romance reader teeth on Maeve Binchy and Jilly Cooper novels, with some Harlequins thrown in for variety. Give her tales about brooding mill owners, oversexed equestrians, and men who can rock an apron, a fire hose, or a hockey stick, and she's there. Now based in Chicago, she writes sexy contemporary featuring strong heroes and amazing women and men who can match their guys quip for quip.

Laws of Attraction

DOWN WITH LOVE

ILLEGALLY YOURS

THEN CAME YOU

Hot in Chicago

REKINDLE THE FLAME

FLIRTING WITH FIRE

MELTING POINT

PLAYING WITH FIRE

SPARKING THE FIRE

FOREVER IN FIRE

Tall, Dark, and Texan

EVEN THE SCORE

TAKING THE SCORE

ONE WEEK TO SCORE

For updates, giveaways, bonus scenes, and new release information, sign up for Kate's newsletter.